Weddings are big business in picturesque Sweetheart, California, and Something Borrowed's rent-a-bridesmaid service is thriving among the Hollywood elite. For the women who work there, a walk down the aisle is just a paycheck—until the right guy makes it priceless . . .

RULE #1: GROOMSMEN ARE STRICTLY OFF LIMITS

Marley Stevenson never imagined her stint as a rented Maid of Honor would practically become a career. Then again, nothing in her life has gone according to plan. At least the money's good—and she needs it to pay off student loans and help out her mom. But the job has rules, which have never been an issue . . . until one encounter with a gorgeous best man—and his swoon-worthy Southern accent—sends Marley reeling.

Determined to get through the weekend with her professional reputation intact, Marley grits her teeth and sends out her best "unavailable" vibes, but Luke Jessup doesn't give up that easy. A former Marine and a current SWAT team officer, his focus is legendary—and it's on Marley. Jeopardizing her job is bad enough, and starting a relationship based on half-truths is worse—yet Marley is beginning to wonder if certain risks are worth taking, especially in the name of true love . . .

Visit us at www.kensingtonbooks.com

Books by Codi Gary

The Rock Canyon, Idaho Series
The Trouble with Sexy
Things Good Girls Don't Do
Good Girls Don't Date Rock Stars
Bad Girls Don't Marry Marines
Return of the Bad Girl
Bad for Me
Don't Kiss and Tell

The Loco, Texas Series
Crazy for You
Make Me Crazy
I Want Crazy

The Men in Uniform Series
I Need a Hero
One Lucky Hero
Hero of Mine
Holding Out for a Hero

The Standalones
How to Be a Heartbreaker

Bear Mountain Rescue
Hot Winter Nights
Sexy Summer Flings

Published by Kensington Publishing Corporation

Don't Call Me Sweetheart

Something Borrowed

Codi Gary

LYRICAL SHINE
Kensington Publishing Corp.
www.kensingtonbooks.com

Lyrical Press books are published by
Kensington Publishing Corp. 119 West 40th Street New York, NY 10018

All Kensington titles, imprints, and distributed lines are available at special quantity discounts for bulk purchases for sales promotion, premiums, fundraising, and educational or institutional use.

To the extent that the image or images on the cover of this book depict a person or persons, such person or persons are merely models, and are not intended to portray any character or characters featured in the book.

Special book excerpts or customized printings can also be created to fit specific needs. For details, write or phone the office of the Kensington Special Sales Manager:
Kensington Publishing Corp.
119 West 40th Street
New York, NY 10018
Attn. Special Sales Department. Phone: 1-800-221-2647.

Kensington and the K logo Reg. U.S. Pat. & TM Off.
LYRICAL PRESS Reg. U.S. Pat. & TM Off.
Lyrical Press and the L logo are trademarks of Kensington Publishing Corp.

First Electronic Edition: August 2017
eISBN-13: 978-1-5161-0229-7
eISBN-10: 1-5161-0229-0

First Print Edition: August 2017
ISBN-13: 978-1-5161-0230-3
ISBN-10: 1-5161-0230-4

Printed in the United States of America

For my editor, Norma.
Thank you for this wonderful opportunity.

Chapter 1

Marley Stevenson was trapped.

If she made a left towards the frozen food section, she was going to have to listen to Mrs. Needermyer go on about her single grandson from Berkeley, who was looking for a traditional wife. Whatever the hell that meant.

If she made a right, however, she would be cornered by Darren Weaver, who had the insane idea that Marley was interested in him. Even though she'd been telling him since he tried to kiss her in second grade that it was never going to happen.

He kept trying though, even after she'd punched him in the nose at an eighth grade dance for copping a feel. They'd both been suspended, but her mom had been proud of her. Her mom had gotten an angry call from Darren's mom about a doctor's bill, but she'd gladly told her to suck it.

Marley loved her mom, but situations like this made her wish she could escape Sweetheart, California already. Living in a small town could be brutal.

Of course, there was always option number three: back out of the store slowly, leaving her meager basket contents behind, but then she'd be stuck buying a sandwich at Subway again, their only fast food restaurant. How she let her refrigerator insides deplete so thoroughly, she had no clue. Maybe because she'd been so busy now that wedding season had officially started, she'd been eating mostly leftovers from caterers.

Those had run out on Tuesday though, and because she'd been in meeting after meeting the last two days, she'd been unable to make it to the store—until now. But thanks to the limited amenities in the small foothill town, she was having trouble avoiding people and places that set her already frazzled nerves on edge. She had to deal with difficult brides at work; she just wanted to breeze in and out of the grocery store without being pestered by annoyingly persistent—

"Marley!"

Damn it. She'd contemplated her escape for too long.

"How are you, dear? How's your mother?" Mrs. Needermyer asked.

Marley pasted on her best smile. "She's good. Busy. You should stop by the café and say hi."

Mrs. Needermyer patted her ample waist, her faded blue eyes twinkling behind her thick glasses. "Would if I could, dear, but I've started a new diet. Can't be going in there, tempted by all of your mama's sweet treats."

Marley smiled politely. Mrs. Needermyer was on a new diet every other week, but nothing seemed to stick.

"I know. I have a hard time not sneaking a few from the pan myself," Marley said.

Mrs. Needermyer raked her gaze over Marley's thin frame—and her look clearly said she had a hard time believing that, but it was true. The difference between Mrs. N and Marley was that Marley was forty years younger, ran five miles a day, and did yoga before bed five nights a week to chill out.

Plus, with Marley's high stress job, she usually only ate once or twice a day. During wedding season she lived on coffee, almonds, and Starbursts. Not exactly the most balanced diet, but the coffee kept her from killing people, the almonds gave her protein to stand up, and the Starbursts…well, they were just freaking awesome.

"Yes, well, you're lucky to be blessed with such good genes, but they won't last forever. After thirty, things will start to slow down and travel south, if you know what I mean."

Please, someone get me the heck out of this conversation.

"Hey there, Mrs. Needermyer."

Marley nearly groaned aloud, and glared at her savior. Darren just grinned at her mockingly.

"I am well, Darren. I am so glad to see you. My car is making the most horrendous sound—"

"If you will both excuse me, I need to get my shopping done and hurry home. Have a good day."

Marley practically ran for the bread aisle, ignoring Mrs. N's huff of indignation behind her. She would probably forget about the confines of her diet just to stop in and tell Marley's mom how rude her daughter was, but at this point, Marley didn't care. She just wanted to get this done, and go home to Butterscotch, her rabbit. She'd saved the orange and white bunny six months ago from Mr. Peltzer, who'd thought rabbit farming would be a lucrative operation. In no time, there were bunnies everywhere, and the town council members decided to close down Mr. Peltzer's rabbit breeding, as they couldn't have the place overrun with rabbits come wedding season.

Marley had been one of the volunteers to help gather them up, and had fallen hard for the tiny bundle of fluff, who had just hopped on over to her and head butted her hand. He was the best man to ever come into her life—that was for damn sure.

Marley tossed a package of milk and honey bread into her basket and rounded the corner, running smack into a hard male chest. When she stumbled back, a muscular arm caught her around her waist, and as she dangled there, leaning back like some historical heroine on the cover of a romance novel, she looked up into a pair of dark, twinkling eyes and a wide, white smile.

"Whoa, there. You okay?"

Marley couldn't seem to find the words, staring up into a face made of granite: sharp cheekbones, a square jaw, and wide forehead. His ears were the only part of him that didn't seem to fit the perfectly proportioned handsomeness; they were a bit large and stuck out a bit, but they didn't detract at all from every other sexy aspect of him. He was built like a mountain, and reminded her of John Cena, especially the way his whole face seemed to get into his amusement.

"Blink once for yes and twice for no," he said.

Shit, he was laughing at her for being all swoony over a pretty face.

"I'm fine," Marley bit out finally, trying to get back up onto her feet. Once there, he released her slowly, those big hands burning through her clothes as they fell away.

She could feel her cheeks heat in embarrassment; she hated to be the butt of anyone's joke, especially some guy who looked like he should be assisting Arnold Schwarzenegger in an Expendable movie. Plus, looking like an idiot in front of an incredibly hot guy is never fun.

"Sorry 'bout almost taking you out there. I was trying to find the cereal aisle and got a little turned around."

Marley had never been one for thinking accents were particularly sexy, but his southern drawl mixed with his smoky deep voice was terribly appealing.

"Is this your first time in Sweetheart?" she asked.

"Yes, ma'am. Don't suppose you could help me out by pointing me in the right direction?"

Marley knew he was playing her. The store wasn't that big and the cereal aisle was just over his shoulder, but she really didn't mind. It had been a while since she'd had a man, who didn't make her want to file a sexual harassment complaint, flirt with her

"Sure, it's just this way. I'm Marley." She held out her hand to him, shifting her basket to her other arm.

"Luke. Good to meet you."

Man, she loved the way he talked. "Where are you from?"

"Mississippi originally, but I've been living in Los Angeles the last eight years."

"No kidding?" She stopped in front of the cereal section, waving her free arm. "Here you go. We don't exactly have a plethora of choices, but we have most of the good stuff."

"What's your favorite?" he asked.

"Hmm, you mean my actual favorite or what I tell people so they don't think I'm immature?"

He grabbed a box of Lucky Charms, shaking it in front of her. "This is mine. Which one do you actually like?"

Marley reached out and pointed to the box of Trix.

When he grabbed it and put the box in his basket, Marley raised an eyebrow. "If Lucky Charms are your favorite, then why are you buying mine?"

"Maybe I'm hoping that you'll agree to have breakfast with me tomorrow morning?"

Marley stiffened. Did he actually think he could flash her a smile and she'd go home with him for a sleepover?

"Thanks, but I'm a strong self-sufficient woman"—she threw a box of Trix into her carton with a sniff—"and I can buy my own damn cereal."

To her surprise, he pulled the box out of her cart and put it back on the shelf. "And while I respect that, I'm an old-fashioned guy. When I ask a girl out, I like to pay."

"It sounded more like a proposition than a date," she said.

He actually looked affronted, but he could just be a good actor. "Then I apologize again. I was trying to be clever, and I guess I missed the mark."

"Hmm…Well, the next time you try to ask a girl out, maybe you should choose a less suggestive meal. Like lunch."

"I'll remember that."

Marley, all traces of the lightheaded excitement gone, nodded. "Well, enjoy your stay in Sweetheart, but I have more shopping to do. By the way, what brings you here?"

"A wedding."

"Yours?" *Oh, why in the heck did I say that?*

That grin was back, 100 percent male and looking self-satisfied.

"No, a friend's. I would never hit on another woman if I was getting married."

She could tell her cheeks were still burning, but she tried to play it through. "Good to know. Well, it was nice to meet you. I'm sorry about the—"

"Hang on now. How about that lunch?" he asked.

Marley hesitated, considering. She didn't get involved with tourists, usually, but it would be nice to go on an actual date.

"How long are you in town?"

"This week, then every weekend until the second weekend in August."

Weekends were usually booked solid for her. "How about Monday? I should be able to meet you around one."

"That sounds good, but can I get your number at least?"

His teasing made her laugh at her own eagerness.

"Absolutely."

After the number exchange, Luke took his phone back, his fingers brushing over hers lightly. That simple touch made her skin light up with tiny tingles, like the bubbles at the top of a glass of champagne.

"I'll see you Monday. It was good bumping into you, Marley."

He walked back down the aisle, and the minute he was out of sight, she picked up the box of Trix again with a smile. She suddenly had a craving.

Chapter 2

Luke Jessup had grown up in a small town a lot like Sweetheart with one major exception...

There was wedding shit everywhere here. Every store had something to do with the big day. His best friend, Brent Harwood had warned him that Sweetheart's main attraction was the wedding destination for the Hollywood elite, and the place was like Santa's Workshop for brides. Brent's fiancée e, Sonora Star, didn't seem to be that thrilled though, if her high pitched complaining was any indication.

"I just can't believe that Belinda flaked! How am I supposed to find another MOH at the last minute?"

"MOH?" Luke didn't know why in the hell he'd asked, considering how her icy blue eyes lanced through him in disgust. That seemed to be the only emotion Sonora could muster for him, and the feeling was completely mutual. Luke couldn't understand how a guy like Brent, who was smart, driven, and above all, a great guy, would take things so far with a has been pop princess with a shady past.

Luke knew enough from the tabloid fodder and from Brent that Sonora had been struggling the last leg of her career. After several singles that flopped, she'd spiraled down to the point where TMZ was calling her the next "Britney 2007." She'd gotten into a Twitter war with Miley Cyrus, and posted a series of Snapchat videos where she was crying, tears and mascara rolling down her face as she'd rambled about how the music industry ruins young artists.

It wasn't until after she'd taken a nose dive while performing at the MTV Video Music Awards and calling Kanye West a no talent hack that her agent had stepped in and gotten her into rehab. When she'd gotten out, she'd been photographed at an SPCA fundraiser, building sack lunches for the homeless and doing several meet and greets for Make a Wish. Even with the good PR, her career hadn't recovered.

A year after she'd gotten clean though, she met Brent at a Feed America charity dinner and the next thing Luke knew, the two of them were engaged. Luke still couldn't figure out how in the hell that had happened.

Fine, so even Luke could admit she was hot. With long, strawberry blonde hair, big blue-green eyes, full pouty lips and a banging body to boot, Sonora could get any guy's motor running.

Until she opened her mouth and made most men want to run screaming in the other direction.

Sonora spun around, giving him an exaggerated eye roll. "Maid of honor! It is a huge responsibility!"

The three of them were heading into breakfast at the Sweetheart Café, and passed by an elderly couple holding hands like a couple of teenagers. Luke and Brent mumbled a "good morning," but Sonora just sniffed like they smelled. It was funny how someone who had pretty much tanked their life and career could still act all high and mighty.

"What about your sister?" Brent asked as he held the door.

"Are you kidding me? Kendall will only sabotage everything! You know she hates me."

"Geez, I wonder why?" Luke mumbled.

Sonora was too busy whining to hear him, but by the warning look Brent shot him, he had.

Luke had tried to be nice, to be understanding and to look deep inside Sonora for whatever drew Brent to her, but all he'd found was a vapid social climber with no talent and even less compassion. The polar opposite of Brent, who along with his two brothers, ran their family's hotel empire. Brent was constantly volunteering or donating to one charity or another.

Sonora, oblivious to them, was still lamenting her lack of bridesmaid. "I guess I'll just have to go through my phone again and see if I can find someone who can fit into Belinda's dress."

"Hey there." A woman in her late forties or early fifties approached, wearing an old-fashioned white apron. Her silver-streaked blond hair was up in a loose bun, and her eyes were lightly lined with crow's feet behind the clear lenses of her glasses. "You can seat yourselves and I'll be right there to tell you the specials."

They found an empty booth at the back of the restaurant, and Luke studied the homey décor as they passed. The red walls were covered in black and white pictures of couples: couples kissing, couples hugging, couples holding hands. Even Luke thought it was a pretty cute setup for a restaurant called the Sweetheart Café.

"God, this place is tacky," Sonora said loudly.

Of course Sonora the Brat would think so.

Several people turned, their expressions ranging from mildly irritated to downright hostile.

"Babe, knock it off." Brent's angry command was so out of character, Sonora stumbled in front of him, and Luke wanted to slap him on the back for finally getting his balls back.

Sonora's mouth opened to say something, but she must have had second thoughts because she closed it with a snap. She slid into the booth first, clearly sulking, and then Brent slid in. Luke did not want to sit next to Sonora, but since Brent wasn't moving, he went to the other side and slumped down.

"Here you go." The server set down three ice waters and three menus. "And today we have our SOS omelet, which is made with jalapeño peppers, bell peppers, onions, pepper jack cheese, and spinach, our 'hot' potatoes, and one of our famous biscuits with jalapeño jelly. If spicy isn't your thing, we have the Sweetheart Hot Cakes, which is a stack of five of our buttermilk and vanilla pancakes, served with your choice of five syrups, whipped cream and chocolate chips, or a helping of our fresh preserves in either peach, strawberry, or blueberry."

"That sounds good to me. Could I add some bacon and sausage to that?" Luke asked.

His friendly tone seemed to relax her, and he wondered if she'd heard Sonora talking shit about the café. "Oh, a big boy like you needs his protein, so I think you should go with this." She pointed to an item in a box on the menu.

Luke read the description aloud. "The Tank, huh? This hefty platter is packed with every food group, and will keep you pumped for battle or spending the day wooing your honey." Luke chuckled. "Well, I don't have a honey, but that sounds good to me."

"And how about some coffee, handsome?"

Luke glanced at her name tag with a grin. "Well, Rose, I think I'll take you up on that. Black is fine."

She winked at him, her green eyes twinkly. "You got it."

When she turned towards Sonora and Brent, her demeanor was more formal, but still friendly enough, even when Sonora started asking for a caloric breakdown of several items and a bottle of spring water.

Rose's expression changed, and she spoke as if Sonora were a child who didn't want to eat her dinner. "You want spring water, darling, you go to Idaho. Our water is filtered, but if you really want a bottle, there's the gas station across the street."

Sonora's face turned bright red and she looked like she was about to stand up and make a scene.

Brent shoved her back down into her seat, flashing Rose a wide, apologetic smile. "The water is fine. You'll have to forgive my fiancée . She got some bad news this morning and—"

"You don't need to make excuses for me," Sonora snapped.

Then she shoved at Luke's shoulder. "Let me out. I need to go to the bathroom."

Luke was tempted to stay put and make her crawl under the table, but they were already the focus of too many curious eyes. He slid out of the booth and let her by.

As Rose gathered up the menus, she gave Brent a dry look. "Nice girl you got there."

Damn, but he liked Rose.

Brent gave her a small, sheepish smile before she walked away. Luke lost all traces of amusement as he focused on his friend's face. He looked exhausted.

"Man, I gotta ask again—"

"Don't." Brent's sharp tone came out like a bark and Luke glared at him.

"Fine, you want to be fucking miserable, that's on you, but I am not going to spend the next two months with her being a bitch to anyone and everyone she meets. I just don't get what you see in her—"

Brent leaned over the table and spoke in a low growl. "Because she meets all of my father's requirements for a wife, and if I want to continue to run my third of the company my way, then I need to fall in line. That means get married, preferably to a woman who will give me children and is willing to stay home and raise them. She should be manageable, and willing to toe the line. Sonora, despite her troubles, has agreed to all of these things, and if she should become difficult at times, well, then I'll just go to work."

Luke couldn't believe this was the same guy he'd met in high school, who'd written bad poetry for a girl he'd been crushing on in their sophomore English class. It was so cold and calculating.

"That's fucked up, man."

"No, that's life. That's business. Not everyone thinks love and marriage have to go hand and hand."

Luke shook his head. He didn't believe a word of the bullshit his friend was spewing, but he wasn't going to tell him how to live his life. Luke wouldn't tolerate people getting all up in his business. It was why he'd moved to L.A. in the first place, to get away from his sperm donor. Luke's lips pinched just thinking of the bastard. Henry Calhoun had been a married, philandering dick when he knocked up Luke's mother, the cook's daughter, who had grown up on his Texas ranch. Kaylie Jessup was eighteen and imagined herself in love with the charismatic Henry, twenty years her senior. The fantasy she had about the two of them being together after he divorced his wife went up in smoke when she told him she was pregnant. He wrote her a check for college, and told her in the nicest way possible to leave and never come back.

So she took his money and bought them a small place in Mississippi. They lived off the money from Henry until Luke started kindergarten and Kaylie got a job as the cook at his school. His mother was his whole world and he adored her.

When he was twelve, his mother was diagnosed with breast cancer. The medical bills were a heavy burden, and Luke found himself mowing lawns and other odd jobs to help his mom out.

But then Henry came looking for them. Turned out his other two sons by his ex-wife wanted nothing to do with him, and he needed someone to take over his business affairs when he died.

Luke's mom told him to go to hell, but he offered to pay off all their medical bills and swore he'd set her up with the best doctors in Houston. Despite everything he knew about Henry, Luke never had a father, and wanted the chance to know him. Luke realized that he was the main reason his mother agreed to Henry's terms.

The next year was like a whirlwind, and when his mother died just two months' shy of his fourteenth birthday, he was left in Henry Calhoun's care. He'd gone to the finest school, where he met Brent and other boys Henry approved of, and he played football and dated the girls that Henry pushed his way. For the next four years, Luke was like a zombie, not really living, just going through the motions.

Then a Marine recruiter had approached him while he was out with friends, and he took the first step to defy Henry Calhoun's plan.

When he told Henry, the old man became so furious, Luke was sure he was going to hit him, but in the end, he just tried to pull every string to keep Luke from going. Only no amount of oil money could release Luke from his commitment and three months later, he shipped off. He did four years and instead of heading back to Texas, he went to New York. After five years working SWAT for the NYPD, he transferred to Los Angeles.

But last December, Henry's oldest son, Michael, called to let him know that Henry had died of a heart attack and for the first time in eleven years, he'd gone back to Texas. He hardly knew his two half-brothers, and after a weekend of listening to them rip Henry to shreds even as they contemplated how to spend their inheritance, Luke had no desire to know them. Ever.

Henry had been a selfish man, but he wasn't a villain.

Of course, once the will was read, there was no use trying to convince the other men of that. Henry had left everything to Luke—his company, his ranch, all of it—and a letter, explaining that even though he'd been a complete disappointment to him, Luke had been the only son he had worth a damn.

What had followed was a whole lot of drama in and out of court as his two brothers took turns suing him, but they both lost, and after they paid court fees, were more in debt than before. Luke hadn't lost much sleep over their predicament though. Instead, he sold off all of Henry's assets, split the money into several money market accounts, and bought a house on the beach.

He'd only been able to take four years of Henry's controlling crap. He had no idea how Brent was still bending over backwards for his family.

"I tell you what. If I ever take that plunge it's gonna be because I am so crazy for the woman, I can't stand to be without her for one more minute."

Brent nodded grimly. "I wish you the best of luck with that."

Chapter 3

Monday morning, Marley's first thought was of her lunch date with Luke. She opened her eyes with a smile on her face. And immediately started screaming.

Butterscotch jumped straight up in the air and took off across the bed, flying down the hope chest and skidding along the wood floor with frantic clicking until he disappeared out the bedroom door.

Marley flopped back on the bed, sucking in air and trying to calm her racing heart.

"Damn it, Butters! You need to stop staring at me until I wake up! It is freaking creepy!"

Of course, she didn't actually expect the rabbit to respond. After six months, you'd think she'd have gotten used to seeing the little white, furry face in hers, but it was still jarring.

When she finally climbed out of bed, she went about her daily routine: filling Butters's dish and rubbing her hand over his soft ears so he knew there weren't any hard feelings. After that, she took a shower and got dressed for work. A chiffon yellow dress and a pair of bright floral heels would work for her meeting with her boss and for her date with Luke.

It took her less than five minutes to drive across town to the office of Something Borrowed Wedding Solutions. Kelly Barrow had started the bridesmaid-for-hire service ten years ago, when she was twenty-one, after all of the bridesmaids for one of the biggest weddings of the season had come down with the stomach flu. Kelly, who had been working at X's and O's Bridal Shop, offered to step in as maid of honor, and called up five local girls who could fit into the bridesmaids dresses.

And the rest was history.

Most weddings that hired them only required a MOH or a bridesmaid, and with the high turnover at Something Borrowed, no one had ever complained about their friends finding out they had to hire someone to be there on the bride's special day. Most of the women who worked at Something Borrowed were twenty-one to twenty-four and only worked one or two summers when they came home from college. Marley was the oldest at twenty-eight, and had been with Kelly for seven years.

If it had been up to her, she would have escaped Sweetheart a long time ago, but she couldn't leave her mom with the mountain of medical bills that had stacked up for her little sister, Bethany. The money she earned had saved the Sweetheart Café and paid off everything insurance hadn't covered. All she needed was one really good summer, and Marley would have enough money to start over somewhere new. To finally go to New York, get an intro job at a large publishing house, and work her way up to a full-time book editor.

Of course, that was just a dream at the moment. Although she had a masters in English, she hadn't quite gotten up the nerve to apply for any jobs yet.

Marley smiled at her friend, Rylie Templeton, who was sitting behind the front desk eating a delicious looking muffin and licking the crumbs from her lips.

"That looks good," Marley called in way of greeting.

"Hey!" Rylie got up and came around the desk, holding the muffin out to her. "You have to try this! I made a bunch last night."

Marley eyeballed the half eaten muffin. Rylie knew that she didn't like to share food. "If you made a bunch, then why do I need to eat yours?"

Rylie's round cheeks turned pink. "Cause I got excited. Come around here and grab one. I think they're my best ones."

Marley came around the back of the desk and picked up one of the big, fluffy muffins and took a bite. A burst of sweet cake and chocolate with just the hint of spice exploded on her tongue.

"Oh my God, what is that?" She licked her lips and hummed in approval as she took another taste.

Rylie was practically squealing, and Marley smiled around the chunk of muffin in her mouth. Rylie was so freaking excitable, it was adorable.

"They're chai chocolate chip muffins. You like?"

The only problem Rylie had was her lack of self-confidence, due partly to her asshole of a boyfriend tearing her down every chance he got. Rylie was three years younger than Marley and had been at Something Borrowed for three years, and in all that time, Marley had never seen Rylie stand up for herself. It was probably why all the clients loved her. She was sweet, bubbly, and didn't rock the boat.

"No, I freaking *love*. I'm going to need another of these bad boys later after lunch."

Rylie was practically bouncing in her ballet flats, her teal skater dress dancing with her. With her chocolate brown hair laced with golden highlights and her big doe eyes, Rylie was lovely, especially when she smiled.

If only she saw herself the same way.

"I'll save one for you."

"Thank you." Marley took another bite of the muffin as she headed down the hallway toward Kelly's office. She stopped off for a cup of coffee, black "like her soul" she always joked, and knocked softly on the closed door.

"Come in."

Marley went inside and held up the muffin. "Have you had one of these?"

Kelly gave her a wide grin and pointed to the small chunk of what was left of her muffin, her hazel eyes glittering. With long straight black hair that drifted almost to her waist, Kelly was classically beautiful, like Elizabeth Taylor, yet Marley had never seen the other woman with anyone in eight years. Kelly had told her that she had a fiancée once upon a time, but he'd gone into the Army, and never came home.

For a woman who made other people's weddings the stuff of dreams, it was strange that she hadn't found somebody to love.

Of course, Marley had no room to judge. The dating pool in Sweetheart was small and she was reluctant to form any attachments, especially since she planned on hightailing it out the first chance she got.

Kelly popped the last chunk in her mouth with a hum. "I swear, that girl is going to end up on one of those reality cooking shows as a judge."

"Seriously." Marley sat down across from her, holding her muffin in her lap. "So, what's going on? Your message last night was pretty cryptic."

Kelly leaned her hip against her desk and clasped her hands in front of her tight purple dress. "Well, yesterday I received a call from Sonora Star."

Marley was surprised. She'd never been a fan, but her sister, Bethany had adored her. "The pop singer? I thought she was in rehab?"

Kelly shook her head. "No, she went to rehab last year. Now she is marrying one of the richest men in America and her maid of honor just flaked."

"Well, from what I've seen in the magazines, I can imagine why."

Kelly gave her a Cheshire cat smile. "Which is why she's hiring a professional. Someone who has the patience of Job and the organizational skills to help this wedding go off without a hitch on August 8."

Marley's stomach sank. "You've got to be kidding. Two months? You want me to organize her wedding in *two months*? Has she done anything?"

"She has the wedding venue, but besides that, nothing."

And yet, Kelly had taken her on, which meant Something Borrowed had gotten a substantial bonus.

"How much did she give you?" Marley wasn't worried about Kelly taking offense. There was a reason she'd chosen Marley; she lacked pretense and didn't pussyfoot around.

"She didn't. Her parents did. Apparently, Sonora's finances took a bit of a hit the last few years, so they will be handling all the expenses."

"What about her fiancée? If he's loaded, why doesn't he pay for some of it?"

"Another reason she wants a professional. Sonora's fiancée isn't aware of her struggle and she'd prefer to keep it that way."

Marley wrinkled her nose in distaste. "That's unethical."

"It's a good thing we aren't the moral police then." Kelly held out two checks to her with a grin. "The first one is your commission and the second is a bonus."

Marley studied the checks, and as she counted the zeros she gasped. They totaled $20,000. She was scheduled on three other weddings this summer and this one paid more than those combined. She'd have more than enough to live on if she needed to supplement her income.

"I can't...I can't believe this." Then a terrible thought crossed her mind as she stared at the checks with only Sonora Star's name on them. "Are we sure it will go through?"

"She assured me we could deposit them immediately, as long as you would meet her for dinner tonight. She wants to get to know you and see if the two of you will suit."

Marley had her doubts, but it still didn't damper the hope that refused to abate. Life had dealt her and her family too many blows.

There was a chance that things could be turning around, right?

"I'll do it."

* * * *

Luke got to the Sweetheart Café first, and took a booth at the back, facing the door. He hadn't talked to Brent since yesterday's awkward breakfast, and had spent the afternoon driving around the area, checking out the river and a few other places that Rose from the diner had suggested.

But it was thinking about this lunch with Marley that had kept him up half the night.

It wasn't like he didn't have a healthy dating life in L.A. In fact, he'd gone out with a woman who he'd seriously thought about seeing again; she was nice, local, and hadn't minded that he was a cop.

Then he'd seen Marley. Her gray stormy eyes and blonde hair, her skin caramelized, as if she spent a lot of time outdoors. It had been an instant zing when he'd touched her, and he'd wanted to feel that again, preferably with his mouth on hers.

She walked through the door, scanning the restaurant until her gaze fell on him. A smile spread across her pretty face and she walked toward him, that soft-looking dress swirling around her long tan legs.

He stood up and held his hand out. "I worried you might not show."

"Sorry, I got caught up at work."

They both sat down, and Rose came over to their booth. To Luke's surprise, Rose leaned over and kissed the top of Marley's head.

"Afternoon, sweetheart."

"Hi, Mom," Marley said.

"Want a water? Iced tea?"

"How about coffee?"

Rose tsked. "You shouldn't drink too much. It will make you jittery."

"It's the only way I survive most days."

Rose shook her head and turned her attention to Luke. The look she gave him was a little less friendly than yesterday. "You want some coffee too?"

"Yes, please."

She nodded and took off for the pot.

"So, that's your mom."

"Yeah, sorry if she seemed a little miffed. She frowns on my caffeine intake. And dating tourists."

"I could always tell her you're my tour guide."

Marley set her menu on the end of the booth with a snort. "She'd never believe you. You're too handsome for this to be platonic."

Luke choked back a laugh. "Thank you?"

"You're welcome."

Damn, he liked the way those gray eyes twinkled like diamonds when the light hit them just right. And he appreciated her lack of filter.

"So, I haven't been shoved into the friend zone yet?"

She shrugged before crossing her arms on the table top. "We'll see how this goes. Who knows, you might end up being in the no zone."

"The no zone?" he asked.

"Yeah, no to everything including friends."

"Ouch. That's the last thing I want."

"Me too."

Her soft admission actually gave him butterflies, like a school girl with a crush.

Rose set down two cups and filled them with coffee. "What do you two want to eat? Not sure how our French Dip goes with coffee, but we can always give it a try."

"You should get it. It's amazing," Marley said to him.

"Then I'm sold."

"Hmm…a man who listens to a woman's opinion and takes it…" Rose teased. "Might be a keeper."

"Okay, that's enough of that. I'm going to have the cobb salad," Marley said.

"With no tomatoes. I'll get you two some waters too."

"Thanks, Rose," Luke said.

Rose went away, and Luke leaned back in the booth. "I'm a little surprised you brought me here. Most women I know don't want me to meet their moms until after date three."

"What, they want to know you can keep up in the sack before they take you seriously?"

Luke almost sprayed coffee out of his nose and mouth. "Yeah, actually."

"Maybe I wanted her to see what you looked like in case I disappear."

"Fair enough." He took another tentative drink, afraid she was going to say something to make him laugh again. When she didn't, he picked up the conversation. "So what do you do?"

"I'm a wedding consultant."

"Like a planner or something?"

"Yeah. How about you?" she asked.

"I'm a cop. SWAT officer."

Marley froze, her coffee cup resting just before her mouth. "A cop in L.A. That's a pretty dangerous job, isn't it?"

"No more than any other big city. I was in New York prior to that, and Afghanistan for four years straight out of high school."

Her frown deepened and he wondered if she was going to hold his job against him. "Were you in the military?"

"The Marines."

For whatever reason, she didn't seem as impressed by his professional history as some women were.

"So, are you a thrill seeker or do you pick these kind of jobs because you genuinely want to help people?" she asked.

Luke had never been asked anything like that and for a half a second, he wasn't sure whether he should be offended. Trivializing his work... that was a bold move.

"I guess it started out as a way to get out from under my father's thumb and from there I just...I wanted to make things better. To protect people."

Marley nodded, and he wanted to ask what that meant, but their food arrived. As they dived in, Luke asked, "Did you always want to consult on weddings?"

"No, not at all. I'm trying to get out of here and go to New York, get a job in publishing. I want to be a book editor."

"Yeah?" Luke studied her, a slow smile creeping across his face. "I don't know. I can't picture you in New York."

"Why not?"

"Because you look like you should be chasing butterflies through a meadow." He caught the shadow that fell over her face and quickly added, "I just mean that you have a soft, happy look about you. It's a nice quality. New Yorkers are tough as nails."

"Yeah, if that was supposed to make things better, it's not working. I'm stronger than I look."

Luke felt his ears and neck warm. "Sorry, sometimes I put my foot in my mouth and it's too big to pull out. New York would be lucky to have you."

A slow teasing smile split her lush red lips and he relaxed.

"That's better."

Chapter 4

Besides that slightly awkward chat about New York, Marley was enjoying herself. Luke was funny, charming, and nice to look at. Of course, as attracted to him as she was, it could never be anything more than a little fun. He lived in L.A. She was moving to New York. And then there was his job...

Not that she didn't think being a police officer was noble, but it was also dangerous. She'd already lost two people she loved: her father, when she was eight and Beth was four. Her parents had been coming back from Jackson, and been hit by a drunk driver. Her mom had been wearing her seat belt but dad had always been bad about that. She hated the fact that something so simple might have saved his life.

When they lost Beth eight years ago, Marley had cut people out, withdrawn into herself for months, and if it hadn't been for her mom, she wasn't sure she would have survived the pain.

There was no way she'd ever get serious about a guy who put on body armor and busted down people's doors in a hail of bullets. She couldn't go through loving and losing someone like that again.

Okay, so she watched too many action films. Didn't mean it changed the score. Luke was a distraction; she could enjoy him, but she didn't need to get attached.

He stood up and put several bills on the table, jarring her from her melancholy.

"Our food was comped, you know," she said.

"Yeah, but this way, your mom gets a nice tip."

Marley had already told him that her mom owned the café, but if he wanted to pay for their free meal, she wasn't going to stop him. As they passed by the glass display, Luke paused.

"What?"

"What the heck are those?" he asked.

Her gaze fell to what he was pointing at and she smiled. "Strawberry cream cheese tarts."

"Yeah, we're getting two of those."

She laughed, and went around to bag up two of the tarts. They were her favorite too.

Luke put another ten up on the counter and she placed the money in the till. As they left the café, she waved at her mom, who gave her a thumbs up. She supposed that meant she approved of Luke, not that it mattered.

"How much longer do you have for lunch?" Luke asked.

"I have another meeting at three, but nothing until then."

Her stomach flopped over as he grinned at her. "Good. Then why don't you point me in the direction of a nice spot to eat these."

"Well, there's a park just up the road along the river."

"Sounds perfect. Wanna take one car?" he asked.

"Sure, I'll drive."

They climbed into her white Malibu, and she headed down the road to the park. Marley laughed every time Luke opened the bag and inhaled.

"God, these smell good."

"If you keep sniffing them, I'm going to let you have them both."

"Cause you don't want to deprive me? You're so sweet," he said.

Marley made a face. "No, so that I don't accidentally eat one of your boogers."

Luke roared with laughter, and when she pulled into the parking lot, he was still guffawing.

"I like that you don't monitor everything you say carefully, afraid of offending someone," he said.

Marley's happiness dimmed a bit, thinking of Beth, who had never pulled any punches. Her sister had always been brutally honest, even when she knew she was about to die.

"If you let mom pick out the dress I'm buried in, I'll come back to haunt your ass."

"Yeah, well, life's too short to pussyfoot around. You got to take it by the balls and enjoy every minute of it."

"Agreed."

"Besides, I spend too much time holding my tongue with clients. No way I'm doing it in my personal life."

Luke climbed out first and Marley followed, trying to push Beth from her mind. She didn't like to think of her vibrant younger sister, who would forever be sixteen. Beth was still the only thing that could break her; just a flash of memory and she'd be weeping into a bottle of tequila like a hysterical baby.

When Luke took her hand, she jumped at the shock that shot up her arm, focusing on his concerned dark eyes. "You okay?"

She nodded. "Yeah, sure. I'm fine."

He didn't push for more, just held her hand as if they were in high school walking to class instead of on their first date. Could it be considered a date, if she knew there was no future? A hangout then. She wouldn't mind hanging out with Luke again, since he was coming back for the next two months. She could show him around, maybe even break her own rules on 'no casual hookups'.

After all, the last time she got laid was last year, when she was dating Garrett Ryan, before he transferred to a fire station in Montana. How was it that she had always seemed to be attracted to guys who put their lives on the line at their jobs?

They sat down on a bench facing the river, and Luke, after inspecting the pastry, handed it to her. "Booger free, I promise."

Marley chuckled softly. "Thanks."

"No problem." Luke took a bite of his, some of the white cream cheese filling smeared across his bottom lip and her fingers itched to reach out and remove it. With just a glide of her thumb across his mouth...

She crossed her legs and moved a bit away, eating her tart silently. Yeah, she was definitely up for a little under-the-covers playtime, but she wasn't quite sure about how to go about it. Although she was outspoken, she had never been the first to make a move. And with Sweetheart being so small, pickings were slim.

"Damn, these are good. Your mom made these?"

"Yep. If you like these, you should try my friend Rylie's stuff. She made these chai chocolate chip muffins that have just about become my new favorite treat."

"Really? Does she have a shop in town?" he asked.

"No, but she wants to open up a gourmet bakery eventually."

"Well, if they are anything like these, then I'm all for it. Sweetness is my weakness."

He popped the last of his tart in his mouth and hummed in clear appreciation. Marley took the bag from him and put the other half of hers inside, full.

"You're not going to finish?" His expression was one of horror, and she giggled.

"I just had lunch. I'll save it for later."

"You're crazy."

"Do you want it?" she asked.

"Hell yeah."

Marley made a face. "You sure? It's got my germs on it."

Luke threw back his head and laughed. Marley's gaze trailed over the thick muscles of his neck as they moved, and she was surprised at how turned on that deep rumble made her.

When his mirth dissolved into a simple grin, her heart skidded a bit.

"Believe me, your germs don't bother me a bit."

Marley swallowed past the sudden dryness in her mouth as his gaze dropped to her lips. "Then be my guest."

He really didn't seem to have any qualms about eating after her, and inhaled the rest of her tart.

"Better?"

"Oh, yeah." He opened his eyes, their brown depths slightly dreamy and it was a warm, soft look that made butterflies erupt in her stomach.

As if sensing her mood change he slid closer, his arm going along the back of the bench.

"You know, I had an ulterior motive for the tarts…"

"And that was?"

He bent his head towards her slowly, giving her every chance to pull away and her breath caught in her throat. Marley's heart beat rapidly as just a hairsbreadth away he whispered, "Because I was hoping you'd let me kiss you. And I wanted it to be sweet."

Marley melted into him as his lips covered hers, a gentle sweep that tightened the muscles between her thighs like corded knots. She leaned into his kiss, her right hand resting on his knee as the hand along the top of the bench came up to cradle the back of her head.

He had been right; it was sweet, and not just because his mouth tasted of sugar, cream, and strawberries. It was the way he lingered, his tongue tracing the inside of her bottom lip until it tangled with hers. Her body coiled up with every stroke, wanting to deepen the kiss and slide her leg across his lap until she was straddling him.

The sound of a car coming down the gravel road to the park reached her ears and she broke away to find Mrs. Baker in her silver minivan staring at them through the windshield, her mouth wide open in surprise. Mrs. Baker had been her freshman English teacher, and Marley remembered her in her early twenties, wearing bright skirts and her hair always perfectly pulled back in neat, intricate styles.

Oh good. Mrs. Baker's four kids were peeking around their mother's shoulder, looking at them too.

"I think I should probably get back to work," she said, softly.

"Only on the condition that you'll have dinner with me tomorrow."

She chuckled, one eye on Mrs. Baker as she opened her door and let her rambunctious brood out. Two seven-year-old boys, a five-year-old girl, and a three-year-old cherub ran by, hollering, "Hi, Marley!"

"Hey guys." Marley smiled at Mrs. Baker, who walked by with a large bag, probably packed full of water and snacks. "Hi, Mrs. Baker."

Since she'd quit teaching to stay home with her kids, Mrs. Baker had dropped the pristine image for a messy top knot, and yoga pants and preferred Marley call her Hailey. But it was still hard to break the habit, even though they were both adults.

"Hey there, Marley. You know you make me feel old when you call me that." She didn't even stop. In fact, she seemed to be jogging to keep up with her kids.

"Bye." Marley shook her head. "Sorry, I would have introduced you, but seems like she's in a hurry."

"It's fine, but what do say about dinner tomorrow night?"

Marley gave him a wide smile. "I guess having dinner with you wouldn't be so bad."

"Now, there's a vote of confidence," he teased.

"No, really, it sounds good. I'll look forward to it."

Luke's arms slipped around her waist before she could start walking back to the car. "Hey we still have a five-minute drive back. The dates not quite over."

"Except I'm not kissing you in front of my mother's café."

Luke gave her a wolfish grin. "Then we might have to make a pit stop."

Chapter 5

Marley walked into Shotgun Wedding Bar and Grill, the blast of a Chris Young song vibrating through the speakers. She was a little surprised that Sonora had wanted to meet here instead of Bow Ties, their upscale Italian restaurant. It wasn't that she didn't love Shotgun or its food, but it was just so...loud.

She recognized Sonora from Beth's old CD covers and the poster her little sister had hung on the back of her door, but honestly, she'd have stood out anyway. While the rest of the patrons were wearing jeans, tube tops and tanks, Sonora was in a flashy silver dress, the thin spaghetti straps showing off her tan shoulders and arms that almost seemed to glitter in the bar lights. Her hair spilled around her shoulders in a fountain of waves and her make-up was on point, highlighting her eyes and lips brilliantly. She was definitely a knockout.

Marley walked over to where the other woman was sitting in one of the booths. She waved at a couple of people who said hi, and stopped next to the table, smiling warmly as Sonora glanced up.

"Hey Sonora. I'm Marley Stevenson. Your new maid of honor."

Sonora's cold blue eyes raked over Marley, who was still wearing her yellow dress. From the frown on her face, Marley had a feeling Sonora wasn't impressed by her.

"Have a seat." The order was dismissive and it grated on Marley. She'd dealt with difficult people before, but she had a feeling this one was going to take the cake.

Sonora tossed her hair, glaring around the bar. "I have been waiting fifteen minutes for someone to come by and take my drink order, but nothing. I thought this place was supposed to cater to tourists."

Marley opened her mouth to respond, but Sonora just kept talking.

"Finally, here she comes."

"Hey there, Marley. How's it going?" Lucy Decker set down a couple of napkins and waters with a smile. In her early thirties with jet-black hair and a full figure in an A-line, she put her hands on her hips. "Are you waiting for anyone else, or—"

"My fiancée and his best man will be here in about an hour, but we would like to eat before they arrive."

Marley was a little put out about meeting the fiancée so soon, as she liked to have a few days with the bride first to really sell their stories. But from what Kelly had told her, Sonora didn't want to be embarrassed by having another friend bail as her maid of honor, since she'd already lost three in the two months she'd been engaged to Brent. She wasn't taking any more chances.

"Alright, well, what can I get you ladies?"

"I want a vodka martini with a twist and…" Sonora wrinkled her nose in what could only be described as distaste, "the Baby Mama Drama Spinach and Strawberry salad."

"Oh, that's one of my favorite things on the menu."

Sonora gave her a onceover, her sharp gaze doubtful. Marley bristled. "And I'd like my dressing on the side."

Lucy kept smiling, and Marley was glad that she hadn't picked up on Sonora's attitude. "Sure thing. How about you, Marley?"

"I'll take the Call the Preacher Bacon Burger with onion rings and a root beer."

"You got it, babe."

Lucy walked away and Sonora sneered. "I think her favorite thing on the menu is what *you* just ordered. I bet she eats two or three a day."

Marley thought that was harsh, but she wasn't there to help Sonora grow a heart size. She was there to plan a wedding.

Marley pulled her iPad out of her purse and opened her checklist app. "We need to get started if your fiancée will be here soon. Since we are just about eight weeks out, it doesn't give us a lot of time to plan. I thought we could start with something fun, like your bachelorette party. What do you think of a spa weekend in Tahoe?"

Sonora made a face. "I was thinking that we could do something exciting, like a cruise to Hawaii or maybe a weekend in Cancun."

Oh, hell no. There is no way I'm going to spend a week babysitting a bunch of drunk women in another country.

"Believe me, I want you to be happy, but most cruises are booked months to a year in advance. At this point, we might be able to find some rooms below deck, but they won't be great. Plus, an overcrowded boat is a recipe for the stomach flu days before your wedding." Before Sonora could argue, Marley rushed on. "Also, a trip to Cancun is going to get expensive, especially a last minute one during tourist season, and your other five bridesmaids might not be able to afford it. At least in Tahoe, we can do lots of fun things and we don't have to pay for airfare."

"Like what?" Sonora asked.

"Well, we could rent a suite, and after our massages we could gamble, go to the beach, the clubs, and—"

"Fine, we'll go to Tahoe." Sonora sat back like a petulant child and waved at Marley impatiently. "What ideas do you have about *my* bridal shower?"

Marley stiffened for a half a second at Sonora's attitude, but she pulled herself together like she always did. She had worked too hard and gone through too much to let one rude bride get to her.

"I was thinking one of the vineyard clubhouses would work nicely. I just need to call in a favor. I understand from your file that you have thirty-five people you're planning on inviting for the bridal shower—"

"No, there are a hundred people being invited to the bridal shower."

Marley blinked at her, reigning in the urge to yell. "I'm sorry, I was under the impression that you were having an intimate bridal shower for close friends and family. A hundred people may be a bit hard to accommodate, especially with the shortened time frame—"

Sonora snapped her fingers at Marley and sat forward, her eyes flashing. "I am the bride, and you are the help. You are paid to make my dreams come true, right? So, why don't you earn the hefty commission I'm paying you and do your job?"

Prickly heat spread over Marley's skin, anger tightening every muscle in her body.

Don't you mean the hefty commission your parents are paying me?

As Lucy came back and set their drinks down, Marley was tempted to stand up and dump hers on Sonora's head. Of all the brides she'd worked with over the last seven years, never had one been so self-centered. Most of them were just stressed or nervous. Sonora was in a class by herself.

Marley could just tell Kelly to ask one of the other girls to take over. So it took a few more months to leave Sweetheart…

"Well, howdy sis."

If Marley thought Sonora's sneer was ugly, the molten rage turning her tan skin purple was vile.

"What are *you* doing here?"

"Mom thought you could use some help." The cute blonde with a sprinkle of freckles across her nose and face ignored her sister's obvious upset and held her hand out to Marley. "Hey there, I'm Kendall, Sonora's younger sister."

"Hey, I'm Marley, an old friend of Sonora's."

Kendall's forehead knitted. "Oh yeah? She's never mentioned you. How do you know—"

"I met her in rehab," Sonora snapped.

Marley's eyebrows shot up. That was not the cover story she'd been given. They were supposed to have met at summer camp when they were kids and kept in touch.

"Oh." Kendall's smile was a little strained. "Sorry. It's really great to meet you. Is it okay if I join you?"

Marley started to say, "Of course," but Sonora broke in. "No, we've got stuff to talk about before Brent gets here."

An awkward silence shifted over their booth and Marley noticed the way Kendall's hands clenched. She wouldn't blame her for punching her big sister. Hell, Marley was tempted to do the honors.

Then again, it probably wasn't a good idea to fraternize with anyone close to Sonora. Getting intimate with friends and family of clients was frowned upon.

"Fine, I'll sit at the bar. I'd hate to cramp your *style*."

Kendall walked away and Lucy brought their food over. Marley didn't say anything to Sonora about the exchange, but she really wanted to. Instead, she devoured her onion rings with gusto until she caught the disgusted look on Sonora's face.

What, do I have sauce on my face? "What's wrong?"

"You eat like a starving gorilla."

Marley stared at her, her temper blazing. That was it, she was going to kick this snotty little princess's ass—

"Hey ladies." A handsome brown haired man stepped next to their table. "Sorry, we're a little early." He held his hand out to Marley. "I'm Brent Harwood, Sonora's fiancée . You must be Marley."

Drawing in a calming breath, Marley took his hand with a polite smile. "It's nice to meet you. I've heard a lot about you."

Not from Sonora, of course. Her sources had been Kelly's file on Brent and several Google searches. She knew that he ran his family's company with his two older brothers, was involved with several charities, and had been featured in *People* Magazine as one of their thirty under thirty to watch.

On paper, she had no idea what he was doing with this diva. In person, well, he was either incredibly shallow or a blind idiot.

"All good, I hope." Brent slid in next to Sonora and kissed her cheek. "How's the food? We didn't have time to eat before we came."

Sonora shot a sour glance toward Marley's plate. "Fine, if you like lots of saturated fat and slow service."

Marley was too concerned with what Brent had said to react to Sonora's sneer. "Who is we?"

"His Neanderthal best friend." Sonora gave Brent a feminine, glossy pout. "For the record, I agreed to have dinner with *you*. Luke is just an unfortunate addition."

Marley's heart started pounding.

No. It couldn't be *her* Luke.

"Could you try to get along with him for one night? I know you two got off on the wrong foot, but he's been my best friend half my life. It would mean a lot if you would try to be civil."

Marley was too busy having a panic attack to listen to Sonora's response. The blood thundered in her ears as she craned her neck toward the door. *Would it be too weird if I just made a run for it?*

"I have the beers and she said she'd be over to take our order—hey!"

Too late. Marley turned and found herself staring up into Luke's dark surprised eyes.

"What are you doing here?"

* * * *

Luke couldn't believe Marley was the old friend from rehab Sonora had told them about. First off, he didn't get that vibe from her. She seemed so down to earth and innocent and beyond that, he couldn't imagine her genuinely liking Sonora.

"I was meeting my friend Sonora for dinner. What are you doing here?"

Why did she sound so irritated? "I'm Brent's best man. I told you I was up here on and off for the next couple months for a wedding." Luke reached out and punched Brent in the shoulder. "The things I do for this guy."

"Oh, I see."

Luke squeezed in next to her, his arm going to rest behind her shoulders. "This is the girl I was telling you about, Brent."

"Ah, he hasn't shut up about you all day. Funny coincidence, you both being in the wedding."

"Yeah, it's hilarious," Marley muttered next to him.

No, he wasn't imagining it. She definitely was not happy to see him. Sonora glanced up from her salad, her eyes narrowed. "You two are involved?"

"No," Marley said swiftly.

"We went to lunch earlier," Luke said at the same time, shooting Marley a frown. Why was she pretending there was nothing going on with them?

Sonora took a ladylike bite of her salad, still watching Marley intently. Luke got the feeling Sonora was silently telling Marley she did not approve.

Marley focused on Brent, ignoring Sonora and him. "I was just talking to Sonora about the things left to do for the wedding—"

"Hey, Sonora, isn't that Kendall at the bar?" Brent blurted, interrupting Marley.

Sonora stabbed her salad viciously. "Yes."

"Why isn't she sitting with us?" Brent's voice was tight and angry, surprising Luke. That was what set him off? Sonora ignoring her little sister?

"Because we were having a private dinner and she just showed up."

"That's bullshit and you know it. I'll be right back." He got up and walked towards the bar.

Sonora tossed down her napkin with a sigh and followed him.

Alone, Luke leaned over her, his lips resting against the shell of her ear. "I missed you."

She jerked away from him. "Stop it."

Completely thrown by her hostility, he asked, "Stop what?"

"We can't do this."

"Do what now?"

She pulled away from him, putting her back to the wall at the edge of the booth. "I can't date you. I'm sorry, but it is just too complicated."

What the fuck? Considering just six hours ago, he'd had his tongue in her mouth, this was coming out of left field. "Whoa, why? Because Princess Sonora won't approve? Who cares?"

Marley held out a hand, as if she was afraid he was going to keep moving closer. "I do. She's my friend and it's her wedding. I don't want to cause any kind of drama for her."

Luke snorted, not believing that for a second. "Please, Sonora creates drama no matter what anyone around her is doing. Besides, I thought things were going good."

The waitress came by and Marley asked for a box before she answered him. Once she was gone, Marley shook her head.

"Look, I knew this was going to be a temporary fling when you first flirted with me, but now, with the wedding and how busy we're both going to be, I think I'd rather just end it before one of us gets hurt and we ruin Sonora and Brent's special day."

Un-fucking believable. He'd been walking around like a sappy, frolicking idiot all day and she was just bailing?

"Don't I get a say in this? How did you know things were going to be just temporary? Maybe I'd fall madly in love with you and follow you back to New York."

"Please," she scoffed. "Don't make this into something it's not. We had one date and as nice as it was, I don't believe for one second that you were ever planning on falling in love with me, just like I wasn't going to fall for you."

"Gee, you're such a sweetheart."

"Don't call me sweetheart."

Their gazes clashed, and Luke was tempted to lean in and kiss her, just to feel her melt against him.

Instead, he turned away and took a long pull of his beer.

The waitress came back and handed Marley her box. As she was packing up her food, Sonora, Brent, and Kendall sat down, Sonora sulking as she was squished between them.

"Luke, have you met Sonora's sister, Kendall?"

He shook the cute blonde's hand and flashed her a smile, aware of Marley stiffening beside him. Did she think he was flirting?

I hope so.

Instead, she gave Kendall a sunny smile. "Here Kendall, you can take my spot. You guys look like a pack of sardines over there. I need to get home anyway."

"But we're not done talking about the wedding," Sonora protested.

"We can talk about it tomorrow. We'll head out to breakfast and go over everything somewhere a little less loud. Don't worry, I've got you, girl."

Sonora shot her a withering look. "I hate being called *girl*."

Luke glanced between them. Something didn't fit. If the two of them were such good friends, wouldn't there be more warmth?

Marley's smile tightened, and he wondered if she was gritting her teeth. "Sorry, I forgot."

Luke slid out of the booth, but he didn't move back far enough. When Marley passed by him, she rubbed against his chest. He ignored the fact that his skin prickled with goosebumps and nodded at the rest of the table. "I'm going to walk Marley out."

She held her box of food in front of her like a shield. "That's not necessary."

"Yeah, it is, so let's go."

Marley rolled her eyes with a heavy sigh and after wishing the table another polite goodbye, headed for the exit. Luke followed her across the bar and out the door. The parking lot was filling up pretty fast for a Monday night, and as they reached her car, he put his hand on the door to keep her from opening it.

She turned toward him, but for the first time, this straightforward girl was avoiding his gaze.

"I don't know what is going on or what she has on you, but I'm not a guy to beg. You don't want to see me anymore, fine, but I know it's not some bullshit about sparing Sonora's feelings. The least you could do is be honest."

Finally, she looked up at him in the fading light and glared. "Ever think I'm just not that into you?"

He stiffened at her cutting words, and then relaxed, a slow grin spreading across his face. He boxed her in with his hands against the top of her car, leaning in. He heard the sharp intake of her breath as his lips descended toward hers, hovering there. His nose nuzzled her cheek, sliding up until his mouth brushed her ear. He felt her sway towards him, her breathing rapid and sexy as hell.

"Nah, that ain't it."

Pushing away from her, he turned and headed back into the bar. He was going to figure out what Marley was hiding, especially if it was something that could hurt his best friend.

And he planned on having a lot of fun doing it.

Chapter 6

Marley sat in the corner booth at the Sweetheart Café, sipping on her coffee as if it was a lifeline. She'd hardly slept last night, unable to stop thinking about Luke and the way he'd hovered over her. Arrogant. Knowing. *Sexy as hell.* Not even snuggling with Butters while watching *Supernatural* had pushed the sensation of his body pressing against her from her mind. She kept telling herself he was just a hot guy, easy to forget.

If only she really believed it.

"Hi. Marley, right?" a voice said above her.

Marley looked up to find Kendall, Sonora's sister, standing at the end of her table, looking adorable in a floral dress and jean jacket, her honey hair pulled back in a messy ponytail.

"Hey, Kendall. How are you?"

"Good. Can I join you?" she asked.

Sonora was due to arrive any minute and considering how she'd reacted to her sister's presence last night, it was probably asking for trouble to say yes.

"Sure, have a seat. Your sister's on her way."

Kendall raised an eyebrow at her. "You actually think Sonora is going to be on time?"

"She was on time last night."

"Maybe, but Sonora is not a morning person. Brunch is breakfast to her."

Marley chuckled, liking Kendall. She reminded her of Beth and the shit she used to give Marley.

A wave of sadness rushed through her as she imagined Beth in Kendall's place. What she wouldn't give for one more breakfast with her baby sister.

"Enough about my sister. I know you're friends, so I'll try to behave."

"That's big of you," Marley said. "What do you do, Kendall?"

"I'm a photographer. That's the only reason I was even invited to Sonora's wedding." Kendall's face scrunched up in a disgusted expression. "She may hate my guts, but she can't ignore free talent. Or actually, my parents can't ignore the fact that I'm one less expense they have to cover."

"I knew they were paying for the wedding." And considering the expense it was going to cost them, she found it odd that they wouldn't pay their other daughter.

"Oh, yeah, anything for their precious Sonora." Kendall sighed loudly and shook herself. "I'm sorry, I said I'd stop. I don't mind doing my sister's wedding. I love my sister."

Marley bit her lip to keep from laughing because Kendall's tone and expression totally belied her words. "I want to see your pictures. Do you have a website?"

Kendall grinned and pulled it up on her cell phone, turning it over to show her. Marley scrolled through the photos, impressed at the quality and lighting. She paused on a photo of a bride and groom running through a field of flowers, the sun setting behind them and the bride turned back, smiling at the camera.

"I love this one." Marley showed her the photo, and Kendall's smile brightened.

"That's one of my favorites too. I actually entered it in a contest last year, and won an award for it."

"Really? That's amazing." Marley handed the phone back. "Where do you live?"

"I still live in Loco, Texas, where Sonora and I grew up."

"You should be in New York or L.A. Your photos are flawless. Better than some of the photographers around here."

"I don't take pictures for the money. I do it because I love creating something beautiful. Capturing moments that people will treasure." Kendall's eyes took on a dreamy quality as she continued. "When I think that people in future generations will look at the pictures I took of their grandparents or parents, it's worth it to me. Plus, I stay so busy I do alright."

Marley shifted in her seat, embarrassed. "I'm sorry, I shouldn't have assumed otherwise."

"Don't apologize. I appreciate someone who speaks their mind. My parents and sister are so fake, sometimes I check for batteries."

Marley choked on her coffee, wheezing with laughter. "Oh, my God, that visual."

"It's true. My parents started the restaurant chain Sonny's Burger Shack. From the time I learned to walk, I knew everything was about appearances.

And once Sonora hit it big, they used her popularity to boost the business. They have pictures of her all over the restaurants even though she altered her last name. She changed it from Stadarski to Star because she knew she was going to make it big, they tell people." Kendall laughed. "Sorry, do I sound bitter?"

She did a bit, but Marley couldn't blame her. It was always hard to live in a sibling's shadow.

"I shouldn't bitch about them. I love my family."

Marley found herself reaching out to take the other woman's hand. "I had a little sister, and believe me, I know how they can drive you crazy."

Kendall met her gaze, her blue-green eyes studying her seriously. "Had?"

Marley realized the door she'd opened too late and her chest tightened. "Beth. She died."

Kendall opened her mouth, probably to offer her condolences, but Sonora chose that moment to breeze through the door in a pair of black shiny shorts, and midriff-baring black and white halter top. The straps of her wedged heels wrapped up her tan, muscular calves, and as she clacked toward their table, she slid her big black sunglasses up, her eyes narrowed on her sister.

Kendall squeezed Marley's hand and pulled away. She probably assumed that Marley was going to let Sonora kick her out of their table.

Not this time.

Sonora stopped at the end of the table and placed her hands on her curvy hips. "What are you doing here?"

"Relax, I just came in to grab breakfast and thought I'd get to know Marley a little." Kendall started to slide out of the booth, but Marley put her hand on her arm.

"She can join us, Sonora. After all, we could use the extra help if you want to get this wedding together in eight weeks."

Marley was sure that Sonora's head was going to shoot through the air, there was so much steam coming out of her ears.

"We can handle it."

"No, we can't," Marley said, firmly.

This was it. Good-bye bonus. She was getting fired and Kelly was going to be pissed.

To Marley's surprise, Sonora slammed her purse down next to Kendall. "Scoot over, then."

Kendall's jaw dropped, but she did as her older sister said.

Once Sonora was composed again, she snapped her menu open and glared at Marley over it. "About my bridal shower…"

Marley waited, hoping for Sonora's concession that one hundred was just too many people.

"My mother sent me a list of additional people to invite, so the count is actually more like one hundred and fifty."

And there it was. Her punishment for defying Sonora's will. To accomplish the impossible.

With a forced smile, Marley pulled out her note pad and a pen from her tote. "I'll figure something out."

* * * *

Luke went with Brent and his other groomsmen to get fitted for their tuxedos before heading out for drinks. Since the tuxes were the only task that Sonora appointed to Brent, he'd wanted to get it done and over with.

Brent's two older brothers, Marcus and Edward sat at the bar, talking shop, while Paul and Wes, two of his friends from college, played darts in the corner of Shotgun Wedding Bar and Grill. They had all taken the week off to help Brent get ready, but now, it just seemed more like a guy's week.

Brent took a long pull of his beer and set his mug down with a thunk. "I am getting married in less than two months."

"I know that, Captain Obvious," Luke said, studying his friend. Did Brent look a little green around the gills? Could be the three beers prior to the one in his hand.

"Yeah."

Brent got really quiet and Luke put his hand on his shoulder, giving him a little shake. "Hey, you okay man?"

"I'm fine. Fine."

Luke wasn't convinced, but he didn't get a chance to question him further before Brent started waving.

"Sonora. Kendall! Hey!"

Luke glanced toward the door to find the two sisters and Marley walking inside. His heart skipped a little at his first glimpse of her in twenty-four hours. He hadn't been able to stop thinking of her, and had looked for her everywhere today, but for such a small town, it had been easy for her to avoid him.

Until now.

Sonora's face was scrunched up like she'd just sucked a lemon, but Kendall was all smiles.

And Marley, well, she wouldn't even meet his gaze.

"Well, hey there," Kendall said. "You a little tipsy, big man?"

Brent grinned. "Men do not get tipsy. We get buzzed."

"Or drunk," Luke offered.

"Smashed!" Paul called in his British accent, making it sound like, *smoshed.*

Sonora pushed next to Brent, her lips pursed. "Sweetie, should you really be drinking? Too much beer will make you bloat."

Kendall breathed out an exasperated, "Geez, chill out, Sonny—"

"Don't call me that!"

Kendall threw up her hands. Luke could tell a fight was brewing between the two, but Marley stepped in, putting her hand on Kendall's arm.

"Come on, let's get some drinks."

The younger sister went with Marley without a fight, and Luke watched Marley lean over to whisper something to Kendall. That was definitely an interesting development.

"Why do you treat her like that?" Brent growled.

Luke swung back to Sonora and Brent, surprised at his friend chastening his fiancée for the second time in two days. And all because of her strained relationship with her sister.

"What? Because I hate being called Sonny? She knows that and only does it to irritate me."

Brent swallowed the rest of his beer and poured another.

"Are you sure you want to do that?" Sonora asked.

Luke got up from the table when Brent gave Sonora a dark scowl, determined to get out of the line of fire. Walking over to stand next to Marley, he couldn't stop from inhaling her soft, floral scent. Was it her perfume or shampoo?

"Mind if I join you ladies?"

Kendall smiled at him around Marley. "Sure, Luke."

Marley took her drink from the bartender, staring straight ahead. Just to bother her, he scooted closer and leaned over to whisper, "You look really good in those jeans, by the way."

A sharp jab to his stomach made him spill his beer all over the floor. She'd slammed her elbow into him.

"Was that really necessary?" he asked.

Marley finally turned, eyeing him over the rim of her beer mug. "Yes, because you were invading my personal space, which I value."

Luke was pretty sure she didn't want him getting close because she liked him there, but he let it go.

"Fine!" Sonora shouted behind them, and they all swung around to watch the drama unfold. "I'm going back to the hotel. You can find someplace else to sleep tonight."

She stomped her black heeled feet right out the door, and Luke watched Brent, waiting for him to get up and go after his fiancée .

Instead, he sat there, tipping back more beer. Luke almost went to check on him when Paul and Wes beat him to it.

Marley stood up. "I better go make sure she's okay, since I drove. Do you need a ride?"

Kendall shook her head, and Luke noticed she was watching Brent too, her face a mask of concern. "No, I'm fine."

Luke got up with her, leaving his beer on the counter.

"What are you doing?" Marley hissed.

"Calling it a night. Figured I'd walk you out."

He could tell by the tight set of her jaw she wanted to tell him no, but didn't. She did do her best to ignore him as he walked along beside her out the door.

"Damn, where did she go?"

Luke scanned the parking lot, but there was no sign of Sonora. "She couldn't have made it far on those heels. Maybe she grabbed a cab or something?"

"There are no cabs in Sweetheart."

Luke watched her nibble her lip nervously. She seemed genuinely worried about Sonora. "Hey, she probably just needed to blow off some steam and started walking."

Marley pulled out her phone. "I'm just going to call to be sure."

Luke waited, thinking she was a better person than he was.

"Hey Sonora, it's Marley. I came after you, but you must have headed back to the hotel. Call me. Let me know you're okay."

Luke waited until she'd slipped her phone back into her pocket to speak.

"Hey, speaking of rides, do you mind giving me one back to the hotel? I rode with Brent, and he looks like he really wants to tie one on tonight."

She hesitated, and he was sure she was going to tell him no.

"Fine, but no flirting."

Luke grinned. "Now, darlin', I can't promise that. You bring it out of me."

Marley rolled her eyes with a grumble, but headed into the row of cars. He followed behind, his gaze traveling down to her ass.

He hadn't been lying when he'd told her how good she looked in those jeans.

She unlocked the doors but before he climbed in, she tapped the top of the car.

"Check out my ass again, and you're going to find your balls in your throat."

The colorful imagery only made him grin wider. "I love it when you talk dirty to me."

Chapter 7

Marley was freaking certifiable. It was the only reasonable explanation for why she'd agreed to drive him back to his hotel.

"Are you hungry?" he asked.

She glanced away from the road for a second to look at him. He was taking up her whole passenger side and his shoulder was edging an inch from hers. Whether he was doing it on purpose or not, she didn't know, but she hated the way his nearness affected her.

A horn blared and Luke jerked up. "Watch out!"

Marley turned the wheel in time to avoid a head on with a silver pick-up, who laid on his horn again angrily.

"I'm so sorry!" Marley panted.

"Jesus, I know I'm distracting, but maybe you should watch the road."

Marley's face burned and she wished that there was some place in her car to hide.

"Or, if you really can't wait to get me alone, you could pull over and—"

"Not. Going. To. Happen," she snarled.

"There she is. Thought you'd gone mute for a second."

"You're a jerk."

"Now, come on. I'm just messing with you a bit. I know you aren't attracted to me."

Marley figured he was fishing, so she didn't respond, even though her first reaction was to tell him not to be an idiot.

"Because if you were attracted to me, then there would be no reason for you to pull the plug on whatever was happening between us."

Okay, that was just about enough of that. She made a hard left into the hotel parking lot. Once she'd slipped her car into an open space, she shoved it into park and turned to glare at him.

"Look, you're hot and I get that you can't fathom one single reason why that wouldn't be enough for most girls to just hop into the sack with you, but I am actually thinking about the big picture here. You are coming up here every other weekend until your best friend gets married, and then you're not coming back again. I am planning to move across the country come September. Sure, I could jump into bed with you and it might be great for a fling, but then again, you might be lousy in bed and then I have to deal with seeing you all summer, and it will be awkward and horrible and I just don't want to take the chance."

Luke had turned in his seat midway through her rant and now, faced her with an annoyingly amused smirk. "I can't believe you imagined me in bed after one date."

Marley wanted to reach out, grab him by those interesting ears and yank. "Out of all that very clear reasoning, all you got was that I imagined sex with you? Believe me, you're not that special. The other night while watching *Supernatural* I imagined a three way between me, Dean, and Sam."

"That's either kinky or disturbed. You know they're brothers, right?"

Marley laughed before she could stop herself. "God, is everything a joke to you?"

"I'm sorry, I just assumed you were joking about fantasies involving fictional characters."

"The actors are real."

"And married," he said. "I never pegged you for a home wrecker."

"I would never! My whole point is that I think about sex with random people, especially if I go on a date with them, but you are my friend's fiancée's best man. That alone is a recipe for disaster. Can you just forget about that one, insignificant date and try to act like an adult about this?"

Luke got a naughty grin on his face, and he leaned forward, his lips mere inches from hers.

"I tell you what. If I kiss you right now, for fifteen seconds, and you feel absolutely nothing, I will treat you like I've never imagined you naked and writhing beneath me."

Oh for the love of chocolate, why did he have to say something like that? The sheer imagery was making her knees tremble... and she was sitting down!

I can do this. I am a professional. It's just one little kiss. Think about the job. The check. Getting the hell out of Sweetheart.

"Fine."

He pressed a finger to her lips. "But if you kiss me back, then you can't keep treating me like a freaky fungus attached to your shoe."

"I haven't—"

The pressure against her mouth increased, silencing her. "You have."

Marley swallowed. Hard. "Then I apologize."

Luke slid his thumb across her cheek as he tucked a piece of hair behind her ear, and she struggled to hide the shiver his touch created. "I don't want your apology, darlin'. I want you."

Marley's heart slammed against her chest as he lowered his head and took her mouth with his.

And kept taking it. His tongue teasing against her sealed lips and she fought the trembles, the shocks of electricity as his hand came up to cradle the back of her head.

Five. Six. Seven. Eight.

Too late, she realized her mouth had opened and his tongue was tangling with hers. She stopped counting as her hands came up, cupping the sides of his head as she kissed him back, forgetting that she was supposed to be resisting his warmth, the spicy scent of his cologne and the deep, rumble in his chest as he groaned.

A loud knock on Marley's window made her jerk away from Luke in horror, while he cursed a blue streak. What the hell had she been thinking? Kissing a man she hardly knew in the parking lot of The Love Shack Hotel?

She rolled down the window and found Dustin Kent standing outside her door, grinning.

"Hey, Marley, I thought that was your car."

Marley's jaw clenched. Dustin knew damn good and well it was her car and had knocked just to be an ass. They had known each other their whole lives, but no one could call them friends. The Kents were the wealthiest family in Sweetheart, owning the Castle Vineyard, and Dustin had become a millionaire by selling an app he designed in college. That and the fact that he resembled Tom Welling from *Smallville*, with his piercing blue eyes, dark hair, and angel face, should have made him the top of any woman's hook up list, but Marley couldn't stand him.

"What do you need, Dustin?"

He raised one dark eyebrow, his blue eyes twinkling. "Aren't you going to introduce me to your boyfriend?"

"No, now what do you want?"

Dustin's lips pressed together and he slid a pair of sunglasses over his eyes like an 80s movie villain. "Oh nothing that can't wait until you're back in the office tomorrow."

What in the name of all that was holy did that mean?

"You two have fun."

He turned away, whistling like one of the seven dwarves as he swaggered toward the silver penis-shaped car he drove.

"Who is that guy?" Luke asked.

Marley closed her window, her back still to him. She could feel the heat in her cheeks and hated that she'd let herself get caught up in him. "An annoyance."

When she turned around to face him again, she expected him to try to kiss her again, but he just sat there studying her.

"So, you work with him?" he asked.

"No I—"

Suddenly, her body went cold. He was going to the office tomorrow. What if he told Kelly what he'd seen? If Kelly asked her who she'd been making out with, there was no way she could lie.

But she couldn't get fired, either.

"Shit. Shit. Shit. I have to go."

"Marley, what is going on?"

"You need to get out."

His expression darkened. "I thought we had a deal about you treating me like a maggot?"

"It was fungus, and this has nothing to do with how I feel about you! This is about me possibly losing my job."

"I don't see how us kissing—"

"I know you don't but you still need to get out!"

She hadn't meant to scream. Hell, she never screamed, even the time that one of her brides had thrown a glass of champagne in her face and told her she was an idiot. But without Something Borrowed, she'd never get out of here.

"Got it." His tone was cold as he opened the door and stepped out. "I won't push you anymore. Despite recent events, I don't normally have to beg women to go out with me."

"Luke, I—"

He shut her door without waiting for her to finish and she didn't have time to melt down, to chase him down and apologize. Besides, how would she explain anyway? *Sorry I can't get involved with you because I'm a fake bridesmaid and I signed a confidentiality agreement that will not only screw me, but my boss if I violate it?*

There was nothing she could do to fix things with Luke now. She had to see Kelly.

She made it across town to the little white ranch house Kelly owned, and pulled right up to the garage like a bat out of hell. By the time she stood on the porch, she was sucking in wind as though she couldn't get enough and knocked hard.

Kelly opened the door, staring out at Marley with wide eyes. "Marley, what's wrong?"

"I have to tell you something?"

"Something that couldn't wait until the morning?"

"No, it can't."

Kelly nodded and stepped back to let her walk inside. The walls were painted a pristine white, with a pine wood floor that shined as if it had just been waxed. Colorful throws covered the back of plain brown couches, and the only wall decoration was one painting of a little girl running through the woods.

"Do you want something to drink? Coffee?"

"Can I just have a glass of water?" Marley's throat was so dry, she was afraid she was going to have a coughing fit.

"Sure, you sit. Relax a spell and just take a breath."

Marley sat on the soft couch, trying to slow her breathing. Without warning, Kelly's black and white cat, Pepper, popped over the back of the couch and slid down. He placed his feet on her lap and demanded pets by bumping her shoulder with his head.

"Hey, Peps. How did you know I needed a little support?"

"He's intuitive that way," Kelly said as she reentered the room. Marley blushed, wishing she hadn't overheard that.

Kelly set the water down on the coffee table and tucked her feet up as she climbed onto the other couch. "Okay, spill. What's got you all in a tither?"

There was nothing for Marley to do but dive head first into the issue. "I met someone a few days ago, and it's been awhile since I had a date, so I went out with him."

Kelly's expression lit up happily and it twisted Marley's stomach up more. "Well, that's great, Marley."

"Yeah, it was, until I found out he was the best man for Sonora's wedding."

Kelly's face fell. "Oh, dear."

"Yeah. And I tried to tell him that we had to pull the plug, but...Dustin Kent saw us kissing. And he said he would see me at the office tomorrow, and I didn't want you thinking that this was deliberate or that it is ever going to happen again, but it was the only way he would stop pursuing me and—"

Kelly reached across the space and grabbed her free hand. "Marley, breathe."

She let out a huge breath.

"Now, I get that you didn't know his connection, and if it would make you more comfortable, I would take you off the account. However, it's a little late for that, so I am going to trust you. You've been with me for a long time and always been the height of propriety and professionalism. I know that you will be able to pull the plug on this, no problem."

Wow, that was easier than I thought it would be.

"But if there's any more impropriety, I'm going to have to let you go. You understand?"

And there it was. She'd worn out her one chance.

"Yes, you won't have to worry. I'll avoid him like the plague." As an afterthought, Marley asked, "Why *is* Dustin coming into the office tomorrow?"

Kelly grinned at her devilishly, and Marley knew she wasn't going to like the answer.

"Because I hired him."

Marley blinked at her in surprise. "For what?"

"Well, Dustin made an excellent point that sometimes grooms need groomsmen, so I've agreed to take him on a trial basis."

"But…he's loathsome."

Kelly laughed, a light, tingling sound that reminded Marley of Christmas bells. "Yes, but he is also loaded, respected, and no one will question him being friends with celebrities if he shows up in their wedding pictures. Besides, it's just an experiment and we could use a little manliness around the office."

Marley didn't bother questioning Dustin's manliness, just nodded in acceptance.

"So, is there anything else we need to discuss?" Kelly asked. "You're all set for the Keller, Vaughn, and Newman weddings?"

Marley nodded. "Yes, we're all good."

"Good, because I've got a row of Oreos and a whole season of *The Walking Dead* to binge watch, so scoot."

Chapter 8

Surprisingly, Luke didn't see Marley again until Saturday morning. Sonora and Brent must have made up after their epic blow up because she'd arranged for the entire bridal party to have dance lessons. She wanted some big, elaborate dance number during the reception. Luke thought it was the stupidest thing he'd ever heard, but he was there.

Which has nothing to do with Marley.

No, he was done playing games. If hot and cold was her thing, then she could do it with someone else.

He sat next to Brent, watching the door. When it swung open, he hated that he sat forward in anticipation, eager to get his first glance at Marley in three days.

Kendall stepped inside with her hair in loose waves around her shoulders, a simple navy dress swinging around her legs.

He looked over at Brent when he shifted in his chair and noticed the way his friend had leaned on his knees, his eyes following Kendall's every move as she came toward them.

Luke didn't have long to wonder about his friend's interest before Sonora and Marley came in, obviously arguing.

"I am telling you what their manager explained to me. They will be out of the country touring, and are not flying back from *Ireland* to play at your wedding," Marley said, her voice strained through her teeth.

Sonora's face was blotchy with temper and she flicked her hair over her shoulder with a huff. "Then call the next contact on the list I gave you. Really, Marley, it's not that hard."

"I called all of them. Every single one and they all said no." Marley seemed to realize her voice had started to rise, and she took it down a notch as she continued, "Why not just go with a local band, or even a DJ?"

"Because I am neither tacky nor desperate."

"All due respect, you are seven weeks out from your wedding so, yeah, you kind of are."

Holy shit. Luke started moving, hoping to pull Marley out of the line of fire before Sonora went bridezilla on her ass.

Brent stepped in just as Sonora's face turned purple. "She's right, babe. It's our fault for putting stuff off. Why don't we have Marley set up a couple auditions with some of the local bands and we'll see if any of them work out?"

Kendall smiled, nodding in agreement. "Yeah, sis, it's no big deal. Besides, a DJ can play everything—"

"Mind your own fucking business!" Sonora screamed. "When I want the opinion of an overrated little nobody, I'll ask for it."

The whole dance hall went dead silent. As if she realized what she'd said, Sonora's eyes widened just before she burst into tears and ran out the door again.

Luke watched in surprise as Marley went to Kendall and put her arm around her. "She's under a lot of stress. She didn't mean it."

"Yeah she did," Kendall said softly.

Luke stroked his chin. Why had Marley comforted Kendall instead of chasing down her distraught friend?

Brent seemed torn, but ended up following his fiancée . Luke waited as Kendall left the room, probably to go to the bathroom. Sonora's other bridesmaids and Brent's groomsmen stood talking in the corner, and he wondered if Marley would ignore him to join them.

"Well, that was dramatic," she said, flopping down next to him.

"Yeah well, that's Sonora."

"I know, but does she have to be so damn hateful to Kendall? I just can't stand the way she treats her."

Again, it was as though Marley didn't even *know* Sonora. He'd been around her less than four months and it hadn't taken him long to realize there was nothing redeemable about her. How had Marley been so blind to her friend for over a year?

"That's how Sonora treats everyone. Kendall just gets it worse than most because they're family. You always hurt those closest to you."

"Not when you know what it's like to lose someone."

Her soft reply ate at him and he wanted to prod, to ask her more about the person she'd loved and lost, but remembered that she didn't want any part of him.

"Unfortunately, Sonora has lived a pretty charmed life."

"Yeah, I gathered."

Luke's brow furrowed in confusion. "You guys didn't talk much in rehab?"

She jerked back for a second and almost appeared offended. Then slowly she shook her head and looked away from him.

"Of course we talked. She was just a different person there, is all."

Luke's bullshit meter was going haywire, but he had no idea why Marley would lie. Most people wouldn't lie about going to rehab...

Unless they had something bigger to hide.

"The Harwood Party?" A robust woman with big hair and plump, dark red lips tapped across the dance floor. "Marley, you're with the Harwood party, aren't you?"

Marley stood up and Luke went with her. "Yes, Delores, but the bride and groom had to step out."

"That's fine, we can get started with just the bridal party. Gather around, gather around." Delores's shirt was covered in sequins and she seemed to shimmer as she moved her arms.

All but Kendall, who was still absent, came out to the center of the room. Delores paired them according to who they were walking with...

Which meant he was going to be dancing with Marley.

Sure enough, Delores grabbed first Marley and then Luke by his arm, flashing him a lecherous grin. "Oooh, you're firm. You two, let's see your form. I'm thinking something fun, with lots of lifts and swinging Marley around. Think you can handle that, Muscles?"

Luke nodded. "Yes, ma'am."

"An accent too? Oh, if only I were twenty years younger." Delores fanned herself, but when she realized they weren't following her commands, she waved her hand. "Well? Put your arms around the girl, and Marley, this isn't your first rodeo. Show us how it's done, baby."

Luke slid one of his arms around her waist and brought her against him, mere inches separating their bodies. With his other hand, he took hers. "How is this?"

"Delightful, except the two of you look as though you're in pain. Come on, dancing is fun. Just wait." She tapped away, calling out, "The rest of you get into position while I find the perfect song to break the ice."

Luke was aware of Marley's floral-scented hair teasing his nose, and the soft skin of her hand against his. Suddenly, "Runaround Sue" was blaring around them.

"Listen to the music and have fun with it. Rock, stomp, twirl. Come on, let's see what you've got."

Slowly, couples around them started to move and Luke took a step to the right. Marley was a half a beat behind but before long, they were in sync and he thought he spotted a ghost of a smile on her lips.

"What did she mean this isn't your first rodeo?" he asked.

She took a step back with a little hop. "I've had friends who have gotten married, and I've been in the bridal party. What did you think that meant?"

"I don't know, maybe that you've had dance lessons?"

"Of course I did. Not much else to do in a small town like Sweetheart but take dance classes at Delores Kingston's Dance Hall." He spun her out and brought her back in, dipping her over his arm and the sweet sound of her laughter rang over the music. "Seems like you might have taken a class or two yourself."

"Maybe." In truth, his mom had taught him, pushing him around the living room until he was old enough to lead.

"Well, whoever your teacher was, you should thank her. She's very good."

He smiled, his body relaxing as they danced around the other couples, her brown hair falling from her simple pony tail and flying as he twirled her. It didn't hurt to talk about his mom, and the fact that she'd given him so much was a blessing.

Plus, it gave him an excuse to hold Marley close.

The song came to an end, and Luke was breathing hard, staring down at Marley as she grinned up at him, her eyes sparkling. Everyone else in the room melted away as he watched her, wishing that he had the right to bask in her joy, to lean over and taste her happiness on his lips.

"What is this?" Sonora practically shrieked.

The spell broke as Marley pulled away from him and the group faced Sonora's wrath, Brent right behind her. His friend's expression was grim, and Luke wondered if he was realizing that marriage to Sonora might not be as smooth sailing as he thought. She seemed to be forgetting all about putting on a charming front for her fiancée .

Delores glided across the room to greet her. "Ah, you must be the bride. I was just getting them warmed up while we waited for you. You have a very talented bridal party."

"Where is Kendall?" Sonora asked, ignoring Delores.

"She's in the bathroom I think. I'll go find her," Marley said.

Sonora shot her a bitter look. "You're my maid of honor. You're here to see to *my* comfort."

Luke glared at Sonora.

She's not your mother, you spoiled little bitch.

"I'll find her," Brent said.

Before Sonora could protest, he was gone, and Luke wondered if she was going to have an apoplectic fit. Finally, she seemed to start breathing again, and addressed Delores. "I have some ideas about the dance numbers. Marley? Can you get my binder from the car?"

Marley broke away from him completely, and Luke tried to tell himself that the moment he'd thought they'd had was just a fluke. Wishful thinking on his part.

He just wished he didn't still want her so damn much.

* * * *

Marley closed the door to her car, Sonora's pink bridal folder in her arms. It was already hot, her hands slick against the plastic, and she could only imagine how she was going to melt later at the Newman wedding. It was the whole reason they were doing dance lessons in the morning instead of this afternoon. Sonora had nearly blown a gasket when Marley told her that she wasn't her only client, but there was nothing she could do about it.

Of course, that hadn't kept Sonora from taking her revenge by riding her about the celebrity entertainment. And despite Sonora's shitty treatment of pretty much everyone, Marley had been nice enough not to repeat the many unpleasant things the musicians and their managers had said about her.

In fact, Marley figured she must be campaigning for sainthood, because not completely turning to goo every time Luke held her in his arms was a feat of strength. She hugged the pink binder to her chest, trying to forget about how good it had felt to just let Luke lead her around the dance floor. To enjoy him, and forget who he was and the damage being with him could cause.

A brief fling wasn't worth her job or her chance to start a new life, and she had to keep telling herself that.

A flash of blue caught her eye and she saw Brent on the side of the dance hall, holding Kendall in his arms. He seemed to be comforting her, and unease made Marley's stomach churn a bit.

Stop it. He's going to be her brother-in-law. There is nothing going on there.

Clearing her throat, the two broke apart and Marley smiled awkwardly. "Sorry, guys, but Sonora is getting us together for some dance number."

Brent ran a hand through his hair. "Yeah, sure. I'll see you two in there."

Marley kept her gaze on Kendall, who was wiping at her eyes as Brent disappeared inside. "Do I look all puffy?"

She did a little, but Marley wasn't going to tell her that. "No, you're beautiful. You ready to go in?"

"I guess." Kendall fell into step beside her, but just as they reached the porch, she blurted, "Is it wrong that I think my sister is a horrible person?"

No, because it is the truth.

"Sisters fight. You two will make up."

"Sometimes I wonder how a guy as great as Brent can stand her."

Marley stopped with her hand on the door, and turned slowly. *Don't ask. Don't you dare ask.*

"Kendall, do you have feelings for Brent?"

Kendall's cheeks turned crimson, and Marley had her answer.

"If I say yes, are you going to tell Sonora?" she asked, softly.

"No. And you don't have to tell me anything. I shouldn't have asked in the first place."

Kendall shook her head, her eyes filling with tears. "You're so nice. I honestly cannot understand what you see in Sonora."

Twenty thousand dollars and a way out of Sweetheart.

Marley squeezed Kendall's shoulder. "Sometimes people lash out because they don't know how to cope with their emotions."

"Or she's just a heinous bitch." Kendall sighed and cracked her neck before blinking her tears back. "Okay, I'm ready to face the dragon."

Marley pulled open the door and immediately, her gaze went to Luke. He was leaning against the wall, watching Sonora and Delores go back and forth, his dark eyes missing nothing. It was probably his cop face, and her stomach knotted up just imagining him storming an armed hostage situation or a spousal dispute. They'd been having so much fun dancing and talking that she'd almost forgotten she was supposed to be keeping him at arm's length.

Even if he hadn't been the best man, it would have been stupid to get involved with him anyway. He put his life on the line every day. Why would she want to risk falling for someone who literally ran toward danger?

Sonora was suddenly in her face, taking the folder from her. "Thank you. Now we can get started."

Sonora spun around on those skinny heels, and Marley's fists clenched.

"Are you sure?" Kendall said.

Marley turned toward the other woman, confused. "Sorry?"

"Are you sure you aren't just pretending to be my sister's friend? Most of Sonora's friends are vapid, narcissistic whores."

Marley burst out laughing. "Tell me how you really feel."

"I mean it. You're funny, down to earth, and seem to care about other people. So what in the heck do you see in my sister?"

As good of a liar as she was, Marley couldn't come up with a single reason. Luckily, they were interrupted by Sonora yelling at them to get the lead out.

This time when she found herself in Luke's arms, she tried to just relax and pretend he was any other guy. Of course, the minute he took her hand, the tingles racing up her arm made a liar out of her.

"What's wrong?" he asked.

"Nothing, why?"

"Because you've got a little wrinkle in the middle of your brow, as if you're thinking too hard."

Marley found herself trying to unwrinkle her forehead, and when Luke laughed, she grinned sheepishly. "Well, that's an embarrassing tell."

"Actually, I think it's pretty cute."

"Wrinkles are cute?"

"When they're on you, yeah."

A ball of warm pleasure settled in the pit of her stomach and spread out through her body. Until she remembered she wasn't supposed to like Luke.

"You shouldn't say things like that to me," she said as he spun her around.

"One thing you're going to find out about me over the next seven weeks is I'm a really honest guy, and I don't hold back. Even when I should."

Marley giggled a little. "Even with Sonora?"

"Fine, I hold back a lot with her, but only for Brent's sake."

"So, you do have restraint. You could stop being inappropriate." He dipped her back over his arm and she added, "You just choose not to."

He pulled her back onto her feet, and leaned down to press his mouth against her ear as the song ended.

"Believe me, being this close and not kissing you is taking all the restraint I have left."

And with that, he let her go and walked away, even when Sonora shouted at him to come back.

Well, that was a bit dramatic.

Chapter 9

Later that night, Marley was convinced if she had to do the chicken dance one more time in her life, she was going to start clucking. This was her thirty-fourth wedding in seven years, and although the people, the menu, and maybe even the floral arrangements might change, there were three things you could count on.

Someone was going to get drunk and piss off the bride.

At least three guests were going to cry.

And the DJ was going to play the damn chicken dance.

The song ended and Sarah Bailey-Newman, the bride at this particular shindig, wrapped her arms around Marley and hung on her like a noose. Sarah was a nice girl, the daughter of a highly religious and conservative Christian movie producer.

And obviously, she'd kicked back one too many champagnes, the only alcohol they'd been allowed to serve.

"I like you soooo much! You did such a good job and I don't know what I'd do without you."

Marley wrapped her arm around the other woman's waist and checked the room for her parents or the groom. The last thing she wanted was for Sarah's parents or her equally stiff groom to notice her current condition.

"I like you too, sweetie, but why don't we sit you down, get you a little water and maybe a cup of coffee?"

Sarah made a scrunched face. "I hate coffee."

"That's blasphemy, but I'll let it go this once."

Sarah weaved against her, giving her a puzzled look. "What?"

"It was a bad joke, never mind."

Marley half dragged, half carried Sarah to the bridal suite. The wedding and reception had been held at Lovers Lane Vineyard, because they had a beautiful chapel a hundred yards from the reception hall. If she could just let Sarah sleep it off for an hour, maybe nobody would notice.

"So, how many glasses of bubbly did you sneak?" Marley asked.

"Hmm, four or five?" Sarah lowered her slurred voice. "I think the server liked me."

Oh, Lord, now was not the time for Sarah to start noticing other men. When she'd first met the nineteen-year-old bride-to-be, she'd been so excited, filled with childlike wonder. The closer they got to the date, the jitterier she seemed to get, though and more than once, Marley had asked her if she was sure she was ready. Sarah had waved her off, and made excuses that she was just tired, but Marley wasn't so sure.

And tonight, she'd gotten hammered in the full view of her parents.

Yeah, she was definitely a happy camper.

Marley opened the door to the salon and laid her on the couch. When Sarah promptly burst into tears, Marley was thrown.

"Sarah, what's the matter?"

"I…I love Ryan, I really, really do, but…"

Marley waited for her to finish but she just cried harder. Marley wrapped her arm around her shoulder and hugged her close. "But what?"

"Do you promise not to tell anyone?" Sarah asked.

"Sure."

Sarah sniffled, wiping at her eyes and dragging black mascara streaks across her cheek. "I'm not a virgin."

Marley sensed that was probably a big deal, but had no idea why.

"That's okay. Did you and Ryan…"

"No, it was with some guy at camp three years ago. I didn't even know Ryan then. He knows what happened and he's fine. That's not the issue." Sarah took in a shaky breath. "I hated having sex. I only did it twice but it was terrible. What if I don't like it with Ryan either?"

Marley almost laughed aloud at the ridiculous situations she was thrown into while working for Something Borrowed. Breaking up fist fights. Having to chase a camel the bride had insisted on riding until it took off with her.

But giving a sex talk? This was a new one.

Marley thought about what she could say, and finally, settled on the truth. "To be honest, most women hate sex the first couple of times. It usually hurts and is messy and if you don't have really strong feelings for the guy, it can be brutal."

She thought back over the handful of partners she had, trying to find the right ray of sunshine, and her mind kept straying to her kisses with Luke.

"But when you are with a guy who knows what he's doing and cares about you, who wants to know what you like and please you, then sex can be amazing. You just have to tell Ryan and don't be afraid to be bossy."

Sarah giggled. "I'm not very assertive."

"Every woman should get assertive when it comes to sex." Marley patted her knee. "I'll get you that coffee."

Marley left the room and grabbed a bottle of water from one of the tables. After she'd poured a cup of coffee, adding a bit of cream and sugar, she snatched up a piece of cake and juggled the load back to the bridal salon.

When she found the door closed, she kicked a couple times with her toe. "Hey Sarah? I got the coffee and even a slice of cake. I figured you hadn't eaten so—"

She heard Sarah giggle inside and then the door was opened by a disheveled Ryan, looking more relaxed than she'd ever seen him.

There was no way...she hadn't been gone that *long.*

"Hey, Marley," he said, grinning.

"Hey. I brought Sarah some coffee, water and a slice of cake. Do you want to..."

"Yeah, sure, I'll take it." Ryan reached for the items, and she noticed his jacket was gone, and the buttons of his white dress shirt were undone. The collar was also hanging open, revealing about five chest hairs.

Marley had to bite her lip not to giggle.

She handed all the items off to him, and he set them down on the table. The door widened to reveal Sarah, holding up her obviously loosened wedding dress and blushing prettily.

Marley had a feeling that Sarah's opinion on sex was slowly changing.

"I'll just leave you two alone and probably call it a night." Marley smiled, turning the lock on the door. "I wish you both nothing but happiness."

The way Ryan looked at Sarah, as if she was everything he'd ever hoped for, made Marley warm to him even more.

She snuck out the side door with a doggie bag from the caterer, and a bottle of champagne. After the night she had, she figured she earned a night to eat, drink, and take a long, hot bubble bath.

She stopped off at the Love on the Corner gas station on her way home. She needed to fill her tank up, and there was a Red Box movie rental outside. She was exhausted, but too wired to sleep and she'd seen everything worth watching on Netflix at least twice.

Plus, she really wanted an assortment of Hostess products. It was that kind of night.

Marley pulled up to pump four and hopped out, fighting with her fluffy purple bridesmaid dress. It had an eight-layer petticoat underneath that was a pain in the ass to drive in, but she'd forgotten to change before leaving.

She walked into the store, and made a face when she saw Darren Weaver at the coffee maker, chatting up Marsha Thornsby. Marsha worked nights behind the register, and didn't seem to mind Darren's attention one bit.

Thank God. Maybe he'll ignore me.

Darren glanced her way, and his whole face lit up.

Damn it.

"Marley. Lookin' sexy."

She snorted. She looked like she'd just stepped out of a prom scene in a bad 80s movie, with her poofy dress, puffed sleeves and French twist, but it had been what Sarah liked and her father had approved.

"Darren. Lookin' stupid."

His face flushed scarlet, and even Marsha snickered.

Marley grabbed one of the arm baskets and headed to the snack food area. Starting with the orange cupcakes, she tossed item after item inside.

When she ran out of room, she turned around and bumped into Darren.

"Jesus, stalk much?"

Darren, who had always been more of an annoyance than anything, grabbed her arm in a painful grip.

"Why are you such a bitch to me?"

Fear prickled her skin, making the hairs on the back of her neck rise up. "Maybe because you won't leave me alone."

The door chimed, but Marley couldn't see who had come in around Darren.

"I'm just flirting with you," Darren said.

"This is not flirting. This is harassment," Marley said.

"I just don't understand why you won't give me a chance. I'm a nice guy—"

"Clearly, because nice guys bruise the crap out of women's arms just to get a point across."

He released her, and threw up his hands. "Fine! I can take a hint."

As he turned around, she couldn't seem to stop running her mouth. "Obviously you can't or you'd have stopped asking me out after I broke your nose in eighth grade."

Darren mumbled something and slammed into the person coming down the aisle behind him.

"Watch it," Darren snarled.

"Sorry, dude, my bad."

Marley recognized Luke's deep voice before she saw him standing there holding a bag of pork rinds. He was wearing a blue T-shirt, cargo shorts and sandals.

"You know the beach is hours away, right?" she said.

He gave her a look with one eyebrow raised. "But you got a river and besides, it's hot outside." He nodded toward the front door as it chimed, signaling Darren's exit. "Friend of yours?"

"A nuisance actually."

"Speaking of odd clothing choices…I thought you were a wedding planner? What's with the prom dress? Costume party?"

Marley rolled her eyes. "I am twenty-eight years old. All of my friends are getting married right now, so I'm expected to be in the wedding. You know what they say, always a bridesmaid."

Luke nodded. "Got it. So, you having a party or just a diabetic coma?"

"What, a girl can't like junk food? We've got to all eat salads and carrot sticks?"

"Whoa, easy! You've got like fifty snack cakes in there. Being funny over here."

Marley hated that he was so damn charming. "Well, I don't find you funny at all."

"No?" he said, a challenge in his voice.

"No."

"Fine, just for that attitude"—before she could react, he'd snatched a package of chocolatey goodness from her basket—"I'm confiscating these Ho Hos."

"Oh hell no," Marley cried, jumping for the white package, which he now held over his head. She tried to bring his arm down by hanging on it but he was too strong. "Give me the Ho Hos and no one gets hurt."

"Nah, I'm gonna keep them. They will go great with my Funions."

"Okay, that's disgusting and it was the only pack left!" She pulled a clear package from her basket and tried to bargain. "Take the Twinkies. I have like six of them."

Suddenly, he stepped into her, still holding her cakes above his head. "And what else?"

"Excuse me?"

"This is a ransom demand. I'll release the Ho Hos in exchange for the Twinkies and…"

His gaze dropped to her mouth and suddenly, she was holding her breath, waiting for him to finish.

He leaned over and her eyes fluttered, waiting for him to kiss her, swaying into him like a bird in a trance.

But the kiss never came.

Instead, he dropped the Ho Hos back into her basket, snatched a Twinkie and Zinger and brushed her cheek with his lips, whispering in her ear.

"Until next time, sweetheart."

She was too blown away to say a word as he walked away, taking her snack cakes and dignity with him.

Chapter 10

Since being back the last few days, Luke had really started to hate L.A. From getting stuck in traffic, to the rude ass people giving him shit for the uniform he wore, he was ready to bust some heads.

As he suited up in the station locker room, he found himself actually missing the quiet, goofy town of Sweetheart. The two lane country roads, no honking horns or city lights at night.

Marley.

He slammed on his helmet, done with thinking about her. What the hell was wrong with him, obsessing over a woman who had no interest in being with him?

Besides, his life was here, seven hours away from Sweetheart and even if she was interested, there was no way he was going to do a long-distance relationship anyway. Those always ended in heartache.

Their team leader, Sergeant Dan Voight came into the room, his dark eyes snapping as he took up the whole entryway with his linebacker shoulders. In his mid-forties, Voight's black hair was going gray at the temples, but that was the only sign of his age. Luke was convinced the man didn't know how to smile, but he'd never tried to push Voight's buttons. "Yo, we got a call to Wells Fargo on West Olympic. Bank robbery in progress, with hostages and shots fired. Let's go!"

Officer Greg Fornier slapped Luke on the shoulder and took a deep breath. "You smell that, Jessup?"

"Yeah, so put on more deodorant," Luke quipped.

"Nah, not that real-man smell my wife loves. I mean the smell of heroism."

Luke chuckled. Fornier was five years older than Luke, with thinning brown hair he kept closely cut, and twinkling blue eyes. The guy was always cracking jokes and keeping the atmosphere light when they needed it, and the guys loved him for it.

"Shit, Fornier, your delusions of grandeur are making you sound like a screwball."

Fornier grabbed his chest as though Luke had broken his heart. "Laugh all you want, but I am telling you, at the end of today, we're gonna have our names all over the news for saving lives and kicking ass."

Several officers around them laughed and cheered, and Luke just rolled his eyes as they jogged out to the SWAT van. While they drove, Voight went over their tactical approach and all thoughts of Marley went out of his head. His mind cleared, just like he'd been able to do since his first combat mission. All emotions turned off, and as they came out of the van and got into position, Luke was ready.

Voight got in front with his shield. "We're going through the side door. The negotiator has been trying to call and no one is picking up. Let's move."

They moved tightly down the narrow alleyway in sync, and then one by one through the door. Two on one side, three on the other. They made it into the main lobby before they heard voices.

"Grant, we're fucked. We got to get out of here." This guy's tone was high and nasally, the type of whine that grated on Luke's nerves.

Another voice, deeper and melodious replied, "There is no way out. It's either a bullet or prison."

"Then let's just walk out of here," the first man said.

The sound of a hard slap echoed through the quiet as a new perp growled menacingly. "Get your shit together, man. I'm not going back to prison."

There were at least three of them. One was ready to die. Suddenly, Captain Rankin's voice boomed from the outside. "This is the Los Angeles Police Department. Send out the hostages and put your weapons down, or we will be forced to come in."

"Jesus, Grant, come on—"

"Shut the fuck up, or I'm going to put you down on principle," Grant the Growler snapped.

The second guy tried to reason with Grant. "He's right. We're done for and I'm not ready to die."

"Then you two walk out like a couple of pussies. I'm getting paid or I'm going down, but I am not letting them put a pair of cuffs on me ever again."

Luke couldn't see any hostages from his vantage point, and shook his head at Voight. Voight cursed quietly over the com, and signaled for Luke and Fornier to get in position on the other side of the room. They crawled behind the teller desks, out of sight of the perps, until they reached the far end. Luke heard a noise, and looked up at what appeared to be an office door. If he stood, the three men would see him, and if he opened the door, they might panic and run, or worse, start firing.

The captain's voice boomed through the glass windows on the front of the bank. "This is your last warning. Give yourselves up or we will take you out."

Voight's voice whispered through his ear piece, "Four bogies at forty-five degrees. Wait for my signal."

Damn, Luke was sure there'd only been three.

"That's it, I'm out of here," the Whiner said.

Luke heard a clattering and then footsteps before the blast of a gun erupted.

"Take them out," Voight said in his ear piece.

Luke came through the swinging door and stood up. He had mere seconds to take in the scene before they noticed him. One man was crying over another, who lay prone and writhing. Two others with guns, standing several feet away, were watching dispassionately and hadn't heard Luke and Fornier move.

Voight and the rest of their squad were moving into position. Luke hollered, "Police! Put your weapons down, and hands on top of your head."

The two with guns whirled his way, and before they could even get their guns all the way up, he fired.

Luke shot the one on the left, and he screamed, dropping his semi-automatic as he clutched his arm. The other man squared off, and Luke could tell he was weighing his chances. This must be Grant.

"Don't do it."

But the man started to raise his gun. Luke and Fornier fired, and then out of the corner of his eye, Luke saw Fornier fall.

Voight and the rest of the squad fired, and Luke blasted until the suspect was on the ground. Then he went to Fornier's side and his stomach sank.

Shit, his neck was covered in blood. The perp had gotten a lucky shot off, right in the throat. Luke put pressure on the wound, talking to Fornier all the while he choked and gasped.

"Come on man, it's just a scratch. You're gonna be fine. Remember, we're going to have our names in the paper. Hell, I bet every news outlet is gonna want to interview us. Your wife is gonna be so damn proud of you."

Fornier coughed and red splattered the inside of his face cover.

"Officer down!" Luke shouted, staring at the blood seeping between his fingers and over the back to drip on the white tile of the bank. "We need an ambo in here now!"

The blast of a gun registered just as something hit Luke in the back, sending him falling forward over Fornier, his slick hands leaving streaks of red over the hard floor. Pain erupted from the spot, and he couldn't catch his breath.

He'd been shot.

* * * *

Marley kept pace alongside a groaning Rylie, grinning at her friend's dramatic carrying on. They'd driven out to Marley's favorite trail behind the middle school, with all of the hills and cross-country trek. It reminded her of running in high school. It was exhilarating and made Marley feel as though she could keep going for hours.

Rylie was less enthusiastic.

"You're fine, we only have a half mile left," Marley said.

Rylie slowed, her breathing ragged. Sweat dripped down her temples and over her ruddy cheeks as she huffed. "A half mile? I can't go another half mile. I'll die."

Marley was tempted to roll her eyes, but managed to control the urge. No sense in pissing off her friend when there were so many places Rylie could bury her body.

"You will not. Besides, you were the one who wanted to come."

Rylie glared up at her as she came to a stop, her hands going to her knees as she sucked in air. "I said I wanted to go for a jog, not the length of California."

Marley jogged backward and the eye roll emerged despite previous concerns. "Come on, I can see where we parked the car. It's the length of a Katy Perry song."

Marley was almost certain he was going to have to carry Rylie back to the car, when suddenly, she burst into a run.

"Katy Perry can suck my balls!" Rylie yelled over her shoulder.

Marley whooped and hollered. "Go, girl, go!"

Picking up speed, she raced Rylie the last fifty feet, and beat her to the fence by several steps. They slowed to a walk as they reached Rylie's car, and Marley laughed as Rylie laid her head down on the hood with a sigh. "Boy, am I glad to see you."

Marley leaned a hip against the passenger side, gulping from her water bottle before pouring some of the cool liquid over her face. As she shook the droplets off, she said, "I take it you're not going to go running with me tomorrow morning either?"

Rylie didn't even lift her head up to answer her. "I'll go running again when hell freezes over."

"Well, I'm pretty sure the devil is alive and well and working at Something Borrowed," Marley said.

Finally, Rylie stretched up, her arms rising above her head as she shot Marley a baleful look. "Oh, come on, Dustin isn't that bad. Plus, he's cute, rich, successful—"

"Egotistical, self-centered, a dick head."

"All I can say is he's been pretty nice to me and as the authority on dick heads, I feel like he's just misunderstood."

The mention of Rylie's abusive asshat boyfriend made Marley grip her water bottle tighter. "Seriously, why don't you leave Asher? He doesn't appreciate you, you're obviously miserable, and frankly, he doesn't deserve you. At all."

Rylie went to the driver's side door and pulled her keys out of the pocket of her sweats. "He wasn't always this way. I guess I just keep thinking things will get better."

"Meanwhile, you're putting your life on hold for someone who needs to have his ass kicked."

Rylie opened the door with a sad smile and hit the unlock button for Marley. "Can we please talk about something else? Like *your* love life for once."

Marley snorted as she slid into the passenger side. "Ha, that's a short conversation."

"Come on. You're hot. You're single and you go to weddings every weekend with tons of single dudes."

"That I cannot date."

Rylie sighed heavily as she started the car. "Oh, what Kelly doesn't know won't hurt her."

Marley almost choked. Rylie would never break the rules; she was too much of a people pleaser, no matter how big she might talk.

"You can run your mouth all you like, tough girl, but I know you. You would never go behind Kelly's back and risk your job."

Rylie's expression changed to one of sadness. "Only because my job is the only thing I have for myself."

Marley reached out to squeeze Rylie's arm, and noticed her friend's wince. "Did I hurt you?"

"I'm a little sore from doing weights last night."

Something told Marley she was lying, but unless she tried to pull off the long-sleeved work out shirt, she couldn't call her out. Marley's jaw clenched in frustration. If Asher was hurting Rylie, there was nothing anyone could do if Rylie wouldn't talk about it.

"You know you can always stay with me, right? If things are really bad."

Marley watched helplessly as Rylie dashed a tear from her cheek. "I'll be okay. Really. I'm fine."

"Yeah, cause that's convincing."

Rylie backed out of the parking lot and headed back into town, ignoring her statement. Marley flipped on the radio, hoping to lighten the mood with some tunes. The lyrics to "Love Shack" pumped from the speakers and Marley grinned, pretending to hold a microphone to her mouth.

Rylie glanced at her then back on the road while Marley belted out the words, and she could tell Rylie was suppressing a smile. When the chorus come on, Rylie joined in loudly, "Well, the Love Shack is a…"

The two were giggling and serenading each other until Rylie pulled up to Marley's place just as the song ended. Marley leaned over and gave her a big hug. "You know I love you, which is why I worry so much. A lot of people would walk through fire for you. You don't have to be alone in this. You can ask for help."

"I know. I promise, it's nothing I can't handle."

"Then I will stop hovering." Marley stepped out of the car, waving as Rylie drove off and went into the house. Her little gray house with white trim was the perfect size at just the right price. She would have saved money a lot faster staying with her mom, but as much as she loved her, Marley liked her own space.

And there was no way she would have brought a guy home to hook up in her old bedroom. The pink canopy bed alone would have been a real mood killer.

She walked through the door and found Butters sprawled on the couch with his legs straight out, his eyes opening slowly as she made her way over to him. Running a hand across his soft fur, she tsked, "You think you run this house, don't you?"

His ears flicked in response and she laughed, stripping off her sweaty shirt when she reached her bedroom. She flipped on the TV as she peeled off her work out clothes and laid out her dress for the day, a teal blue chiffon sundress with lace around the neckline. It was just after nine, so there wasn't much on besides the news. She liked it for background noise.

The minute she turned the shower on, Butters came racing into the room, and sat outside the glass doors, his little tail bobbing impatiently.

"Dude, no, this is my shower. Get your own."

He completely ignored her, of course. With a heavy sigh, she opened the door and he hopped in, shaking and jumping around in the water. It was the craziest thing, but from the first time she'd bathed him in the sink, Butters had loved the water and never passed up an opportunity to sneak in before her.

"Okay, that is enough mister. I have to get ready for work and I prefer my shower hotter than tepid."

Butters hopped out slowly and shook, while Marley bent over to dry him off with a towel. Finally, she was able to take her shower, letting her mind drift as she rinsed off the soap and shampoo.

It had been three days since Luke left, and so far, she'd managed to secure a place for the bridal shower, book the band that Sonora had dubbed the least horrible, and reserve a suite in Tahoe for the bachelorette party. It had taken a lot of finagling and ass-kissing, but she had to admit, she was pretty awesome.

An hour later, Marley walked into work, and found Sonora and Dustin in her office. Sonora was sitting in a chair with her hair swept to one side, showing off her bare shoulders in a creamy white sundress. Her legs were crossed and a pair of strappy sandals encased her delicate feet. Dustin leaned back against Marley's desk, his arms folded over his expensive charcoal gray suit. His blue eyes twinkled when he looked up and found Marley in the doorway.

"Good morning, Marley. We were just talking about you."

Marley's mouth tightened and her eye started to twitch. "Dustin. Sonora. I hope you were saying good things."

Sonora fluttered her lashes at Dustin. "I was just telling Dustin how you've managed to pull so much together in a short amount of time."

Marley doubted it, unless Sonora had told him out of disbelief. "It's my job. Now, Dustin, is there something I can help you with? Because if not, I believe Sonora and I have a meeting."

"Of course." Dustin stood up, nodding at both of them. "Ladies, enjoy your day."

Once he was out the door, Marley sat down across from Sonora, who appeared irritated.

"Did I interrupt something?" Marley asked.

Sonora's face flushed even as she sniffed. "Don't be stupid. I am happily engaged."

Marley sat down in her office chair and spread her hands out. "Then what have I done to piss you off so early?"

Sonora straightened, and pinned Marley with a critical gaze. "I wanted to be sure whatever is going on between you and Brent's Neanderthal best man has been squashed."

Marley fought back the urge to tell her to eff off and it was none of her business, but unfortunately, it was. "Yes, of course. To be honest, it wasn't anything really to begin with."

Sonora cocked her head to the side, but Marley wasn't buying the fake concern bit. "Good. I was afraid you might be upset."

"Upset about what?" Marley asked.

"Oh, there was a bank robbery this morning and Luke's team went to… what do they say? Neutralize it?"

Marley's heart started pounding erratically.

"Anyway," Sonora continued, "I guess he was shot."

Oh my God. Oh my God. Her stomach bottomed out and she waited for Sonora to say more, but instead, she seemed to be studying her cuticles.

Finally, unable to stand it anymore, Marley snapped, "Are you just going to sit there or tell me whether or not Luke is okay?"

Sonora had the audacity to appear smug. "I thought there was nothing going on between you."

"There isn't, but that doesn't mean I can't be concerned."

Sonora stood up with a smirk. "He's fine. All parts in working order. But I forget, you don't care about *that.*"

Sonora headed for the door while Marley's every fiber wanted to know more, to ask a thousand questions about Luke's condition and if he'd be back this weekend.

But there was no way she could push for more with Sonora, and the whole situation made her feel powerless.

"Chop chop! We have lots to do today."

The only satisfaction Marley could hold onto was that Sonora's dress was wrinkly and clinging to her backside in a most unbecoming way.

Chapter 11

On Saturday, Luke winced as he opened the door to the bakery in Sweetheart. He'd agreed to go taste cakes for Brent, who had other wedding duties to perform, but he was still pretty sore from the hostage negotiation. His back had been bruised when the bullet had flattened against his bulletproof vest, but it was a good lesson: Never turn your back on a suspect.

Fornier needed surgery, and although he'd lost a lot of blood, he was supposed to make a full recovery. The whole squad had been in the waiting room while he was in surgery, and when he woke up, he asked for Luke, thanking him for keeping him alive.

That was the part of the job Luke hated. The fact that they were always taking the chance that they wouldn't make it back anytime they left the house. Maybe he was getting old, or the violence was just becoming too much for him. For fourteen years he'd served his country in one way or another, protecting it. It might be time to slow things down.

He figured eating cake for an hour was a great way to start, especially since Marley was filling in for Sonora. Luke wasn't proud that he was excited to see her. It seemed no matter how many times he said he was over it, they ended up thrown together.

A large sign on the wall behind the pink and white counter read I Do... Love Cake, and the walls were pale pink with pictures of cakes, cupcakes, and cookies in spectacular shapes and designs with... puppies and kittens?

That was a little weird. Were they advertising pet hair in their pastries?

The tile floor was white with cake decals and several floor to ceiling display cases hosted an array of sheet and tiered cakes. Luke stepped closer, checking out one of the cakes that appeared to be leaning slightly to the right, covered in a dark blue icing with orange flowers.

Why the hell would someone want a blue and orange wedding cake? Must be Denver Broncos fans.

"Well, hi there." A perky red head popped up from behind the counter, making him jump. "You must be Brent."

Recovering swiftly, Luke held his hand out. "Actually, I'm Luke, the best man. Brent sent me here while he heads over to the caterers."

"Oh, well, glad to have you. I'm Tanya. Is the bride going to make it? I have to admit, I am such a fan."

"Actually, I think her maid of honor is filling in."

The door behind him dinged and he turned around to find a very shocked Marley staring at him with wide eyes.

"What are you doing here?" she asked.

"Filling in. Sonora didn't tell you?"

Her expression darkened. "No. No she didn't."

"Maybe she didn't realize how uncomfortable you'd be."

She snorted rudely. "Oh, believe me, she did this on purpose. This was a test."

"What kind of—"

He didn't get to finish before Tanya squealed.

"Hey there, Marley! Are you the maid of honor?"

Marley glanced around him, even as Luke wondered what she meant by test.

"Hey there, Tanya. Yes, I am. How are you?"

Tanya was practically bouncing, her red braid flopping up and down with every movement. "I'm great. You know, busy."

"I hear ya. Is Betsey in?"

"Nope, she had to go out of town for an emergency and left me in charge." Marley's eyes widened a bit. "Oh, well, that's great. Is she okay?"

"No, her sister is in a bad way, so I'm not sure when she'll be back. But come on and have a seat you two, and I'll bring out some samples. We have some really great summer flavors."

Luke moved ahead of Marley and held her chair out for her.

"Thanks." He went to the other side and sat, cringing as the back of the chair hit his bruise and he leaned forward. "How are you feeling? I heard you were shot?"

Tanya gasped beside the table. "Did you say shot?"

The girl looked as though she was about to keel over with her hand to her forehead. "I'm fine, just a little banged up. I'm a cop, and it just hit my vest. My buddy took one to the neck though."

"I'm so sorry," Marley said.

She'd reached across the table to take his hand and Luke relished the soft warmth of her touch.

"He's doing good now. Doctors said he'd make a full recovery."

She squeezed, her smile bright. "I am so glad."

The air in the bakery grew thick as he found himself stroking the back of her hand with his thumb. "Thanks."

"When Sonora told me, I...I wanted to call but..."

He wanted to know what the but was, except she stopped speaking and glanced nervously at Tanya.

Taking the hint, the woman cleared her throat. "I'll...ahem... be right back."

Marley let him go far too soon and he smiled. "So, you were worried about me?"

"Of course I was."

"That's nice to hear."

Their eyes caught over the table and Marley was the first to look away. "Luke—"

"Here we are." Tanya came back balancing a large silver tray, and Luke was getting a little irritated by her timing. "So, these are the five samples that Sonora chose. Can I get you some water or milk?"

Marley took one of the pink napkins on the tray and laid it across her lap. "Water is great, Tanya, thanks."

"I'd like milk," Luke said.

Tanya disappeared again and Luke picked up the yellow cake with some kind of berry filling. "This looks good."

"Yeah, Betsey is fabulous. She's been baking the wedding cakes around here for fifty years or more."

Luke shoved a large bite of the cake into his mouth and his taste buds immediately protested. The cake itself was flavorless, almost powdery, but the frosting made up for it with the sour, almost fermented tang. His eyes watered and through the blur, he saw Marley pause with her fork a few inches from her mouth.

"What's wrong?"

Luke held up a finger and swallowed, breathing through his nose. When he could finally talk again, he said, "Don't eat that one. It's gone bad."

"It's supposed to be tart." She held up the paper label that read, Raspberry Torte Cake.

"That's not tart. It's toxic."

"Oh, come on, I have never had a bad cake from here." Marley popped a small bite in her mouth, and he knew, the second her eyes went wide, she was going to spew it everywhere.

"Get your napkin," he said.

Marley grappled for it, and spat the cake out into it. She continued wiping her mouth and tongue after the bite was gone, making Luke laugh.

"Oh, my God, that is not how it is supposed to taste. How the heck did you swallow that?"

"Years of tequila shots, and hangover mouth. I told you it was bad."

Tanya came back through the door, and set down their drinks. Marley reached for hers a bit desperately and guzzled half of it. Tanya smiled widely at them.

"Oh, the raspberry torte cake is my favorite. What did you think?"

"It's not my favorite." Tanya looked as though Marley had just kicked her dog, and Luke raised his eyebrow at Marley, who added, "But I'm more of a chocolate person."

Tanya brightened a bit. "Oh, well, Sonora chose two. The tuxedo and the mousse."

Tanya continued to stand next to the table, and Luke had a feeling she was waiting for their reaction to the next bite. Luke grabbed a plate with the tuxedo on it, and held up his fork. "Bottoms up."

He took a bite at the same time Marley tried the mousse and could tell by the green tinge to her skin that hers wasn't any better than his. His was so sweet it made his teeth ache, and there was a funny aftertaste that coated his tongue with a film.

He swallowed, and drained his milk, grateful that at least that tasted normal.

Marley grabbed another napkin and wiped at her lips, making a noise in her throat. Luke was afraid she might throw the cake back up.

She kept it down, and took another drink of water before speaking. "Tanya, did Betsey make these before she left?"

"No, I did. I've been her apprentice for six months, and I know all of her recipes like the back of my hand." She frowned at them, concern in her eyes. "Why? Is there something wrong with them?"

"Pretty sure mine just gave me diabetes," Luke muttered, earning a kick from Marley under the table.

"Why don't you try my mousse, and see what you think," Marley said.

Tanya grabbed a clean fork and took a bite. After a moment of chewing, she frowned. "It tastes fine to me."

Marley looked at Luke, and he mouthed "wow" at her.

"Well, it doesn't taste fine to me, I'm sorry." Marley stood up and Luke took her lead. "Please give Betsey my love, but I think we're going to go with a different baker."

Tanya's mouth opened and closed like a fish, her face flushing. "But… but we're the only bakery in town!"

Luke got to the door first and held it open while Marley turned back. "Then we'll go to Placerville or Jackson, but I am not ordering a cake from here after the way they tasted today." Luke thought Tanya's head was going to explode as Marley added, "This isn't personal, Tanya. It's business."

"What am I supposed to tell Betsey?"

Marley's tone was kind, but firm. "That's up to you, but if she asks, I'm going to be honest."

Tanya's thick brows snapped down over her blue eyes, and Luke could tell this wasn't going to end well. "You're going to get me fired."

"No, Tanya. Like I said, I'm just being honest."

"Well, I honestly think you're a stuck-up bitch, Marley Stevenson." Luke figured it was time to step in before the situation escalated.

"And on that note, we're going to take off. Have a nice day," Luke said.

Luke ushered Marley out onto the sidewalk, noting the pallor of her face. "Are you okay?"

Marley cleared her throat. "Sure. It's not the first time I've been called that."

"But I bet it doesn't hurt any less," he said kindly.

She wouldn't agree with him, but he knew that was the case. Marley might be outspoken and honest, but he could tell that the people of Sweetheart genuinely liked her. The fact that someone she knew didn't probably bothered her.

Not caring if she shrugged him off, he wrapped his arm around her shoulders. "What do you say we drown the memory of the worst cake in history with some tarts from your mom's café? My treat?"

"My food is always free there."

"Then I'll pay double for mine. How's that?"

"Yeah, okay. Thanks," she mumbled.

Luke thought it was a good sign that she didn't try to escape his embrace.

Chapter 12

Marley didn't want to go into the café and be seen with Luke, mostly because she didn't want it to get back to Kelly that they were spending time together. How could she explain that Sonora had thrown them together to be a jerk, and then because Marley hadn't wanted to be alone, she continued to hang with him?

"Why don't you go grab some food, and I'll take you to one of my favorite spots?" she said.

He glanced from her to the front of the café and shrugged. "Sure, I'd love to know more about this town through your eyes."

Marley blushed as he climbed out and shut the door. Leaning back in the front seat, she took a deep breath. She'd known Tanya Jenkins since they were kids, and they'd been friendly. She understood being defensive, but Tanya's reaction to her had been downright hostile. Did she really come off as someone stuck-up? She didn't mean to, especially to people she cared about.

But how could Tanya not taste what was wrong with that cake, unless she had no taste buds whatsoever? As it was, Marley's stomach had roiled in protest after that last bite, and she was already afraid she'd be sick later. There was no way she was going to risk Betsey not getting back and Tanya giving food poisoning to four hundred guests.

Sometimes this part of her job really sucked and she wished like hell that Sonora had just rescheduled the cake tasting. If Tanya thought Marley was a bitch, she wondered what badge Sonora's reaction to the cakes would have earned her?

Finally, Luke came out of the café with a large paper sack, and two drinks. She wondered what he'd ordered for them, until he opened up the door and the familiar aroma of her mom's Heartache Healing Spinach and Artichoke Dip made her mouth water.

"So, I asked them for a bunch of your favorites because you were a friend of mine and they gave me—"

"Did you tell them I was in the car?"

Luke's expression shuttered, and she wished she hadn't sounded so panicked. "No, don't worry. No one will know you're slumming it."

She scowled at him. "That is not why I don't want people to know I am with you."

"Yeah, I know, you don't want to upset Sonora."

Not when she's my ticket out of here.

But she couldn't tell him that without breaking her confidentiality agreement. "I just don't think that the whole town needs to know my business. Okay?"

Luke set the food on the floor in the back and then the drinks in the holders. "You're the boss. Where are we headed?"

"I'll show you." Marley drove out of town and along the windy road. When she pulled off onto a dirt road and kept going about five miles out, Luke asked, "I would ask if this is where you kill me, but I'm hoping that I'm wrong."

Marley laughed as she pulled up to the top of the hill. Two rows of run down wooden buildings bordered the road, and she gestured like a tour guide. "Welcome to Buzzards Gulch, Sweetheart's very own ghost town."

Marley picked up her drink and watched him as he stared through the windshield, trying not to admire his profile. "No kidding. No one has even mentioned this place."

"Because we don't want a bunch of tourists up here traipsing around and destroying it. Pass the artichoke dip, please."

Luke distributed the food with a chuckle, and once she'd taken her first blissful bite, she continued, "Now, as you probably know, this area all the way to Coloma and Auburn was known as Gold Country. 'There's gold in them there hills' should have been our slogan. Behind that hill is the Consumes River and the gold panners used to hike down there, hoping for a big payload." She popped another artichoke dip-covered pita chip in her mouth, and chewed before continuing, "We used to sneak up here in high school at night and scare the piss out of each other. And make out, of course."

Luke chuckled. "You're telling me that a freaky ghost town was your lover's lane?"

"Uh huh. Something about the danger of a spirit coming after us made it hotter."

"I can see that," he said.

They ate silently for a few moments and Marley worried that Luke would get the wrong impression of why she'd brought him up there. "Not that I'm planning on jumping you. It's broad daylight for one reason."

"The thought never crossed my mind," he said, crunching on an onion ring.

Once the food was finished, Marley stepped out. "Come on."

They walked along the right side of the town and Marley told him what each building was. "This was the whore house. Of course, Buzzard Gulch was mostly men, and the few wives that did live here wouldn't have dared complain about a house of ill repute. And back that way is the cemetery."

Marley turned and started walking backwards. "Is this boring for you?"

"Not at all. I am fascinated. Besides, the fact that you're showing an outsider like me this place makes it more special."

A warmth spread through Marley's chest as they walked through the long-broken gate, and headed along the trail through the headstones. "My sister and I used to come here and make up stories about the people's lives."

"I didn't know you have a sister."

"I *had* a sister. Beth. She was four years younger than me." Marley stopped in front of Virginia Rawlins's grave. "Miss Rawlins was brought out here as a mail order bride, but her betrothed was swept down river and drowned before she arrived. Instead of marrying another man, she became the school teacher and lived her life secretly writing fantastic dark poetry."

"How do you know that?"

"I told you, we used to make up their stories. You try it."

Luke walked ahead of her and stopped in front of another grave. "Alan Wick. He died when he was thirty-two." Luke stroked his chin as though he was thinking hard. "He was the brothel owner with a heart of gold who died from an allergic reaction to the barley in his beer."

She laughed as she skipped ahead of him. "Okay, not bad." Marley went to another, and called out, "Fergus McGovern was from Scotland, and was the local sheriff until he was killed in a duel. Before he died, he said, 'I'll haunt ye till ye cock up yer toes, ye filthy bugger.'"

Luke guffawed, shaking his head. "You realize this is incredibly morbid, right?"

"We found it entertaining."

"You don't talk about her much, do you?" he asked.

She stopped in front of the grave of a sixteen-year-old boy and cleared her throat, trying to get past the lump in her throat to speak. "No I don't." Why had she even brought up Beth to him? She hated talking about her with anyone, didn't like the sad, sympathetic looks people gave her.

Silence stretched between them as they continued weaving through the gravestones and then, Luke asked, "Hey, is that bench new?"

Marley nodded. "Yeah, people have been trying to fix this place up for years. For a long time, the town council had talked about restoring it and actually organizing guided tours through it, but the town voted no. Still, people bring offerings up when they can."

"Offerings huh?"

"Yeah, like this bench. And someone keeps the trail to the river clear, and when the roofs and floors collapse, we come up and fix them. If you actually look into a few of the buildings, you'll notice the newer boards."

Luke put his hands up on a low hanging oak tree branch and the smile he sent her way made her stomach flop over. "This is really cool. Thanks for sharing it with me."

Marley's heart skipped as she realized she was actually happy to have shared it with him. She loved the fact that they had this between them, something no one else knew about.

"Consider it an apology for the way I left things in the hotel parking lot. That guy, Dustin and I have never gotten along, and I worried he'd tell my boss I was being unprofessional."

Luke dropped the branch and she noticed he seemed stiff, tense. "Why does he have it out for you? The two of you date or something?"

"Ugh, no! Gross. Are you trying to make me vomit up the rancid cake?"

Luke burst out laughing. "What? Isn't that something guys do when they like you? Torture you?"

"That is a horrible thought, and I curse you for even suggesting it."

He had his hands in the air now, relaxed and smiling, and she found she preferred Luke this way. Teasing easily and playful. She needed it.

"He has always been an obnoxious douche, and just likes to make everyone else feel inferior to him."

"Good." He turned his back on her and walked out of the cemetery.

She hurried to catch up, curious. "Why good?"

"Cause I'd hate to think you were into a guy that wouldn't treat you right."

His soft words were like a sucker punch. Damn, why did he have to say such perfect things?

"I am pretty choosey when it comes to guys."

"I get that."

He didn't say anything else, and she wanted to tell him that her decision not to date him really had nothing to do with him. That she liked him and wished that things were different.

But she couldn't elaborate to make the situation better, so she just left it. "Want to see the river?"

"Sure."

They hiked down the trail and sweat was pouring off Marley by the time they reached the bottom. The sun was straight up in the sky and the temperature had been climbing steadily. She noticed his light gray T-shirt was dark with moisture over his chest, and bit her lip at the way it molded over his gorgeous pecs.

"Whew, now this looks heavenly."

Marley glanced over the swimming hole, and smiled. "Yeah, we used to come down here and jump off that rock into the water during the summer."

Luke eyeballed the fifteen-foot boulder coming out of the water. "Now that sounds like a great idea."

To her utter astonishment, Luke reached down and grasped the bottom of his shirt, pulling it over his head in one fluid movement. Her mouth dried up as her gaze traveled over that rippled stomach.

"What are you doing?" she squeaked.

"Going swimming. It's hot as hell and that water looks mighty refreshing." He kicked off his shoes and when his hands went to the button of his cargo shorts, he raised an eyebrow. "Care to join me?"

"I don't have a suit on."

"Me neither." He pushed his shorts down, revealing the boxer briefs underneath. "But a bra and panties covers the same as a bikini."

Not the set I'm wearing. This morning she'd donned her lacey black bra and matching panty set under her black capris and short sleeved blouse. Not exactly made for concealing.

"Yeah, no, I'm good."

"Suit yourself, but you're more than welcome to put on my T-shirt if you're worried about me peeking."

In the time Marley glanced down at his gray shirt, he'd waded into the water, gliding on his back, the sun glistening off that wet, tanned chest.

Suddenly, the temperature cranked up another five degrees, and she found herself kicking off her shoes. When he stopped to tread water, she paused in removing her capris. "Turn around."

The wolfish grin he shot her turned her knees to mush and she wobbled. "Yes, ma'am."

Once she was sure he was being a gentleman, she shimmied out of her capris and folded them on the rock. She unbuttoned her blouse, and set it on top of her capris. Snatching up his shirt, she pulled it on, breathing in the scent of his cologne and the musk of Luke himself. The shirt went almost to her knees, covering up the sexy lingerie.

"Okay, I'm decent."

Luke turned around, and the look in his eyes made her shiver in spite of the heat.

"Damn, you look good in my shirt."

Marley blushed hard as she stepped down into the water. "Stop it. We're just going to swim—no flirting."

"I agreed to no such thing."

Marley slipped in, sighing as the cool water washed over her heated skin. "This is better than I remember."

"How long has it been since you've been swimming here?"

Since before Beth died.

"Feels like forever."

She drifted closer to him, and when she was within arm's length, he reached out and tucked some wet hair behind her ear.

"I'm sorry," he said.

She stiffened, reading the pity in his eyes. "For what?"

"For how much pain losing your sister brought you."

She didn't want this. She wanted the light-hearted banter. Hell, she'd take the flirtation at this point.

"Yeah, well, it's in the past. Right now, I'm here with you." She splashed him in the face and started swimming backwards. "And you deserve that for always teasing me."

Luke wiped the water from his face, and grinned evilly. "You just remember you started this."

With a squeal she took off, swimming until she felt his hand wrap around her ankle. She was laughing so hard she almost went under, would have if he hadn't slid his arms around her and held her against him. Her laughter died with their faces so close, his lips inching toward hers...

A stream of water flew out of his mouth and right in her face.

"Oh, my God, that is disgusting! Not only do I have your mouth bacteria in my eyes, but you probably have Giardia from drinking river water."

She couldn't see but she could feel his warm breath on her face as he chuckled. "Oh, come on, don't be a baby."

"Seriously, I've been blinded by fish poo water." She sniffled a little for effect. "Oh, my God, my eyes are burning."

His voice was laced with concern now. "Hang on—"

When he released her waist, Marley opened her eyes and jumped him, pushing his head under with all her might. He came up spluttering, and she cackled. "Boom, sucker!"

Luke grinned through the ripples of water on his face. "You're a pretty good actress. No wonder you handle Sonora so well."

"She's pretty easy to figure out. Stay on her good side or she'll make you miserable."

He seemed to be studying her, as if trying to work out whatever she was hiding and it made her heart skip nervously. "One thing I can't wrap my head around is you being in rehab. You just seem so together, I can't imagine you losing control like that."

She couldn't tell him he was right, no matter how badly she wanted to, so instead, she just kept moving. "Strange friendships form when you're thrown together. Just look at us."

"We weren't thrown together. I saw you and wanted to meet you... bumping into you seemed like the perfect solution."

Marley couldn't believe he had orchestrated their first meeting "How did you know I'd bump into you?"

"Just hoping, I guess."

Luke drifted closer, and Marley was so tempted to let him in, to feel his body wrap around hers and let this happen.

Instead, she took off for shore. "We better go. I've got a lot of stuff to do, and now I smell like fish."

She made it to the shore before him, and as he climbed out, she couldn't help but notice that he seemed to be excited and pretty damn impressive through the wet cotton of his boxer briefs.

This time, he picked up his shorts and turned his back on her without being asked. As he stepped one foot and then the other into his shorts, she noticed the way his thighs and butt muscles tightened and moved, and her libido did the lambada.

"You dressed yet?"

Shit. "Almost."

Marley couldn't tell him she'd been so distracted by the thought of grabbing his butt that she'd forgotten to move.

She really needed to stop ogling him. It was destroying her common sense.

Chapter 13

Luke sat in the hotel lobby that night, watching people come and go. Although The Love Shack Hotel didn't look like much on the outside, with its red exterior that could use a new coat of paint, the inside must have had a recent upgrade. The lobby was gorgeous with a gray stone floor, and textured walls the color of eggshells. There was a lounge area with big, comfy couches and chairs, and a bar area around the corner with tables and chairs in dark wood, matching the hardwood floors.

The rooms themselves were clean, with down comforters, and beautiful bathrooms with clawfoot tubs and tiled showers big enough for two. Luke could imagine this was the perfect place for passionate couples to "get together."

But he was bored just sitting in his room, and he didn't want to bother Brent. Sonora and him had seemed pretty cozy after their day interviewing caterers, kind of the way tensions had seemed to ease between Marley and himself.

Not that he wasn't attracted to her anymore, far from it. When he'd seen her step out of the water, his wet T-shirt clinging to her lithe body, he thought he was going to embarrass himself. Instead, he caught her checking out his package, and knew, no matter what she said, that she wanted him too. He just had to let her come to him.

To Luke's surprise, Brent stepped off the ancient elevator, and waved to him as he crossed the room.

"Hey, what are you doing? Where's Sonora?"

"She's got a headache, so she's going to stay in bed and relax. I thought we could head down to Plymouth. Heard there's a fair going on."

"You, big city CEO, want to go to a country fair?"

Brent's eyes twinkled with excitement. "Yeah, why not? Come on, I haven't been to one in years and I am dying for a corn dog."

As much as he loved Brent, hanging out with just him all night eating junk food and getting jerked around on carnival rides was not at the top of his list.

"Why don't we invite Marley? I think she's hanging with Kendall."

An expression he didn't recognize passed over Brent's face and then he was smiling again. "Sure, give her a call. Sounds like fun."

Luke pulled out his phone and tapped on her name. She picked up on the second ring.

"Hey, I haven't talked to you in *forever*."

Luke grinned sheepishly. "Ha, so you missed me, huh?"

"Didn't say that, but your ego is showing."

"You with Kendall?"

Marley drew out her answer. "Yeeeesss, why?"

"Cause Brent and I were thinking of hitting the fair in Plymouth and thought you two might want to join us."

Marley hesitated, then he heard her whispering, but couldn't make out what she was saying. "Where's Sonora?"

"She's resting. So what do you say?"

Luke could have sworn he heard Kendall saying yes emphatically in the background. Finally, Marley said, "Sure. Do you need me to come get you guys?"

"We have a rental, so we can just meet you."

"Sounds good. See you in about thirty minutes?"

"Can't wait."

Luke ended the call with a smile. "They're in."

"Nice. Come on then."

Luke didn't question Brent's eagerness to go, and just followed him out to the car. They ended up getting to the fairgrounds fifteen minutes before the girls. They sat on the front of the rental, scanning the dark parking lot, when Brent asked, "So, what's going on with you and Marley?"

Brent and Luke didn't talk about women and relationships often, but Luke found himself eagerly answering. "No idea, actually. Just trying to go with it. Seems like anytime I try to force more on her, she pulls away. So, I've decided to just wait for her to come to me."

"Sounds like a plan."

Luke wasn't sure about pushing Brent on the Sonora subject again, but he'd noticed his friend's short temper over the last week. He figured it had to have something to do with the six weeks left before he said I do. "What about you? A month out from your wedding. Any second thoughts?"

"I've had second, third, and fourth thoughts, but I'm doing the right thing. We're going to be a good fit."

Luke was surprised by his initial honesty, but the second half didn't ring true. Luke wasn't sure if Brent was trying to convince himself or Luke, but he didn't have time to ask as Kendall and Marley pulled down their aisle and parked. When they got out of the car and headed for them, Luke took in Marley's cut off shorts, simple blue tank and tennis shoes, her long hair up in a sassy ponytail.

And he'd never seen anyone so sexy.

Kendall bounced up to them, wearing jean capris and a pink lacy crop top, her blonde hair hanging around her shoulders in loose waves.

"Hey, guys, ready to have some fun?"

Brent wrapped his arm around her shoulder, sharing in her enthusiasm and shocking the hell out of Luke. "Hell yeah. It's been a long time since I've been to a fair."

"Don't expect too much," Marley said. "It's only a county fair."

They got to the gate and Luke and Brent paid for Kendall and Marley. As they headed down the midway, Kendall asked, "So, should we go on some rides, maybe play some games, or get food?"

"I vote rides before food, but only because I wouldn't want to puke on anyone," Marley said.

"Rides it is," Luke said.

They started with a group ride called the Gravitron, which spun around in a circle really fast, plastering people to the walls as the boards they were standing on slid up. By the time they got off, they were all laughing and massaging the feeling back into their faces.

"Let's go on the Scrambler," Kendall said.

The cars were only big enough for two and as they spun around, they jerked, causing Marley to press into Luke's side. He didn't mind though, and found himself with his arm around her shoulders as she laughed and screamed. They'd finished everything except the Ferris wheel within the hour, and while they waited in line, he got the feeling Marley was nervous.

"Are you scared?"

"No, it's just that it is so high and you know they only had a day to put this together, and all I can imagine is one screw popping loose and us plummeting to our deaths."

"You went on the Zipper and were fine."

"But that goes really fast and the cages spin, so if the cage came loose, it would fly and explode so fast, you wouldn't feel it. This would give you time to think."

Luke took her hand and squeezed. "I'll be with you."

"Unless you're Superman, that isn't comforting." She didn't shake off his hand hold though.

Luke chuckled as Brent and Kendall, who were in line in front of them, stepped onto the platform. They climbed into their bucket, and Kendall waved as the lap bar came down. The wheel started spinning, taking them back, and stopped again with an empty car for Luke and Marley. Luke helped Marley in, noticing the way she trembled against his side and wrapped his arm around her shoulders as the carnival worker secured their lap bar.

The ride jerked into action and as it climbed, he saw that Marley's eyes were closed. He leaned over to whisper, "You're missing the view."

Marley opened one eye and then the other. He felt her relax against him as she gazed out over the fair. "It's beautiful."

Luke stared at her, wanting to tell her she was the beautiful one, but he held back. The ride came to a stop when they were almost to the top. Marley sucked in her breath.

He squeezed her to him. "It's okay."

"I just hate when it stops. I want it to keep going."

Luke tried not to laugh as she buried her face into his shoulder. "They have to let people on and off. Try to think about something else."

"Like what?" she mumbled.

"Raindrops on roses and whiskers on kittens?"

"I hate that song."

His eyebrows shot up. "No one hates that song. It's a classic."

"How do you even know that song?"

"My mom loved that movie. Made me watch it with her every Christmas."

She lifted her head, her lips twisted. "Ugh, I hate it and no offense to your mom, but it is not a Christmas movie."

Luke blinked at her. "Who are you?"

"What? It's not." It started moving again and Marley breathed out hard. Then it lurched to a stop, and she shrieked.

"You okay?" Luke asked.

Marley gripped the bar, her face stricken. "No, why did you convince me to get on this thing?"

He told himself it wasn't funny, but his mouth twitched regardless. "I didn't know you were that scared."

"Well, I am, so shows how much you know!"

"What can I do? I can tell a joke or—"

Luke almost fell back as her lips collided with his. Marley was kissing him. Maybe it was just her panic, but she'd made the move.

Before she changed her mind, Luke cradled the back of her head and kissed her back, his tongue slipping in between her lips to play with her tongue.

He sensed the moment when she started to melt into his kiss and one of his hand glided down, over the smooth skin of her neck. As it molded over her breast, she gasped against his mouth, and he pressed his thumb into her, feeling the hard pebble of her nipple against his hand.

It was probably a bad idea to feel her up in public, but his cock didn't agree. Especially when the couple behind them could probably see them kissing, and he knew Marley wanted to keep everything on the down low.

When the ride lurched into motion again, Marley pulled away, her chest rising and falling rapidly, pressing her breast firmly into his hand.

Slowly he released her, but still didn't move away.

"Do you want to get out of here with me?"

For a few painful moments, he was sure she was going to say no.

Instead, she nodded.

* * * *

Marley still wasn't sure what she was doing. Any minute now, someone might spot her and ask what she was doing sneaking into the Love Shack Hotel's back door.

The door opened and Luke grinned out at her. "I feel like a teenager again, sneaking my friends into a sold-out show."

"Shh, move!" She pushed past him inside and locked the door. "I'll take the stairs. You take the elevator."

"Aren't you worried about someone spotting you on camera, 007?"

"All the cameras are fake. The owner just put them up as a scare tactic."

She started to take off up the stairs, but he grabbed her hand and pulled her against him.

"No, now none of that until we get upstairs," she hissed, breaking away from him.

"You really know how to make a guy feel special."

She didn't respond, just started running up the three flights until she reached the third floor. When she popped her head out into the corridor, she saw no one. Keeping her eye on the moving elevator, she finally came out into the open when the doors opened and Luke stepped out.

"So, if someone comes down the hallway, do you want me to throw you up against the wall and pretend to make out with you so they can't see your face?"

"Why do I get the feeling you're enjoying this?" she hissed.

"Cause, I've never snuck around with a girl before, even as a kid. It's kind of fun." He paused with his key in the door and frowned at her. "You aren't married, are you?"

"Of course not! I just don't want Sonora to find out." *Or Kelly.*

"Okay." He opened the door and she sprang inside. She looked around the beautifully furnished room with a grin, noting the updates. It had been years since she'd stayed here.

"You know, I lost my virginity in this hotel when I was eighteen."

"In this room?"

"No, I think it was the second floor. Kevin Preston. It was not a magical moment. I—"

Suddenly, she was spun around and fell against Luke's chest as he held her in his arms. "I really don't need to hear the details about you and another guy."

Marley blushed. "Sorry, I'm just nervous."

"Why? We're just hanging out. Alone. In my hotel room." He wiggled his eyebrows and she laughed, some of the tension easing out of her shoulders.

"You're right. So you grabbed my boob on the Ferris wheel. It doesn't mean—"

Luke's hand slid forward until it cradled her ribs, slowly making its way up until it cupped her breast. "You mean, like this."

"Yes." That single word almost sounded like a desperate plea.

He leaned over and brushed her lips, creating a train of tingles rolling down her spine. She felt his other hand come up and when he gently squeezed both of her breasts through her shirt and bra, she moaned.

"I have wanted to touch you like this since the first time you went off on me over a box of cereal."

A small smile touched her lips as she murmured against his mouth. "You're a freak."

"With you, hell yeah."

Luke suddenly lifted her up and carried her to the bed. Her heart leaped the minute the firm, squeaky mattress hit her back and her hands went to his chest. He stalled, looking down at her with so much tenderness her breath caught in her throat.

"I just thought you'd be more comfortable this way. Is it all right?"

Her hand came up, cupping his cheek. "Uh huh."

It was like some kind of trigger switch, because his mouth came over hers with more intensity and passion than anyone had ever shown her. Her skin came alive as his body covered hers, and his hands stroked her knee, her thigh, and crept higher.

Her hands slipped under the back of his shirt and she pulled up, trying to get it off his head. He came up onto his knees and tossed it across the room.

Boy oh boy. Luke looked good with his shirt on, but off? Daaaaamn.

When he lifted up her tank and exposed her belly, she thought he was going to push it all the way off, but instead, he curled over and kissed her right above her navel. Her stomach muscles bunched, and she giggled a bit as his scruff tickled her with every kiss downward. When he reached the snap of her shorts, she waited with baited breath.

He actually used his teeth and she laughed. "Doesn't that hurt?"

"It's supposed to be sexy," he mumbled around the zipper in his mouth.

"It's not. Amusing, yes. Sexy, no."

He let it go and leaned up on one elbow alongside her. "This is better for what I'm about to do anyway."

"And what's that?"

He leaned over, his warm breath fanning over her ear. "Watch you come."

Marley had never imagined she'd be into dirty talk, but then again, no one she'd been with had ever tried. When Luke did it though, she actually squeezed her thighs together as a steady pounding started between her legs.

Luke never looked away as he pushed her shorts down and his warm palm rested over her. His finger ran along the lace of her panties, causing friction to explode against her seam. When he dipped his finger under and pressed until he touched her clit, she jumped. That small caress turned into a rapid circle that made her hips arch, her hands gripping the bed spread beneath her as pressure built. She closed her eyes, her breathing coming out in heavy pants, and he kissed her eyelids.

"Don't close your eyes. I want to see everything."

She opened her heavy lids, whimpering as he pinched and rubbed, working her into a frenzy of arousal until finally, a wave of euphoria rushed over her and her legs started trembling.

"Oh, yes. Yes. God."

"That's it, baby, come for me."

Marley's hands started to cramp, so hard were they clenched and as the orgasm passed, she sank back into the mattress with a sigh.

"Damn. If you come that hard with just my hand, I can't wait to get you in my mouth."

Marley's eyes flew open, and as she caught the wicked grin combined with the admiration in his eyes, she giggled. "Has anyone ever mentioned you have a dirty mouth?"

"Stick around a little longer and I'll show you exactly how dirty it can get."

Chapter 14

Luke slid back onto the bed, watching her as she shimmied out of her shorts and tossed her tank across the room. Clad only in her lacy bra and panties, he could feel his cock growing and pushing against the cotton of his briefs. He'd ditched the cargo shorts when she'd gotten up from the bed, and he was dying to see how far this would go.

"I think I should tell you that I'm a classy chick."

Her finger was playing with the strap of her bra and he could hardly concentrate on what she was saying, anticipating the moment she slid it down and exposed those soft, round tits.

"Uh huh."

"No I mean it. I never hook up on the first date, or the third. I wait until the fifth."

Now her hands were sliding along the flat of her stomach and he wanted to leap on her.

"Isn't this like our seventh date?"

"No. Maybe our third."

"So you're saying tonight was a date, huh? And what does one do on a third date?"

Marley climbed onto the bed, her mouth hovering over his crotch.

"Oral."

Have mercy.

Putting his hands behind his head, he tried to appear casual. "I can hang with that."

Marley pulled the waistband of his boxer briefs down, as if she was peeling a banana, and as he waited impatiently, watching her smile, his cock flexed up.

Her hand wrapped around him and he arched off the bed, loving the grip she had on him. He closed his eyes as her mouth slipped over his tip and slid down, meeting her hand and creating a warm, wet pressure that had his balls clenching.

"Now, no closing your eyes." He lifted his head to look at her, and the dark, passionate glow on her face was fucking hot. "I want to see the expression in them when you come."

Having his own words thrown back at him would have made him laugh, except she'd swallowed him up again. He leaned up and back on his arms, watching as she dropped her head and started working him. God, it had been a while since a woman had just given him head without it being a prelude to sex. His breathing kicked up as she moved over him, sucking and doing something with her tongue just below the head of his cock that was almost his undoing.

"Oh, fuck, do that tongue thing again. Jesus yes, God, my—"

She took him all the way in and when the tip of him hit the back of her throat, he was done. Shouting as he came, he threw his head back, shaking from head to toe.

He felt her move as he fell back on the bed. "Sorry I didn't warn you. I didn't expect to come so fast."

Her lips pressed against his and she snuggled into his side. Her silence disturbed him a bit, and he got defensive.

"I'm not a one-minute man, if you were worried."

"I wasn't," she said.

Her tone made him frown. "I'm serious."

"I'm sure you are."

Luke took her chin in his hand and raised her up so he could see her face. She was grinning from ear to ear. "Are you fucking with me?"

"Yep."

"Mean."

She grabbed his hand and circled his thumb with her tongue. "I thought I was pretty nice a minute ago."

He couldn't argue with that.

* * * *

Marley got up and pulled on her clothes. She'd felt Luke drift off to sleep shortly after giving her a warm, lingering kiss and pulling her closer to him. She'd enjoyed the cuddles for a while, but she didn't want to wait too long and run the risk of bumping into Brent or another guest as she was leaving.

Tiptoeing out the door, she figured it was probably safe to take the elevator. She could always say she was checking on Sonora.

As she stood in the hallway, waiting for it to come back up, she heard the click of a door, turned around...

And froze.

Dustin was coming out of a room, looking rumpled. But that wasn't what was so shocking. When Sonora wrapped an arm around his neck from inside the room and pulled him down for a kiss, Marley's stomach rolled.

Sonora was cheating on Brent. *With Dustin Kent.*

Finally, the elevator arrived and she practically dove in. Only she heard Dustin call out, "Hold the elevator please."

Unable to even look at him as he stepped in, she did notice him pause out of the corner of her eye. Maybe he'd ignore her and they could at least pretend that she hadn't seen anything.

"Well, well. I guess I'm not the only one doing the walk of shame tonight." No such luck.

Marley flipped him the bird. "I am not. I was just visiting a friend."

"And I bet I know exactly what kind of friend."

Furious with him, she turned, her hands on her hips and spitting fire. "You're a pig. Don't you get that she is engaged to be married? That you're breaking up a relationship?"

"Relax, that's the best part about it." The doors opened and although Marley tried to get away from him, he kept up with her. "We both just wanted to get off, no strings attached."

"Like I said—pig."

"Oh, and I suppose you and the meathead are soul mates?" he asked.

"Just leave me alone and I'll keep my mouth shut."

"Fine by me. Talking to you is like speaking to my uncle, the priest. Always wants to save my soul."

Marley grabbed her door and jerked it open. "You're the devil. You don't have a soul."

Dustin's grin was unapologetic, and it made her want to punch him. "That must be why I'm so good at being bad."

"Ugh, gross."

Marley stepped into her car, and took a deep breath as she watched Dustin leave. What the hell was she supposed to do? Ignore what she saw?

Twelve hours later, Marley still had no idea. As she sat in her office at Something Borrowed, rubbing her temples and praying for the answer in her black cup of coffee, nothing came to her. She'd hardly slept, and her head felt as though it was about to split open and an alien would pop out.

"Geez, Marley, you look tired," Rylie said.

Marley looked up, knowing that her face was devoid of makeup except for a little mascara. She just hadn't been driven enough to put in the effort this morning.

"Thanks, Rys." Marley didn't mean to sound so nasty, but the last thing she needed was to hear how bad she looked.

Rylie certainly was dressed to the nines this morning. Wearing a black and white striped dress with lemon yellow heels, her hair was in a messy braid and with a little extra makeup, she was gorgeous. She held a white napkin in her hand with a yellow bar perched on top, black stripes covering the powdery white surface of the dessert.

"So, you're dressing to match your baked goods now?" Marley joked.

Rylie looked down at her outfit and laughed. "You know, I didn't even notice. Here, try this. It will make you feel better."

"No, I'm not hungry, Rys. Rys!"

Rylie had come around the side of her desk and she couldn't get away from the lemony looking bar with powdered sugar and chocolate drizzle hanging in front of her mouth.

"One bite," Rylie said.

Marley opened her mouth with a sigh and took a bite. The tart flavor of lemon and the sinful taste of dark chocolate filled her mouth. She licked her lips, and didn't want to admit that the treat did make her feel a bit better.

"Good?"

Marley took the rest of the bar from her and opened her mouth for another bite. As she chewed, her eyes rolled back into her head and she swallowed slowly, savoring it. "You're evil."

Rylie clapped her hands. "Yay, I've always wanted to be evil."

"Mission accomplished. You should just bring whatever is left in the container back to my office."

"Yowza, that bad huh?"

"Yeah."

"I'll be right back with the bars then."

Marley watched her leave the room and debated on whether to tell Rylie what she saw. She didn't want to do anything to void her contract, but her conscience was sickened with Sonora. How could she do that to Brent? A man who despite her many flaws, wanted to marry her. She'd figured Sonora was marrying him for his money considering her financial straits, but it wasn't as though Brent was a toad! And even if he was horrible to her, she could leave him. There was no excuse for cheating.

When Rylie came back in, Marley said, "Can you close the door please? I need to ask you a hypothetical."

"Sure." Rylie shut the door and set the glass Pyrex dish with the rest of the bars on Marley's desk and sat down. "What's up?"

Marley leaned against the edge of her desk and lowered her voice. "If you saw one of your brides or grooms cheating, would you tell Kelly? Or the person's significant other?"

"Who—"

"This is hypothetical."

Rylie's gaze narrowed, but she didn't ask any more questions. "Oh. Well, I guess I'd ask Kelly first and see what she said. I know some clients have a confidentiality agreement, so even if you see them doing something illegal, you can't talk about it, unless they break the contract first."

At least if Marley told Kelly, it wouldn't be on her. "Yeah, I'll do that. Thanks, Rylie."

"Anytime." She stood up, and grabbed one more bar from the pan. "The rest are yours. I don't need them around. Asher keeps telling me that I could lose weight if I wasn't constantly eating."

Marley scowled. "Funny, how he never complains when you make dinner for him. And he's not perfect by any means!"

Rylie appeared so defeated that Marley wanted to personally hunt Asher down and skewer him with a spork.

"He's right though. I have to sample everything, and especially baking all the sweets...I could cut back or start substituting for sugar."

Marley walked around the desk, and bent over to hug her friend. "Rylie, if you want to lose weight, then that is fine and I will support you, but do not change because some jackass thinks his shit don't stink. You are gorgeous."

"Whatever, I'm—"

"Gorgeous, and if you say anything else to the contrary, I will hurt you. I will dump all of these beautiful lemon bars out on my desk and beat you with the glass pan and eat them over your bloody body."

"Okay, okay. Geez, I'm going to get out of here. You're cray cray!" But when Rylie left Marley's office, she was smiling, which was Marley's goal. Then when Marley heard Dustin say hi to Rylie out in the hallway, she went to the door to keep an eye on the dirty rat.

So far, most of the women in the office had fallen under his spell, including Rylie. If she only knew what Marley knew, she'd be just as disgusted with the jerk.

"Hey, Rylie, got something sweet for me?"

Marley wanted to gag.

Rylie took a bite of her bar and held it out to him. "Here. It's the last one."

He leaned close and whatever he whispered, Rylie's cheeks turned bright red.

And she shoved the lemon bar in Dustin's face.

"You're a jackass."

When she spun around, her black and white striped dress flew out dramatically and she stomped back into the lobby in her yellow heels.

Marley started a slow clap, grinning when Dustin wiped a glob of lemon off the end of his nose.

"You seriously think that's appropriate?" he growled.

"Actually, I think they call that just desserts."

Dustin stomped back down the hall. Marley could hear the curses until he slammed his office door. She went back into her office, a smile spreading across her face.

Rylie deserved a gift card to that little baking shop in Jackson she loved. She'd just made Marley's day 100 percent better.

Maybe things were looking up.

* * * *

Luke walked into Something Borrowed with a bouquet of flowers and a wide grin on his face. The front office was relatively normal compared to the décor of the rest of Sweetheart's businesses. The walls had stenciled, curling scripts of romantic quotes and phrases. Not enough to look cluttered or tacky, just homey—down to the plant in the corner and the simple wooden reception desk, which happened to be empty at the moment.

He'd texted Marley this morning about sneaking out on him last night, and she teased that she'd be happy to make it up to him later.

He decided to make later a little sooner by taking her to lunch.

A curvy brunette in a black and white striped dress came down the long hallway to the right. "Can I help you?"

"Yeah, I'm looking for Marley Stevenson."

"And who might I say is asking?"

"Luke Jessup."

Her brown eyes widened and she snapped her fingers. "Oh! You're the best man for the Harwood/Star wedding."

That was a weird way to say it. Maybe Sonora had hired Something Borrowed to help with the wedding details. Or Marley had mentioned him.

That last thought brought a wide grin to his face. "Yes, I am."

"Hang on."

She hurried out of the lobby and Luke frowned. Was it just him or did she look a little panicked?

His suspicions were confirmed when Marley practically skidded into the lobby, looking drawn and pale.

When she grabbed his arm, and started pulling him toward the door, he was completely baffled.

"Hi, what are you doing here?" she asked.

"I thought I'd take you to lunch—"

"Sounds good, let's go."

Luke wasn't a fan of being dragged around, or made to feel like he was an embarrassment, so he dug in his heels. "If I've come at a bad time, I can stop by later."

Rylie stood off to the side, watching them with slack-jawed surprise.

Marley shook her head vehemently. "No! I mean, now is fine. Let's just talk out here."

They walked outside and down the street before Luke finally got a reign on his temper and could speak. "Seriously, Marley, what the fuck is going on?"

"Nothing—"

"Bullshit it's nothing! You just shoved me out of your work like you didn't want anyone to see me. At first, I thought this whole will she-won't she, sneaking around drama was cute, but enough is enough. Now, what is up?"

Marley was biting her lip so hard the area around her teeth went white. Finally, she took a deep breath. "I can't. After the wedding, if we're still a thing, I can tell you, but until then, I just need you to trust me."

Luke shook his head. He wanted like hell to accept that she had a good reason for all of this, but it was exhausting. He liked her. He wanted to be able to enjoy time with her, take her to lunch and dinner and not have to stress about someone seeing them or the town talking or whatever her trip was.

He needed a break.

Handing her the flowers, he said, "Sorry, but I'm suddenly not hungry."

"Luke, please..."

"Unless the next words out of your mouth amount to a reasonable explanation, don't bother."

Her mouth snapped closed and with a heavy sigh, he got into his car and drove. After the fair and last night, the way they talked about dates, he actually thought they were just playing at sneaking around. That they were finally taking a step in the right direction.

Codi Gary

Clearly he'd been wrong. There were three weeks left until the wedding. Did he give her the benefit of the doubt and see what she had to say after the ceremony? Or just try to distance himself and hope he could resist her?

When no sign appeared, he groaned.

Why was it so hard for the universe to give him a straight answer?

Chapter 15

Two Saturdays later, Marley felt like a tractor had run over her head several times and her brain was exposed to an ice pick wielding maniac. God, she hated summer colds. They were always so much worse than winter colds. She'd had the chills for a day and a half, a 101.2 fever, and her nose would not stop oozing. God forbid she sneeze; if she didn't grab a tissue fast enough, it was like a missile of germs exploded from her nose and mouth.

She should have known she was going to get something when one of the groomsman at the Vaughn wedding last Sunday had asked her to dance, then proceeded to sneeze the entire time.

Allergies her great Aunt Petunia!

Snuggling into her down comforter, she opened one eye when something gently nibbled at her hand. Butters watched her with dark brown eyes, his little nose twitching rapidly.

"This is what we humans call a sick day, dude. That means that we sleep a lot and do not want to be disturbed until at least ten."

The stubborn bunny nudged her hand with his soft head, and his ears flicked forward, as if to say, *no excuses, woman. Feed me.*

With a frustrated groan, Marley extracted herself from her cocoon, her head swimming and her nose dripping as she made her way to the bathroom first, and then the kitchen to feed the annoying beast.

She'd just finished putting a kettle of water on when there was a knock at her front door. Kelly knew she was out sick today, and her mom would be at the diner by now. She wasn't close enough to anyone else for them to stop by and see her.

Marley walked across her dining room to the front door. She looked out of the peep hole and backed up with a gasp.

Luke was standing on her door step, looking absolutely healthy and gorgeous, if a tad disproportionate thanks to the glass. They hadn't talked since he'd taken off on her, and she'd been sure he was done with her.

So what the hell was he doing here?

Oh God, her teeth weren't brushed and her hair was a mess and there was probably snot everywhere.

"What are you doing here?" she hollered nasally through the door.

"Checking up on you. Sonora said you were sick."

Marley snorted. When she'd told Sonora she felt like she was coming down with something, the other woman practically sprinted out of the room. She told Marley to get the hell out and get well before she came near her again because the last thing she needed was to catch something.

As if Marley wanted to be sick.

"Yes, I'm very contagious, so you should get out of here before you contract it."

"Just open the door, Marley, I'm not worried about getting sick."

A rush of wooziness overcame her and she pressed her hot forehead to the door. "Please, just go away. I don't want you to see me like this."

"You have two choices. You can either let me in, or I'm going to sit out on this porch all day, singing your name until your neighbors call the cops."

Odious man, he probably would do that.

"Fine, but I warned you."

She opened the door, and waved a hand. "Well, come on in."

As he stepped past, she noticed the two grocery bags and the bouquet of summer flowers in his hand.

"What are those for?" she asked.

He shook his head and held them out for her. "For you, dummy. To make you feel better. I remembered you telling me you liked bright colored flowers instead of roses because the roses always seemed depressed."

She'd told him that when Sonora had been ranting and raving a few weeks ago after Marley had suggested something other than white roses in her bouquet and centerpieces. Marley had backed off, and let her order what she wanted, but she was still convinced the wedding could use some more color.

She tried to ignore the squeeze in her chest because he remembered something so obscure about her. "Thank you. They're lovely."

"Good. Now, where can I set up?"

"Set up?"

"Yes, I brought all the provisions you need to kick this cold's ass, along with some comfort items." Luke headed for her kitchen without her permission, slowing a bit when he spotted Butters eating breakfast. "Whoa, you have a rabbit?"

"Yeah."

"And he just runs around your house? Where does he shit?"

"In his litter box. You can train rabbits, you know."

"Huh. Didn't know that." He set his bags on the counter and squatted down. "What's up, bunny?"

His voice had taken on a creepy, high quality and Marley cringed. "Don't do that voice."

"Why?"

"Because you sound like a serial killer."

To her astonishment, Butters hopped closer and butted Luke's hand with his head, encouraging pets.

"He seems to like it."

Suddenly too weak to stand anymore, she lay down on the couch. "Only because he is a whore."

"That's not very nice thing to call this cute little guy."

"Why are you tormenting me?" she groaned. God, she was tired, and sore, and just wanted to sleep.

When a cool hand pressed against her forehead, her eyes flew open. Luke leaned over her, a concerned look on his face.

"You're burning up. Have you taken any Tylenol?"

"No, I hate cold medicine. It makes me feel drunk."

"Where's your thermometer?"

"In the pink basket in the kitchen cupboard on the far end."

He left her in peace for a few minutes, and came back, pressing the tip of the thermometer to her lips. "Hold this under your tongue."

"I'm not a child."

"You act like it."

"And your bedside manner sucks."

He gave her a dark scowl and she stuck the tip under her tongue, shooting daggers at him as she closed her lips around it. When it beeped, he snatched it from her and his expression darkened.

"Damn. 103.2." He stood up, and pointed his finger at her. "I'm getting you some medicine, and you're going to take it. Then, I'm carrying you back to bed to sleep, and I better not hear any arguing."

"I was trying to sleep when my demon bunny woke me up, and then you knocked on my door and—"

He covered her mouth with his hand. "I don't want to hear excuses."

Her eyes arrowed when she saw his mouth twitch, as if he wanted to smile. When he removed his hand, she said, "You're enjoying having me at your mercy, aren't you?"

"How can you say that about me? I am selflessly sacrificing my own health to care for you in your time of need. I'm a hero."

"Ha! You just want me in your debt."

"Nothing so nefarious. I figured you needed somebody to take care of you."

Marley closed her eyes again, his words hitting her hard. When she moved to New York, her mom would be across the country, and so would her friends. The people who had known her all of her life. She would truly be alone for the first time.

Maybe it was the fever, but it sounded really lonely now.

Luke sat on the couch next to her. "Okay, I'm gonna need you to sit up and take this."

Opening her eyes suspiciously, she saw him holding out a handful of pills and a glass of water. "What's that?"

"Tylenol, just the regular kind, Echinacea, barley green, and elder berry zinc. My mom used to give it to me when I got sick."

"You want me to take all those pills? There's like thirteen of them."

"Don't be a wuss. I've seen you take bigger bites when you eat."

Well, that was a tad insulting, but she still took the pills from him, tossing two into her mouth at a time and swallowing them down with the water he offered. When she finished, she opened her mouth wide, as if to show him she really swallowed and then snapped it closed. "Happy?"

"Yes." He set the glass down on the end table behind her and without preamble, lifted her up into his arms. She turned her face away, conscious of the fact that her breath probably smelled atrocious, and laid her head against his solid chest.

"I hate being sick."

"I don't know very many people that like it."

"It makes me feel weak."

He squeezed her to him. "Which way?"

"My room is past the kitchen. It's just a one bedroom."

Before he lay her down on her bed, she mumbled a half-hearted thank-you.

"If you really don't want me here, I can go," he said.

Embarrassed for acting like a brat, she put a hand on his arm. "I'm sorry. I'm just so used to taking care of myself and everyone else I don't know how to let someone do it for me."

"Maybe because you don't like to let your guard down and trust people."

"I'm not guarded."

He pulled the comforter up over her, giving her a dry look. "Really?"
Too tired to argue, she sank back into her bed. "Fine, but who said I trusted you?"

He raised one eyebrow at her with a smirk. "The fact that you let me in the front door, or that you took pills from me without double checking what they were. Just accept it. You like me and feel safe with me."

"Maybe."

"Without a doubt. If it had been Dustin Kent at the door, you would have ignored him and gone back to bed."

"He's a douche."

Luke chuckled and the sound gooified her insides. "Agreed. Now, do you need anything else?"

"Are you leaving?" Why did she sound so disappointed? He had walked away from her without giving her the benefit of the doubt.

I don't know. If our roles were reversed, I might not have stuck around this long.

"I wasn't planning to. I was just going to sit out in your living room and watch football."

"Oh…I have a TV in here." Now why in the heck had she said *that*?

Because I don't want to be alone.

He didn't ask questions or tease her. "Where's the remote?"

"On the other night stand."

Luke kicked off his shoes and walked around to the other side. He didn't get under the blanket with her, just fluffed the extra pillows and flicked on the TV. She liked that he kept the volume down, and when his hand reached out, rubbing over her sore back, she sighed.

Her eyelids grew heavy to the sound of sports reporters and first and down, but before she drifted, she whispered, "Thanks, Luke."

"You're welcome. Now sleep."

She did exactly that.

* * * *

Luke woke up to unfamiliar surroundings, his arms wrapped around another warm body…

And shiny eyes in a furry face watching him from just a few inches away.

Sitting up like a shot, he hollered, "What the fuck!"

A flash of white streaked off the bed and out the door.

"Was he watching you sleep? He does that. Total creeper."

Marley's calm, sleepy voice brought everything back for him and he released a breathless laugh even as his heart threatened to pound out of his chest. "He scared the shit out of me."

"You get used to it," she mumbled.

Luke shook his head, wondering how anyone could get used to *that*.

"Are you going to come back down here? I was all warm until you freaked out."

Luke realized she knew he'd been spooning her, and lay back down before she changed her mind, his heart racing for another reason. "How are you feeling?" His hand went up to feel her forehead and although she was still warm, she wasn't burning up like before.

"I'm still icky, but not as bad." She took his hand from her forehead and laced her fingers through his, holding it around her waist in front of her stomach. "You'd make a pretty good doctor."

"Naw, I just had a good mom."

"Where is she now?"

His throat lumped up. "Buried in a Texas cemetery."

"I'm so sorry."

"It's okay. I had her until I was twelve, so it's been a while. It doesn't hurt like it used to."

Marley was quiet for several moments and he thought she'd fallen back asleep.

"It still hurts to think about Beth."

Luke was surprised she was willing to talk about her sister, considering how defensive she'd been before.

"I think it always hurts, but it just hurts a little less."

"And the anger? Does that go away too?"

Luke didn't have a good answer. He'd spent many years angry, cursing God or fate or whatever was in control of their lives for taking his mom. When major life moments happened, he still wished she was there, but was that the same thing?

"I think you're always going to wish they were around."

"Yeah. After my dad died, Beth took so many pictures of the three of us. Even when she got sick, she was still snapping pictures and filling up photo albums. My mom and I hardly take pictures anymore."

He kissed the side of her neck. "I'm sorry."

"Thanks." She hesitated, and he waited for what was coming. "I thought after last week you were done with me."

"Honestly, I thought I was too." He paused, debating on how to continue. "But I figured if I'd been chasing you for four weeks, what's three more?"

"Gee, that's sweet."

He squeezed her to him and placed his mouth next to her ear. "Besides, I'm really, really curious to figure out the secret."

Luke was afraid to push her too far and have her kick him out, so he asked, "Are you hungry?"

"A little."

Luke sat up and swung his legs off the other side of the bed. "How does chicken noodle soup and a grilled cheese sound?"

"Pretty good actually. My mom makes a great chicken noodle soup."

He stopped at the end of the bed and put his hand over her foot, shaking it with a grin. "I know. I went by the diner and asked her what you liked to eat when you're sick. She hooked me up."

"Well, aren't you spe—"

A series of wet coughs exploded from her, and as she hacked and gagged, he backed up toward the door. "I'll get you some water and warm up your food."

He walked into the kitchen and flipped on the light. Butters sat in the middle of the floor watching him as he pulled the container of soup out of the fridge and searched through her cupboards for a bowl.

"Look, I'm sorry about scaring you, little man, but you can't get up in someone's face when he's sleeping. You feel me?"

The bunny's ears flipped back and he went over to his food bowl.

"Good talk."

Luke walked back into Marley's bedroom ten minutes later, carrying a tray of food. She'd turned on the light and he could tell she'd combed her hair and washed her face. When he'd first shown up, her hair had stuck up a little on top of her head. She was cute no matter what, though.

"Did I hear you having a conversation with my rabbit?" she asked.

"I was just explaining why you don't stare at a strange guy when he's sleeping."

"Oh, believe me, I've told him not to do it to me many times, and he still does it."

"Stubborn vermin." Luke put the tray with the bowl of soup in her lap. There were a few slices of fresh baked baguette and a spoon on top of a paper towel, and he'd poured her a glass of orange juice.

"Yes, he is." She breathed in the soup with a smile. "Thank you for bringing me the soup. It has healing powers, you know."

"So your mom mentioned." He watched her dip her bread, laughing at the gusto she exuberated. She closed her eyes as she chewed and Luke's gaze hungrily swept over her plaited blond hair, the delicate veins on her eyelids, and pink lips. Her cheeks were flushed, and his lust tempered as he remembered how sick she was.

"Why are you staring at me like that?"

His gaze jerked up to meet hers, and he cleared his throat. "I was just thinking that you look better."

"And not like a snot monster from the black lagoon?"

"Hey, you said it not me," he said.

Marley pointed her spoon at him menacingly. "If I wasn't concerned about spilling hot soup on me, I would smack you. You are not supposed to agree with me."

"I didn't agree."

She cast the stink eye upon him and he chuckled. "Since you're feeling so much better, I guess I should get going."

Did she look disappointed? "Okay. Well, thanks. I appreciate you coming by and staying."

"Hey, if you want me to stick around, I'm happy to. We could find a movie to watch, and I can fetch you stuff while you call me a man servant."

The smile on her face was almost shy. It was charming. "You say that like I won't take you up on it."

He put his hands on either side of her legs and leaned closer. "So, does that mean you want me to stay?"

Just a flutter of hesitation in her eyes, and then she smiled. "Yes. Stay."

Chapter 16

Sonora's bridal shower was held in the Kent's Clubhouse at Castle Vineyards the next Sunday, and the event had come together rather beautifully, considering how short a time Marley was given to organize it. A hundred and fifty of Sonora's closest friends and family were mingling on the gorgeous cobblestone patio and nothing had gone wrong...yet.

Marley hadn't stopped running all morning, and really just wanted to sit down and rub her aching feet. She'd danced for four hours last night at the Keller wedding at the insistence of the bride who adored Marley. By the time she'd gotten home, she'd had blisters on her feet, despite the sensible shoes she'd worn. All she wanted was ten minutes to relax.

But Sonora kept asking for her. Actually, asking was too polite a term. Yelling for her was more like it. She felt a bit like the cartoon version of Cinderella.

Kendall came walking down the hall toward her, a half empty champagne glass in her hand. They'd started serving the mimosas as soon as the guests arrived, and Marley was pretty sure that was at least Kendall's forth one.

"Hey, great party," Kendall said, pulling her in for a hug as she passed.

"Thanks, I'm glad you're enjoying yourself. The guests seem happy."

"Why wouldn't they be? Who's *not* happy? Sonora?" Kendall shrugged. "Eff her then."

Marley glanced around, afraid someone would over hear, but the hum of too many voices drowned out their conversation. "Be careful. You don't want her to overhear and ban you from all the fun."

Kendall waved her empty hand a little sloppily. "Please, I'm about ready to cause a scene just so she'll kick me out. Being here around these snobs is like being waterboarded."

"Okay, I think no more mimosas for you for a while and we should get you some of those delicious little finger sandwiches." Marley took Kendall's glass and led her across the room to the buffet.

Kendall pouted and for a second, she resembled her older sister. "I'm not hungry."

"If you eat some of these, I guarantee you will start to feel better. My friend Rylie designed the menu, and she is amazing."

Kendall popped one of the sandwiches into her mouth and paused chewing, her eyes nearly rolling into the back of her head. "Good God, what is that?"

"Yummy, huh?"

"It's amazing." Kendall grabbed two more greedily.

"I know. She's a genius when it comes to food, so grab a plate," Marley said, pointing to the end of the buffet where the plates were stacked, "and eat up. And stay away from the alcohol for a while."

Kendall made a face at her. "You're bossy."

"So they tell me. I'm just looking out for you."

Kendall sighed, and picked up another sandwich. "I know."

Marley left Kendall and went in search of Sonora, who was probably ready to go off on her for something she thought was wrong with the shower. It seemed as if the closer they got to the wedding, the more demanding and dissatisfied Sonora became.

She rounded the corner and heard Sonora's voice coming from one of the rooms. Just before she opened the door, she heard a man talking and stopped. "Come on, Sonora. It was a little fun. It didn't mean anything."

"It meant something to me. I think I'm falling in love with you, Dustin."

Marley's stomach rolled violently. *Dustin? As in Dustin Kent?*

"You're lying to yourself and to me if you believe that. For one thing, I am not even remotely ready for marriage and if I was, it would be with a simple, docile little woman—not a spoiled, hysterical brat."

"How dare you—"

"You sought me out at my family's vineyard, during *your* bridal shower while you are engaged to another man. Believe me, Sonora, there is no way in hell you will *ever* be more than a fond memory. Don't ruin that by throwing a tantrum." Marley peeked in and saw Dustin chuck her under the chin condescendingly. The move actually made Marley want to slap him on Sonora's behalf, forgetting for a half second that Sonora had cheated on her fiancée .

"Besides, the most important quality I look for in a woman is loyalty to me, and we both know you're as loyal as a cat in heat."

Marley covered her mouth to hold in a gasp as Sonora slapped him across the face.

Dustin rubbed his cheek before giving her a dismissive nod. "Enjoy the rest of your shower."

Marley ducked out of the way as Dustin left the room, and waited for Sonora to come out. When she finally did, she was wiping at her darkly lined eyes frantically.

Marley stepped in as though she'd come from the patio.

"There you are. Are you ready to open gifts?"

Sonora sighed heavily. Must we do it in front of everyone? If I hate something, I just don't think I have the energy to fake it."

Why you self-centered, ungrateful—

Marley meant to take a calming breath and coax her, but instead she snapped, "Stop that. Now you wanted this big party, and all of these people, so put on a smile and open your gifts. Your guests are waiting."

Sonora's blue eyes met Marley's and Marley was taken aback to see tears spilling over her lashes and down her cheeks. "I didn't want this. Any of it. I wanted to continue to hit the clubs with my friends, and focus on revamping my career, but when the great Brent Harwood started looking for a wife, my parents and agent saw a way for me to move uptown. My parents only agreed to pay for the wedding if I reimbursed them with interest and convinced Brent to invest in more locations for their stupid restaurant." Sonora's face scrunched up. "I should just walk out the door now. To hell with all of them. I don't need their money. I'll put out a few singles and be back on top."

Marley's jaw dropped. "Are you out of your mind? Your parents are on the hook for thousands of dollars in deposits. They'll lose all of that if you bail."

"Whatever."

"No." Marley grabbed her arm and squeezed. Dragging her into the nearest empty room, she closed the door and turned on Sonora, furious. "I have taken your shit, and tried to create the perfect wedding day for you, and you will not stick me with having to explain to your guests why you took off."

"Get your hands off me! You're the help—"

"That's right, I'm the help. I am here to help you, and you know what will not help you? Insulting one of the richest and most powerful men in America within hearing distance of over a hundred guests at your *bridal shower*! If you don't want to get married, that's fine. Tell Brent, tell your parents, but you need to give up on this notion of you and Dustin Kent because he is not going to be your knight in shining armor. He's not even a toad in tin foil."

Sonora's blue eyes narrowed into slits. "How do you know about Dustin?"

"Because I saw him coming out of your hotel room a few weeks ago."

Sonora started tapping her nails on the tall glass table next to her. "And are you going to tell someone?"

Marley's stomach twisted. Kelly had told her that she couldn't reveal what Sonora was doing unless she wanted to break the confidentiality clause, so she was stuck keeping her mouth shut.

"No, I'm not going to tell anyone. I just want you to know that if I saw you, other people could too. You need to be careful, especially if you decide you want to go through with this wedding."

Sonora crossed her arms and struck an arrogant pose that told Marley she would not like what came next. "While I appreciate...actually, I don't appreciate your opinion. At all. Here's the deal, Marley. If you say a word about me to Brent or anyone else, I will destroy you and everything you love. Your mom owns that crap diner? I may be broke, but I still have friends in very important circles. If you say a word about any of this, I will bankrupt her."

It was one thing to mess with her, but threaten her mother? Hell no.

Marley stepped into her to the point that she either had to back up or fall over. "Do not threaten me or my family ever again, or I will piss on that confidentiality clause, Sonora. And let's face it, a washed-up diva can only survive scandal so many times before she's done."

Marley expected her to slap her too, but instead, Sonora smiled like a Cheshire cat. It was too damn creepy.

"Well, Marley Stevenson, check out the pair on you. I didn't know you had it in you." She patted Marley's cheek. "But you shouldn't mess with me, sweetheart. I've been chewing up little mice like you since I was in my first beauty pageant."

Marley jerked away. "Don't call me sweetheart."

"Oh, did I irritate you?" Sonora's sweet tone turned into a scoff. "Like I give a shit. Now get out there and make sure everything is just right. If I am going through with this sham of a wedding, then I want it perfect."

Marley left the room, wishing like hell she could just keep walking, but she was only two weeks away from the end.

She could make it. Even if she had to gag and hog tie Sonora to shut her up.

* * * *

Luke was hanging out in his hotel room Saturday evening, looking out the window as he sipped on a glass of whisky. He was supposed to meet Brent at the bar in a few hours, but Brent had been called back to New York for a work emergency. So, he decided to just take it easy instead. He would have texted Marley, but he had no idea how long she'd be at the bridal shower, and he wasn't sure if things were better since he'd taken care of her. He knew he agreed to wait, but it was still weird that Sonora and Brent's wedding was the deadline.

A lone figure in a pink sports bra and black jogging pants ran in front of the hotel, her blond hair swinging as she moved. Luke didn't have to get any closer to know it was Marley.

Setting his whisky down, he pulled on his tennis shoes and ran down the stairs. He raced past a startled couple coming through the entrance of the hotel, hoping to catch Marley before she disappeared out of sight.

When he turned down the way she had, he saw her heading for the dirt road that lead to Buzzard Gulch. Why was she jogging up there?

Luke picked up the pace to catch her before she took that first hill. When he was about ten feet behind her, she glanced over her shoulder at him. Her gaze went from worried to irritated in three seconds flat.

She stopped jogging and yanked out her earbuds.

"What are you doing?"

"Checking on you. I saw you jogging and thought I'd join you."

She was shaking her head before he finished his sentence "No. Not right now. I just want to be alone and run my feelings into the ground."

Without giving him a chance for a rebuttal, she replaced her earbuds and started up the massive hill.

If she'd been anyone else, he'd have given her space, but he didn't like her out here all alone.

So he followed behind at a slightly slower place, smiling as he took in the pretty fantastic view of Marley's tight butt jiggling as she moved.

One thing he would say about Marley was she had stamina. She just kept pushing until she reached the ghost town, and only then did she slow to a walk, sucking in air.

"You do this run a lot?" he asked loudly.

She pulled out her earbuds, still breathing hard. He figured she'd probably heard him, but when she leaned against one of the buildings to take a drink, she looked at him with surprise. "You're still here?"

"Yeah. Figured when you were done working your feelings out, you were going to need a shoulder to cry on."

She slapped her palm against the top of her water bottle, closing it with a snap. "I'm not going to cry. I want to hit something. Pummel it to a bloody pulp."

"Well, in that case," he joked, pretending to run backwards.

"Not you. Sonora." She kicked the side of the building and released a guttural scream. "She's just such a blood-sucking bitch."

"That would explain Brent's Renfield-like behavior."

She gave him an exasperated look. "Can you please take this seriously? She is toxic like a black widow spider and once she has you in her web, you can't escape. Everything is on her terms and she is a horrible human being and I just want to tell her to suck it and—"

He put his hands on her shoulders. "Hey, hey. It's okay. I know better than anyone how fucked up she is. Just take a breath."

Marley did, her breathing labored. "I thought a run would help me blow off some steam, but it seems like it just riled me up more."

Luke chuckled. "I'd suggest another activity, but we still haven't hit our fifth date according to you."

Marley's expression changed and he suddenly understood how prey felt when a predator spotted them.

She came toward him, rolling her hips, her waist appearing longer in the low riding shorts and sports bra. Luke's heart kicked up, and she placed her hands on his chest, running them over his pecs and down…

When she held his cock through his shorts, gently squeezing him, he swallowed hard.

"I think we can go ahead and count you taking care of me as date number four. Don't you?"

"What are you saying?"

Marley stood up on her tip toes as the other hand cupped the back of his head, pulling his mouth down to hers.

"I'm asking where you want to fuck me. Against the wall of one of these old buildings? In the dirt? Down by the river?"

Holy shit! And she accused him of talking dirty.

"Marley, I don't think—"

"Don't think. Please." She released him, and turned toward the river trail. "I'm going down to the water. If you want me, all you have to do is follow behind. If you aren't down there a minute from when I strip off these clothes, I'll know you aren't interested and I'll go for a swim anyway."

Luke watched her and her ass before she disappeared down the slope. If he was a good man, he wouldn't go along with this. He'd wait for her here until she cooled off and save their first time for when it wasn't about her working off her frustrations.

If only he were that good.

Chapter 17

Marley slipped into the cold water, the slow-moving current sliding across her skin as she swam. She wasn't sure if Luke would follow her, and uncertainty started to creep through her frustration and anger at Sonora. She wasn't sure if she actually wanted him to follow her... but what if he didn't?

She rolled over onto her back. Her cheeks warmed just thinking about the embarrassment of throwing herself at him and him not taking her up on it.

She looked up when she heard a thump and saw Luke on the rock, taking off his shoes. Her heart felt as though it were going to explode as he peeled off every layer, revealing the hard, rippled body beneath.

Finally, he slid his boxer briefs down and did a cannon ball into the water from the top of the jumping rock. Marley laughed as water sprayed her the second he connected.

Marley watched him swim toward her under water, waiting for him to break the surface. Strong arms wrapped around her, pulling her down, and she squealed as he came up three inches from her face.

"Hey there."

"Hi."

That seemed to be all either of them could say for several moments, until he smiled softly. "Just letting you know, I decided a swim sounded pretty awesome. It had nothing to do with the fact that I might find you naked."

Marley burst out laughing and wrapped her arms around his shoulders. "Sure it didn't."

He actually looked insulted, which only made her giggle harder. "Are you questioning whether or not I'm a gentleman?"

"Not at all. I am just pointing out that 99.9 percent of single, straight men *would* follow a woman to watch her swim naked. Especially if she hinted they were probably getting laid."

He leaned over and nibbled along her neck. "Oh yeah? And where is this scientific study published?"

"It's just common sense. Everyone knows men think with their dicks first."

Luke pulled back, and she could tell he was pretending to be shocked. "Marley Stevenson, that is sexist. I demand an apology."

"I will not apologize for speaking the truth. Prove me wrong." Her hand slid down between their bodies and she wrapped her fingers around his length. "If you can walk away from what I'm doing to you right here and now, I will take back what I said about men—"

She hadn't even finished the sentence before he pulled away and started swimming for shore. Her mouth hanging open, she watched as he exited the river, droplets rolling down his tan back and over his firm ass. God, she wanted to get her hands on those globes and squeeze.

Maybe men weren't the only creatures to be led about by their hormones.

When he turned around to face her, his arms crossed and his hard on sticking out like a dueling sword, she tried not to laugh.

"You got something to say?" he asked.

"Sure. But first." She swam over to him and climbed out of the water, watching his face as his dark eyes turned black and the muscles in his jaw clenched.

"I am so sorry that I was sexist. Can you ever forgive me?"

She knew that the minute he moved she was about to get a wild ride. Maybe it was animalistic groan as he picked her up, or the way his mouth clamped over her breast, using his teeth and tongue to make her whimper with pleasure. All she did know was that when he stuck his fingers between them and found her clit with two of them, it didn't take too many strokes before she ignited. The fire of her orgasm rushed through her body, warming her from the inside out, and she leaned her head back against the rock he had pushed her up against, riding the sensation out until she was trembling with aftershocks.

"Fuck," he groaned.

"What?"

He pressed against her, and she could feel the rub of his dick against her slit. "I wasn't expecting this and my wallet is back at the hotel. No condom."

"I'm on the pill. If you're clean…"

"I'm clean."

She wrapped her arms around his shoulders and kissed him, pulling back far enough to whisper, "Then don't stop."

Marley's gaze held his as he reached between them and adjusted his cock. Then he was sliding inside, stretching her until her eyes closed and her lips parted in a low moan. She kissed him hungrily, messy and wet as he pressed all the way in. His hands moved around to grip her ass. She gasped into his mouth as he pulled out and slammed back in.

Her nails dug into his shoulders as he repeated the motion, slowly out and swiftly returning. It was magic and she could feel another orgasm building inside, her muscles squeezing him and throbbing around his girth. She let him set the pace, holding on as he bounced her up and down on his dick.

When he picked up speed and his motions became unsteady it hit her, stars exploding behind her closed eyelids as she pulled away from his mouth, crying out.

"Oh, shit. Fuck. I'm coming."

He pressed her harder into the rock wall and hollered. His body shook against hers, his orgasm seeming to sap his strength as he sank against her, breathing raggedly into her ear.

His lips moved over the skin underneath and he whispered, "Are you okay? Was I too rough?"

At that moment, all Marley felt was euphoric and she smiled. "Uh uh."

He continued to lean against her, and she noticed that her skin seemed to be tingling, as if a hundred tiny wings were kissing her skin.

"Uh, Marley?" he said.

"Hmm."

"You've got ants crawling all over you."

Marley's eyes flew open and she glanced down. The sensation she'd thought was afterglow was actually a swarm of ants all over her chest.

"Off, off!"

She pushed him away, and he slipped out of her. She didn't stop to see if he was okay as she ran back into the water, rubbing at her skin and dunking her head under the water.

When she came up for air, she frantically looked down at her body for any more insects. "God, are they off? Ugh, this is horrible."

She glanced toward the shore and scowled when she saw Luke rolling on the ground with laughter.

"They're probably on you too, jackass!"

He sat up with a wheeze, wiping at his eyes as he continued guffawing. He stood up, and walked into the water with her, stopping a few inches away when he was waist deep.

"Come here and I'll make sure they're gone," he said.

"No, you laughed at me. You just keep your distance."

"Oh, come on! It was hysterical. My first time having wild, passionate sex by a river and it ends up being an orgy with a bunch of ants."

"You are not funny," she said, her mouth twitching as she suppressed a smile.

He reached out and pulled her to him. "I'm kind of funny."

Marley let him inspect her, mostly because it felt good to have his hands all over her. He spread the strands of her hair and ran his fingers through them, rubbing her shoulders and easing a bit of her irritation with him.

When they finally climbed out of the water, the sun was starting to set and the sky was turning an orangey pink. Marley picked up her clothes and groaned.

"They're covered in ants."

"Mine too," he called from the top of the rock. He hopped down, still nude. "Naked run for it?"

"You are so crazy. Let's try shaking them off. We can shower when we get to your hotel," she said.

"Fair enough."

When she didn't see any more crawly creatures she put her clothes back on, and shook her head. "I think all future sexual exploits should occur in a bed."

"Sounds good to me." He grinned and took off at a run. "First one to my hotel gets to be on top!"

Marley laughed, chasing after him. "I didn't agree to that!"

"Don't be a sore loser!"

* * * *

Luke let Marley pass him before they reached the lobby doors of his hotel. "Hey, did you let me win?"

He leaned his hands on his knees, breathing hard. "Me? I am the most competitive person you will ever meet. If you beat me, it was fair and square."

"Hmm." She started walking around to the back staircase and he frowned. "Are we still sneaking around?"

Marley turned, a flush in her cheeks. "It's just for two more weeks."

"Yeah, I know." He opened the door and walked into the lobby, pausing when the door opened again behind him. Marley caught up and warmth spread through him. He figured holding her hand would be pushing it, so he held back.

"Hey Turner."

Turner, the owner of The Love Shack Hotel, was a balding man in his early fifties who spent most of his time behind the desk reading. He looked up from the James Patterson novel in his hands and nodded. "Hey, Marley. Mr. Jessup."

Luke said hi, and they continued to the elevator. When they stepped inside, Marley slipped her arms around his waist and leaned her chin against his chest. "Are you happy?"

"Just about." The minute the doors closed he kissed her, hard and fast and he actually felt her stumble when he released her. "Even better now."

The doors opened and he led the way to his hotel room, hurrying with the door before she bolted.

When Marley made a beeline for the bathroom, he went to kick off his shoes and lie down on the bed.

"Aren't you coming?" she asked from the doorway, dropping her sports bra on the ground.

He paused, watching as she bent over and discarded her shorts and underwear. "Figured you'd want some privacy."

"And I thought we'd have a shower and then get very, very dirty again. With me on top, of course."

Like he was going to say no.

Two hours later, Luke lay on his back with Marley sprawled out across his chest, her deep, even breathing telling him she was asleep. As he stroked her hair, he wondered what it was about her that was so different. From the moment he'd met her, he'd been drawn to her like a bear to honey and now, he didn't want to ever be without her.

Which is why the reason behind why they couldn't go public bothered him so much. For the first time in his life, he was falling in love. Imagining a future, marriage, kids...

And she wanted to move to New York and start her life.

He didn't want to go back to New York and he definitely didn't want to raise a family there. But if it was what Marley wanted, and she wanted him too, was he really going to not follow her?

Why was he even thinking about this now? They had two more weeks. Then they could talk about life after Brent and Sonora's wedding. Right now, he should just enjoy what they had.

Too bad his brain wouldn't shut the hell up.

Chapter 18

The next Friday was the Bachelorette party, and Marley was already exasperated with Sonora. Tahoe was bustling in the summertime, and as Marley and Kendall walked behind the group of scantily clad bridesmaids led by tiara and boa wearing Sonora, Marley had a sudden urge to disappear into the crowd.

"I guess no one was interested in my spa idea," Marley said.

Kendall smiled and nudged her shoulder. "I was, but I was outvoted."

Instead, the girls had all decided they wanted to go dancing and get hammered. Forget dinner or gambling—Marley was still going to end up taking care of a bunch of drunk girls all night.

They walked into Harvey's and through the lobby until they reached the club. Marley could feel men's gazes following them as they passed, and it made her feel like a slab of beef on the grill. Damn, when had she gotten so old?

Sonora walked right up to the VIP booth, and flashed a smile at the bouncer, whose eyes widened in his dark face. "You're—"

"Yes I am. You should have us on the guest list."

"Of course I do. Come right in." The bouncer pulled back the rope and stamped each of their hands in turn with a little neon yellow bumblebee. They followed him into the club as another thick-necked man took over the booth. The club was dark, with strobing lights, and women in go-go boots and silver miniskirts and bras dancing on a catwalk above their heads. A couple of shirtless guys in fedoras and metallic MC Hammer pants danced and gyrated along with them.

"Here you go. Enjoy," the bouncer said, waving them up to a secluded table behind a roped off section.

"Thank you," Sonora said sweetly, nodding back at Marley. Marley pulled a five out of her pocket and gave it to the bouncer, who frowned.

"What?"

"I think you're a little short," he said.

Marley took back her five and slapped a twenty on his palm. It wasn't her money, at least.

The man gave her a gap-toothed grin. "Pleasure."

Marley walked away from him and sat next to Kendall, grumbling.

"Someone flag down the server! We need shots!" Emma, an actress that Sonora had been friends with since they were both on the Mickey Mouse Club, bounced in her seat until her short black skirt was practically at her waist. Marley wanted to reach out and yank it down, but she didn't know the girl that well.

"God, you are shouting right in my ear," Sonora griped, before waving at Marley. "Go get us some drinks."

"I think they have bottle service. If we wait just a minute, I can probably flag someone down."

"Do you have to argue with me about everything, or maybe, for once, can you just do what I ask without being a giant pain in the ass?"

Sonora's two friends giggled, and Marley felt like she was back in high school, trying to be friends with the popular kids and getting shit on again.

Marley raised her eyebrow. "Do I look like your bar wench?"

"No, you look like my maid of honor, whose sole purpose of being here is making me happy as a clam, so how about you run along and do that?"

Marley gritted her teeth and stood up, heading down to the bar on the far side of the club.

Kendall caught up alongside her. "Why do you let her talk to you like that?"

Because it's part of my job.

"Because she's right. It's her last night of freedom and I signed up to make sure it goes off without a hitch."

"Seriously, though, she is such a bitch sometimes."

Marley grinned at her. "Only sometimes?"

"Okay, all the time, but that doesn't mean we have to bend over and take it. One of these days, I'm going to let her have it."

"And I will pay to see it."

They got in line and the guy in front of them with slicked back hair and a smarmy grin said, "Well, hey there, ladies."

"Hi," Kendall and Marley said politely.

"Are you having a good time?"

"We just got here," Kendall said.

"Me too. It gets busier as the night goes on. Can I buy you a drink?"

"Thanks, but there's a group of us, and we're in charge or procuring liquor for them."

The lined moved, but Casanova hadn't given up yet. "Oh, yeah? You guys here for a bachelorette or a birthday party?"

"Bachelorette party. My sister's," Kendall said.

"Nice, either one of you married?"

"No," they said at the same time.

"But we both have really big, burly boyfriends who're in court-ordered anger management," Kendall added.

Marley laughed as the guy turned away from them, probably figuring he wasn't getting laid by either one of them tonight.

"Gee, was it something we said?" Kendall said.

"Maybe he's just not into drama."

"Shame, cause it seems like we got nothing but drama."

"Amen, sister," Marley said.

By the time they made it back to the table with six shot glasses, there was a bottle and glasses already on the table. They set them down and Sonora took one. "We flagged down a server while you were gone, since it took you forever."

"Well, I'm sure you'll drink it," Marley said, irritated.

The night just went downhill from there.

Maybe it was the fact that she was the only sober one; even Kendall had started taking shots and had deteriorated into a giggling whoo-hooer. Or that the drunker Sonora got, the meaner she became.

Either way, by midnight Marley was ready to go back to the hotel and sleep.

Fiona, one of Sonora's back-up dancers, sat down next to her, weaving a bit in her seat. "I don't feel good."

By the green tinge to her skin, Marley had a feeling she was going to blow. "Okay, let's get you to the bathroom."

Marley put her arm around the stumbling redhead and they managed to get to a bathroom stall in the nick of time. She spent the next thirty minutes holding Fiona's hair while she puked. When Fiona finished, she could hardly stand, and Marley ended up practically carrying her back up to the room to sleep it off.

When she got back to the club, the bouncer stepped up to her, and her eyes narrowed.

"Seriously?"

"What? I ain't ever seen you before."

"Then what is this?" She waved the stamp on the back of her hand at him.

"No ins and outs. Those are the rules."

Marley gave him another twenty with a slap in his hand, and headed back in to make sure everyone was still in one piece. She found Emma and Caitlyn, Sonora's cousin, grinding on the floor to the delight of a group of salivating men. Kendall was at the bar, laughing with some guy who looked like he should be modeling underwear for Calvin Klein and Sonora...

Shit.

Sonora was up in someone else's VIP lounge, sitting on some guy's lap.

Marley made a beeline for them, and when she came up alongside them, one of the other men at the table laughed. "Whoa, sweetheart, no need to look so cross. It's a party."

"Don't call me sweetheart." Standing over Sonora with her hands on her hips, she said, "Come on, let's get you some water."

"Fuck off, I'm talking to Gregg."

Marley grabbed Sonora by the arm and lifted her off the man's lap. When he started to protest, she stared right at him, and snapped, "So help me, if you touch her again, I will bust your nut sack with my three-inch heels."

Gregg threw his arms up and shifted away. Marley pulled Sonora along behind her.

"You big pussy, she isn't even wearing heels!" Sonora hollered over her shoulder. She started fighting Marley at the bottom of the stairs. "Get off me, you aren't my mother."

Marley let her go and squared off with her. "No, and I shouldn't have to be, but you were about one lap dance away from ending up on TMZ, and then there's no way Brent would marry you. So, maybe instead of acting like an idiot, you might want to thank me for making sure you still have a fiancée in the morning."

"God, you are such a buzz kill!" Sonora stomped out onto the dance floor to rub up on Emma and Caitlyn, and Marley climbed into their own VIP booth, where Kendall was sipping on a drink.

"Everything okay?" Kendall asked.

Marley flopped down with a groan. "Yeah, except your sister can't hold her liquor."

"Sorry you have to babysit all of us."

"It's my job. I just wish she didn't make it so hard."

"It's not your job. Who designated you the sober sister?" Kendall leaned over and poured Marley a drink. "You deserve to drink and have fun too."

Marley shook her head. "No I can't. If I get drunk, who is going to make sure we all get back to the room safely?"

"They are adults. If they can't take care of themselves, then they shouldn't drink."

Marley considered the shot, and sucked it back before she changed her mind. One shot wouldn't kill her.

* * * *

Marley blinked her eyes open against the blinding light in the room, groaning at the piercing throb in her head. Her stomach was twisting on top of itself, and the rancid taste of her mouth caused bile to rise up in the back of her throat.

"Oh, God."

"Already there," another voice mumbled.

Marley turned her head and found Kendall face down in the pillow next to her. Her blonde hair looked like a bird's nest and she still appeared to be wearing her halter top from the night before.

Marley came up on her elbows, and glanced around. "What the hell happened?"

"We're idiots who can't hold our liquor?" Kendall offered.

Marley started to laugh, then moaned in pain. "Don't make me laugh, dude."

"Sorry."

She got up and swung her legs over the bed. When she stood up to go to the bathroom, her head spun like a tilt-a-whirl and she barely managed to stumble to the toilet before she was dry heaving.

I am never drinking again.

After she finished her business, she came out to grab her toiletry stuff and something was off. It wasn't just that the suite was quiet. It was that it was *too* quiet.

"Where is everyone?" Marley asked.

"Probably still asleep."

Except Caitlyn was supposed to be sleeping in the other bed in their room, and it was empty. Marley walked out into the open area, but there was no Fiona or Emma on the pull out. She knocked on Sonora's door and when she didn't answer, she opened it up.

All of her stuff was gone, and the bed was empty. The clock on the nightstand said 1:00 p.m.

She stomped back into the room to find Kendall sitting up, staring at her phone.

"What's wrong?"

Kendall held out the phone screen and Marley wanted to throw something against the wall: **Have fun finding a ride home, bitches!**

Sonora had left them there.

Marley went to sit on the other bed and dialed the hotel phone.

"Front desk, how may I help you?"

"Hi, this is room 1411, and I was just wondering if the rest of our party left us a message."

"Let me check, one moment please." After several moments of listening to her click around on her computer, she came back on the line, "I'm sorry, but Ms. Star checked out and canceled the reservation you all had for tonight. If you would like to stay, I can reinstate the reservation for an additional charge, but as it is now, you're going to have to pay for late check out."

"Oh…okay. Sure, we'll do that. Thank you."

"My pleasure."

Who the hell says my pleasure after they shaft someone?

As Marley hung up the phone, it really sunk in. Sonora had let them oversleep and canceled their second night.

But why? "I am going to fucking kill her. Why would she do this?"

"Maybe because I called her an evil skank monster from hell who didn't deserve Brent?" Kendall offered.

Marley paused, her jaw dropping to her chest. "You said that? When?"

"When she started yelling at you about how you sucked as a maid of honor, and you told her she had no honor and she called you a really nasty name and I went off…you really don't remember any of this?"

"Shit. Shit." She was so screwed. She wouldn't be surprised if Kelly fired her after this. She should not have let her guard down.

Who was she going to call to bail them out?

Scrolling through her phone, her thumb landed on Luke's name and before she could really think about the repercussions, she hit call.

He picked up on the second ring. "Well, hey there. How's the bachelorette party?"

"Actually, it kind of sucks. Sonora took off and left Kendall and me."

She had to hold the phone away when he shouted, "What?"

"She took the car, left us in the hotel room, and we're completely stranded. I was hoping maybe—"

"I'm on my way."

Marley released the breath she didn't know she'd been holding. "Thank you."

"Hey, if I get to see you, it's worth the drive."

Marley's heart skipped, and her cheeks warmed. When she hung up the call, Kendall was just coming out of the bathroom.

"Who did you call?" she asked.

"Luke."

Kendall's grin was brilliant. "Aha! I thought something was going on there."

Marley shot her an alarmed look. "Has anyone else said anything?"

"Who, like Sonora? Please, she'd so self-involved she wouldn't notice the sky was falling."

Marley was relieved for a half second and then it hit her. If she was fired from Something Borrowed, she wouldn't have to sneak around anymore with Luke. Maybe instead of New York, she could apply for internships at publishing houses in L.A. There were several in that area and—

Marley shook her head, realizing that she was actually thinking about rearranging her entire future for Luke—a guy she'd barely known two months and wasn't even sure where or what they were.

It was official. After twenty-eight years of sensibility, she'd lost her damn mind.

* * * *

Two hours later, Luke stood on the other side of the hotel room door, a big grin on his face as Marley swung it open. The pure relief on her face was worth it, and as angry as he was with Sonora for ditching her and Kendall, he did like getting to save the day.

"Thank you so much."

"Hey, I love being your hero," he said, leaning over to give her a kiss on the lips. He pulled back and noticed her eyes were bloodshot and there were dark circles under them. "Rough night, huh?"

"Can't you tell by the fact that we were left stranded?"

"That was a dick move by her. I don't care what you did to piss her off."

"I called her an evil skank monster from hell," Kendall called out. She was sitting on the bed with her shades on watching TV.

Luke stared down at Marley in surprise. "Did she really?"

"Apparently. It's all a big blank for me. I guess Patron and I are not a good combination."

Luke squeezed her shoulder and gave her a kiss on her forehead. "Well, let's get your stuff and get you home. No point in staying around here to lose money."

Luke walked in and picked up their overnight bags.

"Was Brent happy that his princess was coming home?" Kendall's tone was mocking and angry, which surprised him a little. She always seemed so cheery.

I guess everyone can have their sunshine stolen by a hangover.

"Actually, when I told him what she'd done to you guys, he seemed pretty pissed. He wanted to come with me, but I wasn't sure it was a good idea."

Kendall grabbed one of the pillows, squeezing it viciously between her two hands. "I hope he rips her a new one."

"He did call her before I left. I guess they headed to Reno this morning to spend the night and will be back tomorrow."

"Gee, that's nice.

Kendall turned off the TV and they followed him out the door silently, so he filled it. "The good news is Sonora had booked the suite for two days, so you didn't have to pay for it."

"Except she canceled the second night and stuck us with a late check out," Marley said.

Shit, he was hoping she wouldn't have to know about that.

Luke pressed the elevator button, trying to sound casual. "It's okay, I called and paid for the second night before I left."

"You didn't have to do that," Marley said.

"I know, but I wanted to. You'd already had a rough one. So, if you want to stay and enjoy it—"

"No!" The two women shouted at the same time, then groaned simultaneously.

"Okay, all right, we'll get the hell out of here," Luke said, suppressing his laughter.

They stepped into the elevator, and Luke liked that Marley leaned her head on his shoulder with a sigh. "I am so tired."

"I'm hungry," Kendall chimed in.

Luke chuckled. "We can swing through a drive-through on our way home."

"Sounds good," Marley said, yawning.

As the elevator doors opened and they entered the lobby, Luke led them out into the parking garage. Once Kendall was settled in the back and Marley in the front, Luke did what he promised and pulled through the McDonalds drive-through for them.

"Greasy food is the best thing to combat a hangover," he said.

Marley looked at him with a soft smile, and it was like basking in the glow of the sun.

"Thank you."

Luke took her hand and didn't release it the entire drive home.

Chapter 19

Marley walked into Something Borrowed on Sunday and headed straight back to Kelly's office. She'd been expecting to get home last night and have a message on her answering machine from Kelly, telling her to get her butt into work so she could fire her in person, but there was nothing. It wasn't like Kelly to avoid a problem.

As Marley passed by her office, she thought about the last seven years of working there. Although there had been some tough clients and times when she wished she didn't have to always put on a happy face, it felt like she was leaving her home. The faces at Something Borrowed might change frequently, but she knew the business backwards and forwards. It was bittersweet to say good-bye.

Not to mention she was going to have to pay back the commission check on Sonora's wedding. With only six days to go, that was a bitter pill to swallow.

She knocked on Kelly's door.

"Come in!"

Marley opened the door with a tentative smile. "Hey Kelly, how are you?"

"I'm good." Kelly tilted her head to the side, looking confused. "Shouldn't you still be in Tahoe for the bachelorette party?"

It was Marley's turn to be surprised. "Didn't Sonora call you?"

"No, why would she?"

As Kelly waited expectantly for an answer, Marley's brain scrambled to make sense of what was happening.

"Oh, just that I got food poisoning from one of those seafood buffets and had to come home early. I know we're supposed to stay with our brides the whole time and keep an eye on them, but—"

"Marley, you can't help getting sick and I've had food poisoning. I know how horrible it can be. Are you feeling any better?"

Marley had a feeling Kelly was asking since she'd walked in wearing yoga pants, a Harley T-shirt, and no make-up; not her usual business attire.

"I'm still a little queasy, but I couldn't wait until tomorrow if you were upset with me."

"Not at all. Things happen and you've done a fabulous job on this. Sonora sings your praises."

That made Marley uneasy. "She does?"

"Yes, she says you're so helpful and organized. She even said it feels like she's known you forever."

This is too reminiscent of a spider playing with a fly. What's the catch?

"Well, great. I guess I'll go home and rest then."

Kelly stood up and came around the desk. When she took Marley's hand and squeezed it, Marley was taken aback by the emotion in Kelly's hazel eyes. "You take care of yourself, Marley. You know how much I need you."

A lump of guilt lodged in Marley's throat. Kelly wasn't just her boss; she was her friend too. And she was lying through her teeth about everything, including Luke.

Just six more days and it will all be over. I can't blow this.

"I promise I will."

Marley walked out of Something Borrowed and once she was safely in her car, she dialed Sonora.

"Hello?"

"Sonora, it's Marley."

"I know, you're programmed into my phone."

Ignoring Sonora's *you're an idiot* tone, she pressed on. "I just wanted to apologize for Friday night, and thank you for not telling Kelly."

"You think I did that because I *like* you or something?"

Marley could feel the muscle under her eye start twitching. "Actually, I have no idea why you did it."

"Because as long as you work for me, you're bound by confidentiality to keep your mouth shut. So, it behooves me to keep you on as my maid of honor."

"Lucky me," Marley muttered, but Sonora heard her.

"Oh, you have no idea how lucky you are. It would have been so easy to screw you over when you were passed out drunk with my idiot sister."

Forgetting that she was supposed to be kissing Sonora's ass, she snapped, "You mean stranding us and making us pay for an already booked hotel room wasn't bad enough?"

"No. No, I could have left you passed out in our VIP booth. Who knows what would have happened while you were drunk and defenseless?"

Marley's blood chilled. "You wouldn't do that to anyone, even your worst enemy."

"I'd do worse to an enemy. Thank your God or whatever you pray to that I find you just a mild annoyance."

Sonora wasn't just a self-centered bitch. She was psychotic.

"Now, we're going to get through this week. I'm going to marry Brent and become his perfect little trophy wife. And you are going to help me every step of the way because that is what I'm are paying you to do. Right?"

"You mean your *parents* are paying me."

Sonora hissed into the phone. "And they'll snatch it all back if you screw this up. So shut the fuck up and do your job, or I will make you regret it."

The call ended, probably because Sonora had hung up on her. Marley stared at the screen, her mind whirling.

This wasn't what she had signed up for when she'd started at Something Borrowed. She hadn't expected to get pulled into duping a perfectly nice man into marrying a heinous gold-digger.

With her hands shaking, she pressed on Luke's name.

"Hey. How's it going?" he asked.

"Oh, fine. Have you left for the airport yet?"

"Not yet. My flight doesn't leave until five. I was actually hoping to spend a little more time with you before—"

"Yes. I'll pick you up."

* * * *

Luke knew there was something going on with Marley from the minute she picked him up. The car ride was pretty quiet and when they walked inside her place, she was on him before the door fully closed.

He caught her in his arms, and dipped his head so he could meet her lips. Her mouth moved hungrily, desperately under his and he didn't fight it or try to ask her what was wrong. He reached around and gripped the globes of her ass in his hands and lifted her. She wrapped her legs around his waist as he carried her back toward the bedroom. He half expected to step on her rabbit, who liked to get under his feet, but he made it to the edge of the bed safely.

He lowered her back onto the bed and pulled up enough to strip off his T-shirt.

"I swear, every time your shirt comes off, it's like angels start singing in my ears," she said, grinning.

Luke laughed as he tossed his shirt to the side and climbed onto the bed with her. "Oh yeah? So being with me is like a religious experience?"

"Easy tiger, I didn't say that. Just meant I like your rippling pectorals."

"Well, that's a good thing." He took the bottom of her T-shirt and pulled it up and over her head, determined to lighten her mood and keep her smiling. "Because I have to tell you, I like your pectorals too."

Marley laughed, her "pectorals" jiggling above the cup of her blue bra. "They're called breasts, dude."

Luke bent over and kissed each one, following her when she lay back with a sigh. His lips trailed up over her collarbone and to the crook of her neck, where he nipped lightly.

The sensation of nails slicing across his back made him jerk up with a yowl and he twisted around to see what had happened.

"Are you okay?"

Luke finally spotted Butters at the head of the bed, his little nose twitching as he watched Luke with beady eyes.

"Bunny."

Butter's ear flicked, but he didn't move.

"What did he do?" Marley asked, her voice laced with laughter.

"He jumped across my back and clawed the shit out of me."

"Oh, poor baby. Let me see."

He got up on his knees and turned his back toward her. He felt her fingers glide across his skin gently as she tsked behind him.

"He broke the skin, and there's a little blood. I should probably clean them."

She slid off the bed and went into the bathroom. While she was gone, Luke glanced over his shoulder at Butters, who had stretched out on his stomach, his paws straight out in front of him.

"Are we going to have a problem, Punk?" Luke joked.

Butters hopped up and came up along his side. Luke stroked a hand over his ears and back, the soft fur tickling his palm.

"Ah, I'm just kidding. I know you didn't mean to hurt me."

"Of course he didn't," Marley said as she came back into the room. "He was probably just trying to get to the other side and you were in the way."

"Cool, so I'm a bunny obstacle course. Good to know."

She climbed up behind him with a first-aid kit in her hand. "It's just a few little scratches. Stop being a whiner."

"Geez, and you talk about my bedside manner."

He heard a paper package rip open before a cold, wet wipe ran over his back.

And then it started to burn.

"Ow, ow, dammit woman, are you using alcohol on me?"

"I am disinfecting the wound. Chill out." She blew over the alcohol, soothing the sting a bit. "Better?"

He grunted in response. She rubbed something slick on his skin, and he felt the tape of a band aid before she swung around to straddle his lap. "There. All better."

He slipped his arms around her waist, pretending concern. "So I'm gonna be okay, doc?"

"Hmm, you might need bed rest, but I think you'll pull through."

She kissed him, and he couldn't believe how lucky he was. There was something about Marley and him that just worked. If they could just get beyond the shit she was keeping from him, he knew they could be something special.

If only he could convince her to really trust him.

Chapter 20

The day of Sonora and Brent's wedding was scorching by nine in the morning. This did not help the mood of the bride, who had been biting people's heads off for hours. It was almost four and they'd just finished pictures, for which Marley was thankful. The last thing she wanted was a photograph of her on top of Sonora, choking her out.

Since their phone conversation, Marley had been trying to concentrate on making it through every task Sonora asked of her. Picking up the wedding favors at UPS an hour away when Sonora wasn't around to sign for them. Grabbing Sonora's honeymoon outfit from the drycleaners because she didn't have time. All week she'd run her errands and taken her insults and kept a button on her emotions.

Today though, it was 105 degrees outside, she was wearing powder pink itchy taffeta, and the sound of Sonora's bitching was grating on her one last nerve.

"God, it is so fucking hot, I'm melting," Sonora screeched. "Someone turn on the fan." When Emma, one of her other bridesmaids did, she jumped up from the bridal vanity. "Don't turn it on me or my hair will be ruined."

Marley could tell the other women were frazzled and felt their pain. Times ten.

"Are you stepping on my dress, you drunk hippo?" Sonora stood up from the vanity, and whirled on poor Fiona. "If there is a footprint on my one of a kind Vera Wang, I will personally take that ginormous size nine heel of yours and shove it up your—"

"Okay, that's enough!" Marley shouted.

All the bridesmaids swung around to stare at her in horror.

"What the hell did you just say to me?" Sonora hissed.

Ignoring her, she addressed the stricken bridesmaids calmly. "Why don't you guys head to the kitchen and get Sonora a cup of iced tea, and—"

"I don't want iced tea!"

"At this point, I don't care what you want! You are being terrible to all the people you call friends and I am sick of it."

Sonora stood up with a sneer. "And I'm sick of you acting as though you're so much better than me, like I'm just some dumb pop star who doesn't get exactly what you think of me."

"Everyone out. Sonora and I need to have a talk."

They escaped as fast as their five inch heels could carry them, Emma the last one through the door.

"Bring me back a bottled water," Sonora yelled.

When the door closed and they were finally alone, Marley advanced on her. Sonora's eyes widened, and Marley thought she spotted real fear in them. Did she think Marley was going to hit her?

Tempting.

"Now, you and I have this last day together and then I don't have to deal with your poor me, no one understands why I'm such a bitch attitude."

"How dare you—"

"I dare because you treat your fiancée like a dog you need to train. I dare because you don't give a flying fuck about your little sister, who happens to be a warm, caring person who is taking your wedding pictures for free, despite the shit you put her through. Because your parents are paying for this extravagant wedding and you don't have the decency to be grateful. You've threatened me, kicked me, and tried to break me when all I wanted to do was help you—"

"Please, you were just working for a paycheck. You didn't give a shit about my happiness."

"You are absolutely right. Because from the moment I met you, there wasn't one single redeeming quality that made me feel an ounce of compassion for you. You're in a position to actually make a difference to someone; a kind word or action from Sonora Star would be something people could hold onto. Women idolize you, until they actually meet you and find out what you're really like."

Marley could tell Sonora was reaching the boiling point but she was too far gone to care. All the threats, all the abuse… it was too much and someone had to put an end to it.

"You do not have the right to belittle anyone else's existence. You're a former drug addict, a has-been, and a cheater. You're just as flawed as all the people you look down your reconstructed nose at."

Sonora's face turned cherry red. "You're fired!"

"Fine by me. You go out and explain why you lost another maid of honor."

Marley headed for the door, picking up the taffeta skirt to quicken her steps. As she left the door to the bridal suite, she slammed it and released a whoop. She'd just officially screwed herself; there was no way Sonora wasn't telling Kelly about *this*.

But Marley had fulfilled her end of the contract. She'd organized and made sure that Sonora a beautiful wedding. Even if Sonora's parents made Marley give back her bonus, Kelly got to keep the money for Something Borrowed. She was protected from brides firing their bridesmaids and maids of honor the day of the wedding in order to get out of paying full price. If the firing had been unjust, Marley could have fought for her bonus, but she was just glad it was over.

At least she was free. Free to leave this train wreck, free to go home and never have to deal with the wicked bitch of the stars again...

Free to see Luke out in the open if I want.

Marley rounded the corner with a definite skip in her step, but slowed when she heard hushed voices. She scooted closer to the closed door, curious. She recognized Kendall's husky tones immediately, choked with tears.

"I don't understand how you can marry her. I know you feel something for me. I feel it every time we're in the same room together."

"I do have feelings for you." Marley covered her mouth to smother a gasp. That was *Brent*. "If I had met you first, I'd have married you within the first week. But despite your sister's faults, I made a commitment to her, and I am not going to humiliate her by leaving her at the altar to run away with her sister."

But Kendall persisted. "Isn't it better to end it now, rather than to get divorced later when it doesn't work out? You're both going to get hurt, and despite the situation we're in and the differences we may have, I love Sonora. I don't want to hurt her, but I do *want you*."

"It's just better if we forget whatever it is we think we feel."

Marley didn't believe him, and clearly neither did Kendall. "Better for who?"

Brent didn't respond for several heartbeats and then, his voice choked with emotion, muttered, "I'm sorry."

Marley ducked around the corner when she heard Brent's footsteps coming toward the door. She watched him, her heart aching as he took a shaky breath and ran a hand over his eyes.

Oh, my God, he's crying.

Whatever had been going on between the two of them this summer was no longer one sided. Brent cared about Kendall too.

And she was right. He *was* about to make a really big mistake.

Marley waited until he was gone before she snuck into the room.

Kendall glanced up, her pretty face streaked with tears, and she frantically wiped at them. "Marley. Sorry, were you looking for me?"

Marley sat next to Kendall on the loveseat and held her arms out. "You look like you need a shoulder."

Kendall's face crumpled and she threw herself against her. Marley stroked her hair, whispering nonsensical encouragement. When Kendall's tears finally slowed, she sniffled. "Were you sent to find me?"

"No. Actually, I was leaving. You sister just fired me as her maid of honor."

Kendall pulled away. "What? Why would she do that?"

Marley grinned mischievously. "Because I finally went off on her and told her what a horrible person she was."

"Wow. You would think she would learn that you just have to be nice to keep friends."

Marley tucked one of Kendall's blond curls back into place. "Well, to be honest, we were never really friends to begin with."

"What do you mean?" Kendall asked.

Marley opened her mouth to tell her everything, but someone knocked on the door. Luke poked his head in, and Marley's heart flipped just catching a glimpse of that lopsided grin. After she'd dropped him off at the airport on Sunday, she'd missed him like crazy. Sure they'd Skyped at night before bed, and she'd even put on a little show for him, but it wasn't the same as having him there with her. They hadn't gotten to see each other last night because he'd been out with Brent and the other groomsmen having a guy's night before the big day.

"Hey, ceremony is about to start and they're looking for Kendall," Luke said.

Kendall wiped at her cheeks once more and took Marley's hands. "Do I look like I've been crying?"

"Yeah, but it's okay. You're supposed to cry at weddings."

Kendall squeezed her hands. "Thanks." Then she got up and left the room.

When Kendall was gone, Luke shut the door behind her and locked it.

"What are you doing? You have to get out there."

"They can wait." He stalked around the back of the loveseat and sat down next to her. "God, I missed you."

His hands cradled her face and as his lips brushed hers, she closed her eyes. "I missed you too."

His kisses trailed over her cheek and down her neck until he buried his face in her chest with a groan. "I want to toss up this ridiculous princess skirt and have my way with you right here."

"We can't," she murmured, arching her neck.

"I know." He lifted his head and ran his thumb across her lips. "To be continued."

As he left the room, she sank back into the couch with a sigh. "I hope so."

As the silence around her became suffocating, she got up and headed for the exit. Life wasn't fair. Sonora had cheated on Brent, had only decided to still marry him because Dustin had rejected her, while Kendall and Brent were miserable. And there was nothing she could do.

Her footsteps slowed as she realized that wasn't true. Now that Sonora had fired her, the confidentiality clause was null and void.

Besides, if being sued by Sonora meant Kendall and Brent could be happy, she was all for it.

* * * *

At the front of the church beneath the arbor, Luke stood up with his best friend as they watched the bridal procession. Neither Brent nor Sonora were religious, but for some reason, Sonora had insisted on being married in a non-denominational church by a minister. It was strange, but the setting was gorgeous with the high vaulted ceilings and stained glass windows.

Luke glanced over at Brent and realized that he was deathly pale. His normally smiling face was pinched and grim, and his eyes appeared red rimmed.

"Man, are you okay?"

"No." That was all Brent said, and Luke frowned.

The music changed to the wedding march and everyone stood.

As Kendall came to the front of the church Luke noticed the splotchy puffiness of her face. She'd been crying, and he noticed she kept looking away from the bridesmaids coming down the aisle to look at Brent. His friend never took his eyes off the back of the church.

When the ring bearer and flower girl, Brent's niece and nephew, came tripping down the aisle as fast as their little toddler legs could carry them, Luke realized that Marley had never come down the aisle.

Maybe she's after the kids.

Then Sonora came into the open doorway on her father's arm. She wore an off-white mermaid style dress and long veil, making her look like she just stepped out of a magazine cover.

Catching Kendall's eyes, he mouthed *where's Marley?*

Kendall nodded toward Sonora. As the bride walked slowly, smiling and basking in the attention, Luke knew what Kendall's nod had meant: Sonora had finally run Marley off.

Luke fumed, wanting nothing more than to walk out of the ceremony to go find her, but he couldn't ditch Brent during his wedding.

The minister went through his introduction and Luke found himself tapping his shoe impatiently. The bride and groom had not prepared any special vows, just two simple 'I Dos.'

The minister's clear, soothing voice called out, "If anyone here feels that these two should not lawfully be joined, let them speak now or forever hold their peace."

"I've got a buttload of reasons," Marley's voice rang out.

Every head swung around to the back of the church, where Marley stood in that awful puffy pink dress. All of the guests watched Marley marched up the aisle, their jaws slack with shock. Even Luke was thrown by the determined set of her jaw as she squared off in front of Sonora, who looked as though she were about to beat Marley over the head with her bouquet.

"What the hell do you think you're doing?" Sonora shrieked.

"I'm saving him from marrying *you*." Marley turned towards Brent, lowering her voice a bit. "I can keep this for your ears only, or I can tell everyone in the room. Your choice."

Brent glanced at Luke who shrugged. He had no clue what was about to happen.

"If you've got something to say, then say it," Brent said.

"Fine." Clasping her hands in front of her, she shot Luke a small, apologetic smile. "I was hired to be Sonora's maid of honor. She'd run off several maids of honor with her attitude, and her parents thought a professional was the way to go. She made up the story about us meeting in rehab."

Luke nodded as she continued to watch him. He'd known there was something off about her story, but he'd never figured her for a professional bridesmaid.

"I went along with it because it was only eight weeks. Eight miserable weeks of listening to her berate and belittle everyone around her. I put up with it because her parents were paying me handsomely."

Marley paused, and it was as if the entire church moved, leaning forward so as not to miss the punchline.

"Until she fired me this morning for telling her that she should be nicer to her friends and family."

"You threatened me!" Sonora said, and Marley scoffed.

"Please, you were the one who said you would destroy my mother's business if I told anyone that you'd slept with another man while you were engaged to Brent."

This time, the crowd erupted and Luke's jaw hit the floor. Sonora was a lot of things, but she wasn't an idiot. Why in the hell would she cheat on Brent?

But Marley wasn't done. "If you're wondering why she'd do that when Brent is the whole package, it was because the other man was loaded and less like a…what was it, Sonora? A caveman?"

Sonora paled, and turned to face Brent, stuttering, "She's lying, baby, you have to believe me."

Brent stared first at Marley and then at Sonora. Everyone seemed to be holding their breath, including Luke.

"I don't," Brent said.

Sonora's eyes widened, and then her face flushed purple. She whirled toward Marley. "You!"

Luke was already in motion as Sonora headed down the stairs straight for Marley, her fingers curled into claws.

"I'm going to fucking *kill* you!"

But to Luke's surprise, Kendall beat him there.

"Back off, Sonny."

"I told you never to call me that!" Sonora screamed, spittle flying out of her mouth.

"And under most circumstances I would respect your feelings, even though you've never considered mine. But not today. For years I've made excuses, loved you in spite of the horrible way you treated me. But you aren't going to hurt Marley. She is a true friend. She could have stood by and let Brent marry you and you would have made him miserable." Kendall looked up at Brent, her expression softening. "And my heart would have broken every day seeing him like that."

Luke realized what she was saying and his breath whooshed out. "Damn, there is a lot of drama going on in this room."

Sonora whirled on him, her eyes wild. "Shut up, you idiot!"

Kendall jumped to his defense, and he had to admit, watching her let it all out on her sister was a sight to behold. "No, you shut up, Sonora. I would have let you have him, stepped back and allowed you marry the man I love because despite your obvious personality flaws, I didn't want to hurt you. Today, I don't care. You are a mean, selfish woman and I hope that someday you grow up, or you're going to wake up years from now and realize you're all alone."

When Brent moved, it was like watching a movie in slow motion. He stopped at Sonora's side and took her hand. For a brief moment, Luke watched her face soften, and he thought Brent was going to forgive her.

And then Luke noticed Brent was holding her ring hand.

She seemed to realize what he was doing a moment too late as he slipped the large diamond engagement ring off and held it between two of his fingers.

Then he dropped it into his pocket and held his hand out to Kendall. "I'm hungry. Want to grab some dinner?"

Kendall's smile was massive. "Yeah, I do."

"What? You can't do this!" Sonora wailed. "She's my sister!"

The two of them walked down the aisle, ignoring Sonora as she cried, cursed and screamed. Luke came down the stairs past her to stand beside Marley.

"So, does this mean we can be seen in public together?"

Marley nodded enthusiastically, and without warning, he flipped her up and over his shoulder.

"What are you doing?" she asked, her voice shaking with laughter.

"Taking the conquering hero somewhere I can have her all to myself."

Chapter 21

Hours later, Marley snuggled deeper into the warmth of Luke and the smell of his skin. On the drive back to her place, she'd explained everything: how she started at Something Borrowed to pay off all of the medical bills that had piled up during her sister's care. That she wanted to date him, but the no-fraternizing clause made it impossible because she would have lost her commission. Luke had taken it all in stride, and she was actually relieved that he wasn't furious with her over her ruse.

She was just drifting off to the steady thump of his heart when the sound of her phone ringing in the quiet of her bedroom startled her.

"God, why can't we just have a moment's peace?" she grumbled.

"Um, babe? We've had eight hours and forty minutes of sweaty"—he kissed her shoulder—"peaceful"—kissed along her neck—"bliss."

"Still not long enough." She picked up her phone and answered sharply, "Hello?"

"Marley? It's Fire Chief Riggs."

Marley jerked up, her heart skipping nervously. "Chief Riggs? Is everything okay?"

"No, Marley, it's actually not. Someone set fire to the Sweetheart Café."

The world tilted on its axis and Marley gripped her cell harder. "Oh God—"

Luke sat up, putting his hand on her naked back, smoothing his hand in small comforting circles.

"That's not all. Your mom was inside when the fire started. She'd fallen asleep while baking the daily pastries. We got her out, but she's been taken to Marshall Hospital for smoke inhalation."

No. No this wasn't happening again. Not again. She couldn't lose her mom too. "Is she going to be okay?"

"I think so, but Marley, we couldn't save the café. It's gone."

Tears spilled over, mostly relieved that her mom was going to recover but also heartbroken. Her mom had put everything she had into the café. Hell, Marley had put a lot into it too. All her money, time, blood, sweat, and tears? How was her mom going to feel when she found out her livelihood was gone?

"Do you know who did it?" Marley wanted them tarred and feathered. The hair from their bodies plucked slowly and painfully.

The chief hesitated, clearing his throat. "The police have a suspect in custody, but I don't think that's what you need to be worrying about now."

"Who is it?" The knot of dread in her stomach already knew though.

"Marley, you don't need to worry about it."

"Who *is* it?"

The chief sighed through the phone. "Sonora Star. She was pulled over up the road for a DUI and they found gas cans in the back of her car."

Marley's chest tightened and breathing was becoming an issue as the truth sank in.

This is all my fault.

"Marley? Marley are you still there, sweetheart?"

Marley didn't bother correcting the chief, who had known her since she was in diapers. She sucked in several breaths, trying to speak, until finally she managed to wheeze, "Thank you, Chief. I better go so I can be with my mom."

"Of course. I am so sorry. I wish I had better news."

"Thanks."

Marley hung up the phone, guilt chewing at her chest, causing sharp pinches. She got up from the bed, and went to her drawer to grab some clothes, dazed.

"Marley, what happened?" Luke asked behind her.

"Sonora burned down the diner. My mom was inside."

Luke jumped up from the bed. "Oh my God, is Rose okay?"

Marley shook her head. "I don't know for sure. The fire chief thinks so, but I need to get to the hospital." Was that her voice? Why did she sound as though she was a robot?

"I'll drive you. You're in shock and shouldn't get behind the wheel."

"That's fine, just hurry." She could see him pause out of the corner of her eye, but she didn't feel bad for the sharpness in her tone. She was already too sick and caught up in her own emotions to worry about his.

The whole drive up to the hospital, Marley couldn't speak, and thankfully, Luke didn't try. She couldn't believe that her mom had lost everything…because of her. Because of her mistake. She had been stupid and reckless, thinking only about herself. Sonora had warned her she'd go after her mother and she'd still taken her on. She had every chance to quit that wedding and instead, she kept going, challenged Sonora and acted as though she were bulletproof.

She thought that Sonora might try to sue her, but set her mother's restaurant on fire with her mother inside? Even if she didn't know that it wasn't empty, it was someone's livelihood. What kind of sociopath does that?

Luke dropped her at the front while he went to find a parking space, and she practically ran inside. A tall, pretty brunette sat behind the reception desk and looked up with a blank stare as she approached.

"Hi, can I help you?"

"I'm looking for Rose Stevenson? She was brought in by ambulance about an hour ago for smoke inhalation."

"Rose Stevenson." The receptionist tapped along her keyboard, her eyes on the screen. "Are you family?"

"I'm her daughter. Marley Stevenson." Marley showed the brunette her driver's license just as the doors opened behind her. She glanced over her shoulder and nodded at Luke before facing the receptionist once more.

"Hold tight, I'll find her for you." She typed away at the computer, and finally looked up with a smile. "Good news, she's in recovery. I'll have an orderly take you to her. Is this your husband?"

"Just a friend."

The receptionist addressed Luke. "I'm sorry, family only at this time. You can have a seat, and wait if you want."

Luke rubbed Marley's back. "If you need me—"

"I'll be fine," she said.

Luke hesitated briefly, as if he didn't really believe her, but ultimately walked away. When the orderly called her name, she breathed out, as if relieved to get away from Luke.

That's not fair. The fire isn't Luke's fault.

No, but he was another mistake. She had started to think that once she finished Sonora's wedding and quit Something Borrowed, they could be together. That she could have everything; the career, the guy, and the life she'd always dreamed of away from Sweetheart.

She'd been willing to risk her reputation, her relationship with Kelly and her professionalism for him, and because she'd been so distracted, she'd almost lost her mother.

She was twenty-eight years old, and after everything she'd lost, she should have known that life wasn't about your dreams coming true and having it all.

Believing that utter bullshit had almost cost her the most important person in her life.

Marley walked through the door of the hospital room, her mother was lying with the bed elevated and oxygen tubes in her nose. When she saw Marley, she held her arms out, her eyes filled with tears, and Marley broke. The zombie state she'd been in cracked, and she cried out as she threw herself into her mother's arms like she was seven years old.

"Oh, baby, I'm okay. I just woke up and it was so smoky I couldn't see very well, but I made it to the front door. I'm alive."

Her mother's words made her sob harder. "I am so sorry. So very sorry."

"Hey now, what are you sorry for? This wasn't your fault." She felt her mom's lips brush her forehead and pulled back, needing to get the truth off her chest.

"Yes it was. The fire was deliberate, and I caused it."

"How could you have caused it?" her mom asked.

"Because I humiliated Sonora Star last night, and she burned down the Sweetheart Café for revenge."

Her mom cupped her cheeks and pulled her up to look at her. "All I heard is that Sonora Star is more than just a spoiled little princess, but crazy to boot. I don't care what you did, her actions have nothing to do with you and everything to do with her being a deranged individual." Her mother squeezed her in a fierce hug. "I'm just glad it was the café, and not anything that couldn't be rebuilt."

Marley wasn't going to try to argue. She was just relieved to feel her mother's warmth and know she was going to live.

Nothing else mattered.

* * * *

It was almost dawn. Luke sat in the waiting room, texting Brent and Kendall to update them on Marley's mom. Slowly, the whole waiting room filled with Sweetheart residents, waiting on an update about Rose Stevenson. Turner and Delores were the only ones Luke knew by name, but he'd seen most of them around. Perks of living in a small town it seemed; everyone knew everyone.

Luke hoped Rose was okay, but he was also concerned about Marley. He tried not to take her cold behavior personally, knowing she'd been dealt the shock of her life and especially after everything he knew she'd gone through.

But she'd hardly looked at him, and he could have sworn she'd flinched away when he'd touched her.

When Kendall and Brent came through the door, Luke was pretty glad to see them.

"Is Marley's mom okay? Is Marley?" Kendall asked.

Luke shook his head. "I don't know, she went back a while ago and hasn't come out to update us."

"I can't believe this," Brent murmured.

Luke bristled at his comment. Brent had always been blind to Sonora's faults.

"What? That your crazy ass ex-fiancée e almost killed Marley's mom?" Luke asked.

Brent stiffened, but before things escalated, Kendall stepped in.

"Hey, okay, tensions are high, but let's keep things in perspective. She's my sister and I can't imagine her doing this. So let's not start throwing blame around."

Luke ran his hands over his head with an exhausted sigh. "I'm sorry man, I'm just on edge."

Brent nodded. "I get it. You don't have to apologize."

They went and sat in the corner, hardly speaking. When Marley's friend, Rylie, came running through the door with Dustin the Douche behind her, Luke frowned, wondering why the guy was even here.

The receptionist stood up and hollered, "Okay, now, I get that you're all worried about someone close to you, but you can't all be here. It's family only, and you are gumming up my emergency room. So either take it home and wait for a call or take it outside."

"We aren't going anywhere until we know Rose is okay!" Turner called out, and the other town members agreed.

The receptionist made a call and a few minutes later, Marley came through the door, her eyes red and swollen. Luke stood up and made a move toward her, but Kendall put a hand on his arm. He paused, frowning down at her, but all she did was shake her head.

"Thank you all for being here," Marley said, her hands clasped in front of her. "They're going to keep Mom for a few more hours, and then we'll be heading home. I promise to let you know the moment we get in."

Marley disappeared into a sea of heads and hugs as the people of Sweetheart swarmed around her. When only Rylie, Dustin, Brent, Kendall, Luke, and Marley remained, Luke ignored Kendall's warning look and made a beeline for her side, only to be blocked by Rylie giving her a hug.

"I am so very sorry," Rylie said.

"Thanks."

When it was Kendall's turn, she sobbed uncontrollably and Marley looked pained.

"I can't...I am sorry."

"It's not your fault. Don't blame yourself," Marley said.

Finally, Luke stepped up to hold her and she held up her hand. "Can we talk for a moment?"

He nodded, a lump of dread balling in his stomach. Everyone seemed to be looking anywhere but at them, and he had a feeling they all knew what was coming next.

They stepped outside and he watched Marley wrap her arms around herself, as if she was mentally putting up a wall between them.

"You should catch a ride back with Brent and Kendall. I'm going to stay with my mom and I'll be fine to drive us back."

He wanted to reach for her so badly, but he knew she was distancing herself from him. He just had no idea why. "I don't mind being here for you."

"I get that, but I do mind." Her voice was harsh and raspy. "I want to be alone with my mother. I want you to leave."

Even though he'd known the words were coming, hearing them aloud didn't hurt any less. "So, that's it? You're back to pushing me away?"

"I'm not pushing you, I'm telling you that I don't need or want you here right now. I want to be with my mother, and I don't want some guy I've fucked a couple times on weekends hanging around."

Luke's cheeks burned and his stomach churned with humiliation and anger. "I understand that your mom had a close call tonight, but taking it out on me—"

"You don't understand anything or you would know that this"—she waved her hand emphatically—"right here, is not about you. It's not about how you feel or what you want. It's about me. It is about me spending all summer trying to avoid getting involved with you so that I wouldn't lose my job and the biggest account I've ever had. Money that would guarantee me a new life, and I blew all that. But it isn't just that. My actions tonight— telling off Sonora, stopping the wedding when I outed her, taking you back to my place—all had consequences. Nearly fatal consequences. Whatever we had has been tainted and I can't..." Her voice broke and he wanted to hold her, to take her in his arms and forget about everything she'd just said.

And then she finished her sentence, crushing him into a pile of dust. "I can't even look at you right now."

After several excruciating moments, Luke cleared his throat, trying to hide the cuts of pain every vicious slice of her words had caused. Digging into his pocket, he pulled out her keys and held them out to her. "Here."

When she tried to take them, he circled her wrist with his other arm, holding her there. She tugged, trying to get away, but he was too strong.

"Let go of me, Luke."

"Not until I have my say." He was trying to hold it together so she wouldn't hear the hurt, but he wasn't that good of an actor. "I get that you have lost people you loved, and that tonight you almost lost Rose. I understand that I might just have been some guy you fucked a few times, but that isn't all I was. And you can't admit it now because you're blaming yourself and you're looking for a way to punish you and me and everyone, but you weren't just a bit of fun for me. You were more than that. When all this shit blows over and you realize that you didn't have to give me up, and throw away whatever we could have had, I want you to remember that I wasn't the one who hurt you."

He let her go and walked off into the parking lot, pulling his phone from his pocket to text Brent. He took a deep, shaky breath, fighting back the tears. He hadn't cried since his mama's funeral, not since Henry had told him that real men don't show weakness.

I need a ride. In the parking lot waiting.

He stopped under a parking lot light and the emotions rushed to the surface, making him tremble. Fury, disappointment, rage, bitterness all rose like bile in the back of his throat.

Before he thought it through, he hauled off and smashed his fist into the metal pole. Pain radiated from his knuckle up his arm and as he cradled his injured hand against his chest, a single tear escaped, the wet drop trailing over his cheek.

That's it. All she gets of me.

Chapter 22

Marley sat in Kelly's office the following Wednesday afternoon, waiting for her to say something about the events over the weekend. She'd taken several days to be with her mom, but Kelly had called her last night, telling her they needed to talk. She knew she was fired; even if Kelly could forgive her for lashing out at a client and outing her for cheating, she couldn't ignore what Marley had told her about Luke. That they had carried on an affair despite Marley's assurance that she would pull the plug.

Marley had tried to push Luke from her mind the last two days, especially that last look in his eyes. Anguish. He didn't even have to tell her, although he had. In a long, articulate speech that had chipped away at all the blame she had toward him. She'd been the asshole.

She didn't deserve him.

Kelly sat behind the desk, steepling her hands and watching Marley with a combined mix of disappointment and pensiveness. The company's lawyer, Christian Ryan, stood next to her in a gray suit and light blue tie, perfectly matching the icy blue of his eyes. His hair was blond and spikey, and every time she was around him, she wanted to call him Ken because he reminded her so much of Barbie's boyfriend.

Marley knew he was more than a pretty face though. Christian was ruthless when it came to business, and Marley knew it was bad if Kelly had needed to call Christian.

Finally, Kelly sat forward and started talking. "Well, the good news is that the Stadarskis are willing to not sue Something Borrowed for violating the confidentiality clause in the contract—"

"There was no violation. Sonora had fired me thirty minutes before," Marley broke in.

"According to you, but since there were no witnesses and Sonora denies firing you, they would have grounds." When Marley opened her mouth to say more, Kelly held up her hand. "Like I said, it is a moot point considering the current circumstances. Instead, they are offering to pay a generous settlement to your mother."

It was just like that family to use money to solve their problems.

"In exchange for what?" Marley growled.

Kelly's expression turned grim. "The D.A. has offered Sonora a very generous deal. Sonora agreed to plead guilty to arson. The Stadarskis want to make sure you won't contest it."

Marley scoffed, knotting her hands in her lap. "What does she get? Probation?"

"And her license revoked."

Marley slammed her hand down on the desk, fury roasting in her belly. "Forget that. That psycho almost killed my mother. She should rot in prison."

"She told the D.A. she was drunk and high. She didn't even fully understand what she was doing and she didn't know your mother was inside," Christian said.

His calm, matter of fact tone exasperated her anger. "So, she gets a pass? Because, what, she bribed someone? This is bullshit."

Kelly sat forward, her eyes blazing. "I agree. I hate this and I hate that woman almost as much as you do. Her sister came to see me Monday, told me everything you took while working for her and I need you to know that had I known, I would have never accepted her as a client."

Marley wanted to believe her, but money had a way of shifting priorities. As much as she loved Kelly, she wasn't so sure her friend was above it all.

Marley shook her head. "I will give her parents every penny of my commission back, plus interest, but I want her punished. She is a monster, and will never change if she doesn't pay for the full extent of her crimes."

"Unfortunately, it's not up to us, and since I work for Kelly, I must advise her as to what is in the best interests of Something Borrowed." Christian came around the desk with papers in his hand and set it before her. "This is a contract that states you will accept the settlement and agree to not contest Sonora's plea deal nor speak about what she did to any press or media outlet. It also includes a clause that Sonora cannot come back to Sweetheart, or contact you in anyway and vice versa."

"Oh, I will accept it, huh?" Marley stood up, ready to walk. "You represent Kelly, not me, and I don't have to accept this."

"You're right, you don't," Kelly said. "But Sonora going to prison is not going to help your mother rebuild her café or get you to New York.

You need to move past your anger and find that level-headed woman I've come to respect these last seven years."

Kelly's words struck a nerve and she sat down, weighing the truth to it. "What happens if I do contact her or tell the world what she did?"

"You'll be in breach of contract and you will have to return the settlement, plus damages."

Marley looked at Kelly, and even though she saw the regret in her eyes, she didn't care. "You're really okay with this? With letting her skate on everything?"

Kelly spread her hands out, as if to signify she had no other choice. "This is my livelihood, Marley. I have to do what is best for Something Borrowed's future."

Marley almost snorted, but held it in. "Give me the pen."

Christian pulled one from his pocket and held it out to her. She signed the paper, stabbing at it with the pen, as if that would somehow make all of this better.

It didn't, but she had a feeling nothing really would.

She stood up and headed for the door without saying a word.

"You're forgetting the check," Christian said.

Marley didn't even look at him; all of her disappointment and rage was directed at the woman she'd considered a friend. "I worked with you for seven years. I confided in you, shared my dreams with you. I know I made a mistake, but what you're doing? What you're accepting from the Stadarskis is exactly why so many of the horrible women who come through here as brides think they can treat us any way they want. They don't see us as anything but the help, and undeserving of basic common courtesy. And you see them as dollar bills. A way to keep your company afloat. I get it, it's business, but I don't have to be a part of it."

"Marley..." Kelly started, but she cut her off.

"You can keep the check; I'll help my mother rebuild, without the Stadarskis thinking they can buy their troubles away. All they care about is money; just like you."

Kelly stood up, her face sheet white, but Marley didn't care what she had to say. She was done with all of it.

She passed by the reception desk, but didn't stop to talk to Rylie or Josephine, their newest hire. She needed air.

The minute she hit the sidewalk, she started running. Past the charred remnants of the Sweetheart Café. The Love Shack hotel. Honey-Moon Intimate Apparel. She kept running out of town and up the hill to Buzzard Gulch, her lungs burning as she cried, gulping for air. She finally slowed as she reached the center of the old ghost town and screamed, using whatever oxygen was left in her lungs. She railed until she was hoarse, cursing Sonora, Kelly, the Stadarskis...

"Damn you!" She threw her hands up in the air, staring into the dark clouds forming above and yelled again. "Damn you! What the hell did I do? What did my family do? Are you even up there listening? Is this a joke to you? Is my life and my failures some kind of entertainment you can't stop watching?"

There was the distant rumble of thunder, but nothing else. She collapsed in the dirt, her shoulders shaking violently, unable to stop the sobs.

The storm drew closer, but she paid it no attention, wallowing too deep in her troubles.

If she'd been smart, she would have taken the money. Insurance on the diner wasn't going to be enough to cover all of the equipment that they needed to replace. Her mom was going to have to take out an equity line of credit, if she even qualified, and Marley had already given her every penny she'd ever saved. No more New York.

The funny thing was, that as she sat there, hysterically losing her shit, she didn't have any tears for the dream she'd clung to for nearly ten years.

Maybe because my dreams changed.

The crack of thunder above pulled her out of her meltdown, and she climbed to her feet as huge drops of rain started falling. Splashing her cheek, her shoulder, running down the back of her neck.

Just what she needed, to run home in a thunderstorm.

Suddenly, the sky lit up and a bolt of lightning hit the saloon. Sparks shot up out of the center as the ground shook beneath her feet. A high-pitched sound rang in her ears and she realized it was her screaming in terror.

She held her hand over her chest, her heart pounding against her palm, and then it stopped altogether when she saw the first flame climb up over the second floor, like a long arm waving. Inside the windows were no longer dark, but an eerie glow of yellow, orange, and red danced behind the dirty glass and it finally sank in.

The fire in the saloon was spreading quickly. Too quickly.

Marley pulled her phone out of her pocket, and dialed 911. Another lightning strike hit just over the hill and she shivered as she realized how close she'd come to being struck.

When the dispatcher picked up, another rumble above her head told Marley she needed to find shelter. Fast.

"Hi, this is Marley Stevenson, and I'm up at Buzzard Gulch, the old Ghost Town above Sweetheart? A bolt of lightning just struck one of the buildings and it's burning." Smoke billowed and now the flames were gathering on the roof. "Hurry, before it all burns down."

* * * *

An hour and a half later, the storm had passed. Marley sat on the boardwalk in front of the old town hall, a blanket wrapped around her shoulders. Rylie had come to get her an hour ago, but Marley refused to leave until she saw all the damage.

Men and women from the El Dorado County Fire Department meandered around now, after managing to put out the flames before the fire spread too far.

They hadn't been able to save the saloon though. There wasn't anything left of her favorite building but a few boards and the front sign, which was a little charred on the top.

"Honestly, they should just bulldoze this whole thing," one of the firefighters said to another.

Marley stood up angrily, shaking under the blanket they'd given her. "Are you kidding me? This is a historical landmark."

The guy shot her a look of disbelief. "It's a death trap, lady."

Rylie put her hands on her shoulders and pulled her back. "Just let it go."

She took a shaky breath and let Rylie lead her to the car. Once she was in the seat, she stared out the window as they drove down the hill back toward Sweetheart.

After several moments of silence, Rylie spoke, "You know, if they could just find a little bit of money to restore it, I bet Sweetheart could use it as a wedding venue. It has beautiful views of the Sierra Mountains, the river, and the rolling hills. Plus, people would pay a buttload to have a themed wedding up there, if it was all painted and landscaped."

Rylie's words sunk in. A little bit of money and Buzzard Gulch could be beautiful. Sure, the town had blocked all attempts to update it, but if it was privately owned…

Marley smiled for the first time in days. "I need you to drive me out to Kelly's."

"Now?" Rylie asked.

"Right now."

Rylie made a left at the stop sign. "Why do you want to talk to Kelly?"

"Because I have a business proposition for her."

The minute Rylie pulled into Kelly's driveway, Marley leapt out without waiting for her to even put the car in park. She jogged up the front steps and started banging on the front door.

After knocking for several minutes, Kelly finally opened the door in just a robe, her long hair wet and dripping around her shoulders.

"Marley, what are you doing? I was in the bath."

"Sorry but it couldn't wait." Rylie came up alongside her, panting, and Marley continued, "Can we come in? I have proposition for you."

"Really, Marley, I've had a long day and I think we both need some time—"

"Just give me five minutes, and if you don't like what you hear, we'll go. No harm, no foul."

Kelly glanced over at Rylie, who shrugged. Finally, with a heavy sigh, she stepped back to let them pass. "Come on in, I guess."

Kelly and Rylie sat down on the couch under the window, but Marley was too wired to sit. "You still have the money from Sonora's parents, right?"

Kelly frowned. "Of course, it's your money. Did you think I would really do that to you?"

"No, that's not what I meant. I just wanted to know if you gave it back to them," Marley said.

"I thought when you calmed down, you might need it."

"I do need it. Badly." Finally, she sat, both of her hands on her knees to keep her legs still. "I want to invest it in the restoration of Buzzard Gulch."

Both Rylie and Kelly blinked at her in surprise, but it was Kelly that said, "I beg your pardon?"

"And I want you to invest with me."

A laugh burst from Kelly, until she seemed to realize Marley was dead serious. "Why would I want to invest in an old ghost town?"

Marley gleefully clapped her hands. "Because we're going to buy it from Dustin Kent and turn it into a premiere wedding venue. Rylie had the fantastic idea of restoring it all to its former glory, and we can charge people to use it. Comfort meets the old west. Plus, there are gorgeous places for pictures up there and Rylie pointed out that you have three different geographical views that are sure to delight people. It's the perfect solution. Keep and maintain a historical landmark and make oodles of money to boot."

Kelly held up her hands. "Okay, I can tell you're excited about this, but several hours ago, you hated my guts. Why would you want to go into business with me?"

"I didn't hate you Kelly. I was disappointed, but I could never hate you. But to answer your question, you know the wedding business inside and out and I love Buzzard Gulch. It's special to me, just like it was special to my sister. I'm doing this for her."

Kelly's wariness melted into a sad smile. "Marley, I want to make amends with you so badly my heart hurts, but—"

"Before you say no, it wouldn't just be you. I'd want Rylie in in on this deal."

Rylie's eyes about popped out of her head. "Me? But I don't even have a quarter of what I'd need in my savings to invest in something like this!"

"Maybe not now, but if we turn this into a tourist attraction, we're going to need a caterer on the payroll. Sweet Eats, the caterer we normally use, has been inching up their prices lately, haven't they, Kelly?"

"That's true," Kelly mused.

Sensing that Kelly was warming to the idea, Marley plunged on. "And after my last trip to Betsey's, I wouldn't order anything there if it was the last cake on earth." Marley got up again, standing behind the back of the couch. "We could transform Something Borrowed from a simple bridesmaid-for-hire business to a complete wedding service. And we'd pull in a lot more money keeping those services in house."

Kelly seemed to be considering. "How are we going to convince the Kents to sell?"

Marley rubbed her hands together like a Disney villain. "Oh, I think Dustin is going to be more than happy to help us. Just leave him to me."

Chapter 23

Once Marley was 99.9 percent sure that Kelly was on board, she dragged Rylie back to the car and over to Dustin's place. Dustin lived in a gorgeous four-bedroom home on a lane with no close neighbors and surrounded by trees. Considering what an attention whore he was, Marley was surprised he lived so far out of town.

Rylie parked in his driveway and as they got out, she hissed, "Maybe we should have called."

"Why?" Marley asked.

"What if he's got company?"

"Please, I'm sure she can wait for the extreme disappointment he's sure to give her."

Rylie blushed hard in the porch light as Marley rang the bell.

Dustin answered the door in nothing but a pair of boxers and Marley almost rolled her eyes. Like he hadn't looked out the window and known it was them.

"Ladies, what the hell are you doing here?"

"You need to put some clothes on before you open the door," Rylie scolded.

Dustin flashed her a lopsided grin, his gaze lazily traveling over her from the top of her messy bun and down to the simple black ballet flats she was wearing. "Why is that, Rylie-cakes? Don't you like what you see?"

Rylie appeared mortified, and Marley sighed loudly, trying to get the conversation on the right track. "We don't have time for this. Let us in."

Dustin folded his arms over his chest, still blocking the entryway. "I don't know, I might be too tired for a three-way, although with a little creative convincing, I might be able to muster to-oomph!"

Rylie smacked him in the stomach with her purse, putting a halt to his suggestions. "Knock it off, you perv. This is business."

Dustin rubbed his injured six pack with a frown. "What kind of business?"

"We want to buy Buzzard Gulch," Marley said.

Dustin actually laughed at them. "And I want my own island with unlimited sushi and women. What's your point?"

"God, you're a pig," Marley said.

Rylie jumped in. "We want to buy it so we can restore it. You probably know there was a fire there tonight?"

"So? That land is worth more than the two of you make in a year and it would cost about that to fix it. How are the two of you going to do all that?"

"It's not just us. Kelly is going in with us." Marley pretended to be studying her nails as she added casually, "Besides, you're going to give us a screaming deal."

"Oh, yeah? Why is that?"

"Because I know that Sonora taped your little tryst and she owes me," Marley lied. "One call, and it gets leaked." Giving him the full effect of her mock sympathy, she continued, "How do you think your mother would feel to watch another scandal unfold? I know what a stickler she is for propriety."

Dustin's expression darkened. "You're bluffing."

Turning to her friend innocently, she held her hand to her chest. "Rylie, am I bluffing?"

Rylie actually seemed to consider her question before answering. "No, she is not."

Dustin glanced between them, before running his fingers through his hair with a frustrated groan. "Why do you want it?"

"Because it has sentimental value," Marley said.

Dustin didn't look like he was buying it. "Maybe that's part of it, but it isn't all of it. Kelly wouldn't be in without there being some kind of monetary recovery to it. So, if this is a business venture, then I want in."

Marley glared at him. "That's not gonna happen."

"Hear me out. I already have the deed. I can just add your names to it, and then you've got another backer with a head for business. Despite your objections to my morality, I'm a pretty smart guy. You might need me."

"Like a hole in the head," Rylie mumbled.

Marley narrowed her eyes. "I want it in writing, and our names on the deed by Monday."

"Done." Dustin held his hand out. "Partners?"

Marley glanced at Rylie and the three of them shook. "Partners."

* * * *

On Saturday after work, a bunch of the guys from the precinct headed over to Fornier's house to check on his recovery, and enjoy a family friendly barbeque. Luke wasn't really in the mood to socialize, but Fornier's wife, Maria, had insisted he come.

Now, as he stood off to the side, drinking a beer, he'd wished he'd been able to turn her down. Watching the men around him with their wives and kids was painful, like a thousand tiny needles stabbing him in the eyes and heart. It reminded him of the moments when he'd been with Marley and however briefly it may have been, he'd imagined a future with her. Marriage and 2.5 rugrats.

All he had to look forward to when he left was a pint of Half-Baked ice cream in his fridge and a new *Chicago PD* episode he hadn't watched yet.

"Hey, Luke!" Fornier said, making his way over to him. He still looked the same as he always did, except for the red, puckered scar on his neck. "What are you doing, hiding over here?"

"Just staying out of the way. I'll come out of hiding when those burgers are done."

"My brother-in-law is the one manning the grill and he does make a kick-ass bacon burger. Don't ever tell him I told you that, though."

Luke chuckled good-naturedly. "Your secret is safe with me."

Fornier slapped his arm and nodded toward a couple of empty lounge chairs. "Come on, let's take a load off."

Luke followed him, figuring he'd have a little conversation, eat a burger, and when everyone was distracted, sneak out the back.

"Oh, and don't think about sneaking out later, because Maria baked you a whole dessert assortment. She'll be pissed if you don't take it with you."

Luke had seen Maria when she was fit to be tied. She seemed taller than five-foot-one, had this huge vein that popped out of her neck, and she started cursing in Italian.

It was actually pretty funny, as long as her fury wasn't directed at you.

"I'll be sure to say good-bye to her before I leave."

"Good." Fornier smiled, and Luke followed his gaze to the lanky boy of about nine. He had on a ball cap, jean shorts, and was currently showing off his dance moves to a couple of the cops' wives, who laughed and cheered in delight.

"Is that your oldest with the killer moonwalk?" Luke asked.

"Yeah, that's Kenneth. Lilly and Paula are inside having a tea party with some of the other little girls." Fornier sank back into the chair, his expression somber. "I think about how close I came to missing all of this and...I don't know, man. It puts things in perspective."

"What do you mean?" Luke asked.

"Maria doesn't want me coming back to SWAT."

Luke wasn't surprised, but he was a little thrown by Fornier's tone, as if he was considering calling it quits.

"What does she want you to do? Parking duty?"

Fornier chuckled. "Probably, but I'm not that out of the game yet. I was thinking about taking the detective exam."

"The hours are crazy though. If Maria wants you safe and spending more time at home, that isn't going to help matters," Luke said.

"Probably not. And Lord knows I live to make sure that woman is happy." Fornier shook his head. "The strange thing is, I'd actually be okay walking away from being a cop, but I don't know what else to do with myself. I've got to work, can't afford to go back to school..."

"You could take online classes. Take a desk job, or a dispatch position. That would definitely be a safe gig."

Fornier roared with laughter. "Jesus, could you see me trying to talk down some panicking woman on the telephone? I'd be fired within the hour for cracking some inappropriate joke."

"Naw, you'd be great at it. You're good with people, you know how to work under pressure, and you're patient. Hell, you'd have to be to wrangle those three kids the way you do."

"Thanks, man," Fornier said. "So, what about you? Ever think of hanging it up?"

Luke took a swig of his beer. "What for? It's about all I have going for me right now."

"No one special then?"

Marley's face tried to swirl to the surface, but he pushed her back down. "Nah, not a one."

"That's too bad. I think you'd make some woman very happy."

Luke coughed, covering up the lump of emotion at Fornier's words. Damn, what was wrong with him? If he got all blubbery over a compliment, the guys would never let him strap on a vest again.

Swinging his legs over the side of the chair, he held his hand over his heart. "Fornier, I say this with the utmost respect and love, but if you try and kiss me, I'm going to kick your ass."

"Don't kid yourself, Jessup. If I kissed you, you'd swoon like Scarlett O'Hara. Just ask my wife."

"What the hell are you two talking about?" Voight had come up behind Luke sometime during the conversation, and Luke had no idea how much he'd heard, but he and Fornier both started busting a gut.

"Crazy as hell," Voight muttered as he walked away.

They finally stopped laughing, and before Luke knew what he was doing, he asked, "Was there ever a time when you thought you and Maria might not make it?"

Fornier turned his face toward him, and Luke watched a shadow pass over it. "Marriage is hard. It has its ups and downs, but we've managed to pull through."

"What if she told you she didn't care or need you around?"

"I'd know she was either lying through her teeth or it wasn't real to begin with."

Luke's heartbeat picked up speed. "Why do you say that?"

"Love's not complicated. I believe when two people are right for each other, shit will work itself out. Sometimes it's harder, but at the end of the day, if being without that person is like trying to get around while it feels like half of you is missing, then that's true love. And you don't walk away from that easily."

Fornier's words cut him to the quick and he drained his beer. "Some people do."

Chapter 24

On Monday, Marley was curled up in her favorite chair reading a book when someone knocked. She set her book down and stretched as she stood up. She had to admit that after working seven days a week for seven years and being at other people's beck and call, just staying home and being able to read one of the many books she'd been collecting for years was very relaxing.

Don't forget lonely.

Marley frowned, hating the sadness that kept creeping over her at the most inopportune times. She missed Luke.

Her eyes started filling again, and she blinked back tears. She didn't want to cry anymore. She'd spent days crying, doing anything to distract herself from the fact that she had totally screwed up something good. Something that could have been amazing.

With a deep, steadying breath, she opened the front door, expecting it to be Dustin with the deed to Buzzard Gulch in his hand.

Instead, she found Kendall standing on her porch with her hands on her hips, looking irritated. Marley hadn't seen her in over a week, and apparently jetting off with Brent to some unknown location had agreed with her. She was tan and gorgeous in a blue wrap dress and simple ballet flats, her blond hair in waves down her back.

"Do you know I have called you four times and no answer?" she said.

Marley rubbed at her swollen eyes, trying to wipe away the evidence that she'd been crying over Luke. So many times she'd almost reached for the phone to call him, but words failed her. The only thing that had kept her sane was worrying about the Sweetheart Café, her mom, and the new business venture.

"Sorry, been a little out of it."

Kendall reached for her hand, taking it with a squeeze as she came into Marley's home. "I heard about Luke leaving. I am so sorry."

"It's okay, I ended it." When Kendall swung around, her mouth hung open in surprise. "It was doomed from the beginning, anyway. It cost me my job, the café—"

Kendall broke in with a cry, "How did your being with Luke cost you the café?"

"Because if I hadn't been with him…"

"You could have what? Followed Sonora around all night?" Kendall shook her head. "It was nobody's fault but my sister's. It especially wasn't Luke's."

She knew Kendall was right, but hearing the words aloud just made Marley's eyes mist, and she rubbed them again with a sniff. "I know. But if I don't have a reason to justify sending Luke away, then I'll never get over him."

"Why do you need to get over him? Just call him and tell him you're sorry and you love him. I know he'll forgive you."

Marley laughed bitterly. "Really? Because he practically told me that I had screwed him over, and he would never forget it. So, I'm not so sure."

"But—"

"Please, Kendall, can we just save the drama for another time? I haven't seen you in a week and I want to hear about you."

"And I want to know what is going on with you!"

Marley shook her head, giving up. "Fine, but my life is definitely not all hugs and puppies. It turns out the insurance money won't cover all of the remodel, so my mom is thinking about not rebuilding."

"Yeah, I talked to your mom yesterday after you'd ignored my call twice." Kendall reached into her purse and held out a white envelope to Marley. "Here."

"What's this?" Marley opened it up and when her eyes scanned the check inside, she started coughing. When she finally stopped, she wheezed, "What is this for?"

"It's an advance. I want you to be one of my bridesmaids and Brent wants you to edit the tell-all book he's writing."

Marley gaped. "Brent is writing a tell-all?"

"He's tempted, especially after Sonora just got offered a huge advance for her version of what happened this summer. I'm betting she's going to leave out her little fling with Dustin Kent and burning down your mother's café."

"Probably," Marley said.

Kendall shook her head. "I still don't understand why she'd make a move on Dustin when she had Brent. It is incredibly mind boggling, especially since he's so..."

Kendall's voice trailed off and her cheeks turned bright red. Whatever she'd been about to say was obviously very naughty.

Which Marley didn't need to know anything about.

"Some people are never satisfied, I guess." Marley slipped the check back inside the envelope and held it out to her. "I can't accept this. I no longer work for Something Borrowed, and even if I did, I would be your bridesmaid for free. You're my friend."

Kendall pushed it back towards her. "Which is why I am giving you this. Brent and I talked and we agreed that if it wasn't for you speaking up before the wedding, Brent would have married Sonora and been miserable until he divorced her. Now, we get to be happy together, and for that, you deserve every penny. Plus, I thought you could use some of it to fix up the diner and the rest for your move to New York."

Marley walked into the kitchen, turning her back on Kendall. "I'm not going to New York."

"What? But you said it was your dream!"

"It was, but dreams change. I changed this summer. With the loss of the café and my mom getting hurt, I realized that I was just running from memories. Running from the constant reminder of what I'd lost and ignoring everything I've gained." Marley turned on the coffee maker, her third cup of the day, and turned to Kendall with a reassuring smile. "I can be an editor anywhere, even if I go into business for myself, but this place? This is home. And I used the money your parents gave me for not contesting Sonora's sentence to restore Buzzard Gulch."

Kendall tilted her head to the side, her brow furrowed. "What is Buzzard Gulch?"

"It's an old ghost town on the hill. My business partners and I are going to restore it and turn it into a wedding venue. In fact, we were talking about how nice it would be to have more in house services for Something Borrowed, and we could really use a talented photographer."

"I thought you didn't work there anymore," Kendall teased.

"I don't, but Kelly, Rylie, and Dustin are my business partners and I spent seven years at the place. I want to see it grow and thrive." Marley listened to the bubbling brew boil behind her, music to her ears. "Do you want some coffee?"

"No, I'm okay," Kendall said.

"Anyway, Kelly and I are on good terms, especially with the changes she's making to Something Borrowed."

"Oh yeah?"

"Yeah. Kelly has put into place a code of ethics in the contract for future brides. Any harassment and degradation of a Something Borrowed employee will result in termination of the contract with no refund."

Kendall sat down at her dining room table, her face brightening. "Wow. And you're really going to stay here?"

"This is where my family and friends are." The coffee pot beeped, signaling it was done and she filled her *Coffee, I love you* cup three quarters of the way full. "This is where I want to raise my children and build a life with the person I love."

"And who is that?" Kendall asked.

Marley shot her a dirty look as she leaned against the counter. "Don't be cute."

"I'm always cute. I'm just saying that you've got this great plan, but what if you just let the love of your life go—"

"I didn't let him go. I chased him away."

Kendall sat down at the table, staring at her. "Do you even know why?"

A thousand lies threatened to roll off her tongue, but instead, she told the truth. "I was afraid of getting too close? Of putting myself out there and losing him? Of getting my heart broken when he didn't feel the same way."

"Well, that's dumb," Kendall said.

"Gee, tell me how you really feel."

"I'm serious, you are an idiot. I mean, I was in love with my sister's fiancée , about to watch him pledge to love her for the rest of their lives, and just before the I dos, he came to me and told me that he loved me too. And when he was still going to go through with it because of obligation, you saved the day. I lived with heartbreak for a year and now I'm the happiest I've ever been. Life is crazy and you have to embrace it, the good with the bad."

Marley reached down to pick up Butters, who was nibbling on her toes. When he nuzzled into her neck, she sighed at the warmth his small body brought her. If her life had gone differently, she wouldn't have been here to rescue him.

"He lives in L.A. and I live here. It wouldn't have worked unless one of us was willing to make a change and I finally know where I belong. I can't leave."

"But did you ask him to? Did you say, 'Luke, I love you and I want you to stay and be with me?'"

"I couldn't ask him that," Marley said.

Kendall looked like she wanted to choke her. "Why the hell not?"

"Because it isn't a fair question. Relationships are about compromises. It isn't right if one person sacrifices everything for the other."

"What isn't fair is making him think he doesn't have the option to decide."

Marley carried her mug over and sat across from Kendall, Butters against her chest. "I can see we're just going to keep arguing about this."

"Only because you're being a giant dumbass."

Marley set her mug down and picked up the white envelope, waving it at Kendall. "Can we get back to this ginormous check and how I can't accept it?"

"Just accept the help." Kendall reached forward and wrapped her hand around Marley's, crinkling the envelope. "I love you, no matter how you came into my life. You were always supposed to be my friend, no, you're more than that. You're my guardian angel, cupid, and fairy godmother all in one. And you deserve to find your happiness."

Marley's eyes pricked with tears. "I love you too."

Kendall wiped at her own wet eyes with a laugh. "Now that that's settled, let's talk wedding details. We're going to do a small, private ceremony in two weeks at the Kent's Winery, and I want to do a fall theme. Very simple and lots of DIY. Are you in?"

Marley went to Kendall and gave her a big hug, making Butters squirm between them. "So in."

* * * *

Tuesday night in L.A., Luke met Brent for drinks at Casey's Irish Pub, Luke's favorite bar, celebrating Brent's engagement to Kendall. Luke was putting on a good front, but the truth was, having Brent there made him think of Marley. How she smelled, how she felt held against him. The way her smile could light up her whole face.

He missed her like crazy and there wasn't a damn thing he could do about it. She didn't want him. Had pushed him out of her life.

Luke held his glass up to Brent, forcing a smile. "Congratulations on marrying the right girl this time."

He took a deep draw of his whisky, but noticed Brent wasn't drinking.

"What's up? Not going to toast your own good fortune?"

"How are you doing, man?" Brent asked.

"I'm good. You know, just working, eating and sleeping. Don't have time for much else."

"That so? Because Kendall talked to Marley."

Luke needed another if they were going to go down this road. Signaling the bartender, he didn't respond, and Brent pushed forward.

"Seems like she's pretty miserable without you, man."

"That was her choice, not mine."

Brent swirled his glass. "Maybe so, but I think—"

"Drop it, okay? I don't need to hear how she regrets the whole thing and that I should call her. I'm not interested in anything she has to say."

"Really?" Brent's sarcasm grated on Luke. "You don't want to know that she made a mistake and that she thinks she lost the love of her life?"

Hope stung Luke's heart despite all his bravado, but he squashed it before it could fully bloom. "Did she say that or did Kendall?"

"I think Kendall interpreted it from all of Marley's weeping and woe-ing."

Luke laughed. He couldn't help it, although the thought of Marley weeping because she missed him did soothe him a bit. "Woe-ing? Really?"

"Just what a little Kendall bird told me."

Luke tossed back his whiskey, and set his glass down on the bar with a thud. "Well, she can stop putting herself in the middle of the drama and let it go."

"Come on, you don't mean it. I saw the way you were with her."

Luke didn't want to discuss the fact for a few, blissful weeks, he'd thought maybe he'd found the one. But it was going to be painful enough being around Marley without Kendall and Brent playing matchmaker.

"I'm assuming Marley is going to be at your wedding?" Luke asked.

Brent had the good sense to appear uncomfortable. "She's the maid of honor."

Luke took Brent's glass of whisky and downed it. "Swell."

"Just talk to her. I think that she was freaking out a bit and is scared you won't forgive her."

Luke stood up, ready to get the hell out of there and go home to his apartment, where there was no one reminding him of the woman who broke his heart.

"She's a big girl. If she wants me, she knows where to find me."

* * * *

Marley sat at her kitchen table that night, a dozen balls of paper littering her feet. She'd been sitting there for hours, trying to pen the perfect apology letter to Luke.

Only words seemed to be failing her.

Smoothing her hand over the white sheet, she closed her eyes and released a calming breath. She thought about the emotions that had been swirling and twisting inside her for the last week. The regret, and the sadness, lonesomeness and heartbreak. She pictured Luke standing before her, that broken look in his eyes...

And started writing again.

Dear Luke,

I am so sorry that I hurt you. You were right. It only took a few days for me to realize that nothing that happened was your fault, and that I was taking out my anger at myself on you. It was my choice to disregard the rules of Something Borrowed and start seeing you in secret. It was on me that I called out Sonora in front of all of her wedding guests.

And I wouldn't change any of it.

I should have probably told Brent sooner than his wedding day, but as for the stuff between you and me, I wouldn't have done it any differently, except for the way I treated you that last night. You were so patient and supportive and I shit on you. You told me how you felt and I let you walk away thinking that you meant less than nothing to me.

I wish I could expunge that from your memory. I wish you were here now, so I could share all of these feelings with you and all the things that have changed.

I'm not moving to New York. I am staying in Sweetheart, and putting the settlement money Sonora's parents gave me to restoring Buzzard Gulch. I'm going to start a freelance editing service, and Kendall and Brent have generously helped my mom rebuild the Sweetheart Café. She'd almost considered not rebuilding because she didn't want to take money from me, but it all worked out.

Except between you and me.

But if there is anything I've learned this summer it's that I am lucky. I've been lucky in this town. With the friends I've made and most of all, I was lucky to have found you.

This letter has probably come too late, but I didn't feel like a phone call would do everything I needed to say justice and I was afraid if I showed up on your doorstep, you might call the cops. They'd probably get there fast since you're one of them.

I understand if you can't forgive me. I just wanted to say that this summer was the best and worst of my life, but I owe all the best parts to you.

Your Sweetheart, Always,

Marley

Chapter 25

Two weeks later, Marley walked down the hallway at Castle Vineyard, a nervous wreck. Not because she thought Brent and Kendall were making a mistake getting married. No, she knew they were completely gone for each other and going into this with open eyes and hearts.

She was a frazzled bundle of nerves because she hadn't seen Luke yet. She'd sent him the letter two weeks ago and hadn't heard a word about it, even from Kendall or Brent. She figured if he cared at all, even if it was just to be pissed off, he would have at least told his best friend.

Instead there'd been nothing, and she wasn't sure what to expect today when they stood up with Brent and Kendall. Would he ignore her still? Be civil for their friends' sake?

God, was it too late to run away and let Kendell hold her own bouquet?

Knowing damn well that it was, Marley stepped into the bridal suite and held up the veil she'd run to fetch. "Got it."

Kendall sat at the vanity, smiling beautifully into the mirror. Marley was the only bridesmaid she had, mostly because Kendall's family had opted out of coming, including her parents. They thought that she was betraying her sister by marrying Brent, even after Sonora had cheated on him.

Assholes.

Kendall's blonde hair was up in a top knot with curls cascading down, and her makeup was light. The simple A-line gown fit her perfectly, and once Marley placed the veil over the curls, she looked as though she belonged on the cover of a magazine.

"I am so sorry the rest of your friends and family couldn't be here."

Kendall tried to put on a brave face, but Marley could tell she was hurt. They might not have known each other for very long, but Kendall wore her heart on her sleeve.

"It's just so crazy, you know?" Kendall said hoarsely. "Sonora played a part in everything that went down, yet everyone feels bad for her. I'm the horrible sister who stole her fiancée ." Kendall grabbed a tissue from the box on the vanity and dabbed at her tear-filled eyes. "Brent and I didn't do anything except have feelings until *after* he called off the wedding. She actually slept with someone else."

"I know, love," Marley said.

Kendall chuckled bitterly, and blew her nose. "It's all right though. Brent's family has been amazing, and his older brother offered to walk me down the aisle, but I kind of thought you and I would just walk together." Kendall turned and took Marley's hand. "I don't know why, but from the first time we met, I've always thought we were kindred spirits, like Anne and Diana from *Anne of Green Gables.*"

Marley squeezed her hand. "How did you know I loved that book?"

"See? Kindred spirits."

"Well, sister from another mister," Marley said, pulling Kendall to her feet with a laugh. "What do you say we walk out there and get you your happy ending?"

"I am so ready."

Marley looped Kendall's arm through hers, and they left the bridal suite, heading down to the double door exit out onto the veranda. Even in late September, the weather in Northern California was still summery and Marley could feel the warmth from the afternoon sun beating through the doors. Droplets of sweat rolled down her temple, and she told herself it had everything to do with the heat and was not because just beyond that door, Luke would be waiting.

Two of the attendants opened the doors and the music from "God Bless the Broken Road" played over the outdoor patio. As they stepped down, the guests stood, but both Marley and Kendall were focused on who was waiting at the end of the aisle.

The minute that Marley saw Luke, her chest tightened and her breathing grew unsteady. Her heart kept slamming against her breast bone, and she had to tell her feet to slow down, not to run into the arms of the man she loved.

Loved.

Kendall had mentioned it, browbeat her with the truth, but it was the first time that Marley had ever let herself think it. She was in love with Luke Jessup.

Luke wasn't looking at her as though he was happy to see her, and her stomach knotted. Instead, he smiled at Kendall, not even casting his dark eyes Marley's way through the whole ceremony and she resisted the urge to run weeping back inside.

It's not about me or us. It's about Kendall today. Tomorrow, I can cry.

* * * *

Luke fought the need to stare at Marley as the officiant pronounced Brent and Kendall husband and wife. She looked so happy for them, her smile nearly splitting her face, her soft blonde curls pinned back from her face and the simple silver dress fanning out to below her knees. It was modest and sexy all at the same time.

Luke wanted to get her alone and his hands under it.

Don't rush into anything.

When he got her letter, he'd gone through several stages of emotions. At first, he was pissed that after almost two weeks, she sent him a damn letter instead of picking up the phone. He tossed it in the trash and went to work, biting heads off the whole day and making pretty much everyone miserable.

Then he came home, dug it out of the trash and read it, sadness wrecking him all over again. He'd almost called her, but then fear settled over him. What if he called her up, told her he forgave her and she hurt him a second time?

It was why he hadn't been able to respond, and he still hadn't figured out what his next move would be.

Until he saw her, staring down the aisle at him with so much joy that it knocked the wind out of him. It took all he had to not meet her in the aisle, wrap her up in his arms, and tell her he forgave everything.

But he wasn't going to just fall to his knees for her. She could work for it. He'd chased her all summer.

She could sweat for a couple of hours.

He held out his arm to her, and she took it silently, placing her hand on his forearm. As they followed behind the bride and groom, she asked, "How are you?"

She sounded so casual, he almost tripped. Here he was practically coming out of his skin and she was cool as a cucumber.

Well, he could play it close to the breast too. "I'm fine. How are you?"

"Okay." She paused, smiling and waving at several guest before adding, "Did you get my letter?"

"I did." That was Marley, right to the point. He liked that she was still direct, but damn, he did not want to have that conversation in front of all of Kendall and Brent's guests.

She seemed to be waiting for him to say more about it, and when he didn't, she mumbled, "Oh. Good."

They made their way out to the back lawn for pictures. As the photographer, a friend of Kendall's from college, directed them on where to stand and pose, neither Marley or Luke spoke.

Then Kendall decided to meddle. "Darcy, I think we should do a couple of casual pics, you know? Lighten the mood and loosen us up."

Darcy nodded, her gray eyes twinkling behind her glasses and Luke wondered what they had planned.

"Luke, cradle the back of Marley's head and dip her as though you're dancing. You two were really good together as I recall." When Marley shot her a glare, Kendall added, "At dancing, of course."

Brent bent down, and Luke could almost imagine him telling her to leave them alone, but she wasn't having any of it. "Chop chop, the photographer is waiting."

Luke did as she asked, wrapping his arm around Marley's waist and cradling her head. As he dipped her toward the ground, it was so reminiscent of the day they met in the grocery store that he smiled.

Her green eyes stared into his, as if trying to read his thoughts. "What are you thinking about?"

"Trix and you."

Marley's cheeks turned pink. This close he was overwhelmed by the scent of her, the lithe body he thought he'd never hold again stirring a rush of desire through him. Before he knew what he was doing, he was resting his forehead against hers and releasing a shaky breath.

He didn't say anything, and was shocked to his toes when she squeezed his shoulders and whispered, "I've missed you so much."

Luke pulled away then, needing distance before he did something crazy like tell her he missed her too or God forbid, kiss her.

Setting her on her feet away from him, he asked, "Are we done? Cause I need a drink."

Without even waiting for them to protest, Luke walked back up the stairs and into the great room where the reception was being held, finding the bar as fast as he could. Taking the Jack and Coke the bartender handed him, he downed the entire contents of the glass and asked for another. It was an open bar after all.

After Kendall and Brent were introduced to the room ten minutes later, he found Brent standing next to him, frowning.

"Kendall sent me over to find out what you're doing to Marley."

Luke was on his third glass and drinking it a lot slower than the previous drinks. "I'm not doing anything. At the moment, I am enjoying a Jack and Coke." He caught sight of Marley standing next to Kendall, scanning the crowd. Luke nodded in their direction. "As far away from her as humanly possible."

"That's what I mean. One second you've got her in your arms, acting as though you can't get enough of her, and then you're running away."

To hell with slowing down. Luke took a swift gulp and set his glass on the bar. "I need to figure out what I want without you and your wife getting in the middle and causing more drama. Just enjoy being married and let us figure things out for ourselves."

Brent shook his head grimly. "In that case, I am also required to inform you that my sweet, demure bride will 'rip off your junk' if you hurt her MOH."

"Is that a direct quote?" Luke asked, grinning.

"Yes, and it was painful to deliver."

"You can assure Kendall that hurting Marley is the last thing on my mind."

Kissing her was another story.

Chapter 26

Marley finished her toast to the bride and groom and once she was out of the spotlight, she downed her champagne like a glutton. For the last hour, she had tried unsuccessfully to get Luke alone and he'd somehow managed to elude her every time.

If this was the way the rest of the night was going to go, she was definitely in need of something stronger.

She crossed the room, the soft fabric of her silver dress swishing around her legs. She ordered an apple martini at the bar. When she heard the DJ on the mic call Luke's name, she turned around to watch.

Luke walked out into the middle of the dance floor, looking so handsome in that tux. His hair seemed longer than the last time she'd seen him, making his ears stand out less and it was disappointing. She loved his ears.

Luke took the mic and mumbled, "Good evening."

The crowd murmured their response, and Luke continued.

"Brent and I have been friends since high school, and I can easily say, I love the guy like a brother."

"I love you too, buddy!" Brent hollered, making the guests chuckle.

"And I can't tell you how happy it makes me that my friend has found a woman who loves him as much, if not more, than I do. A woman who is kind, compassionate, funny, and smart. Because she realized, even when others didn't, that Brent is a great guy."

Every word was obviously coming straight from his heart.

"God, isn't he fantastic?" Kendall's friend Darcy asked, having come up beside her without her knowing it.

"Here's your drink, miss," the bartender said.

Marley picked up her drink and shot Darcy a small, forced smile. "He's definitely something."

"He is just so delicious."

Back off, sister, he's mine.

Marley ignored Darcy, her attention focused on Luke as he continued his speech. "When we think about love, parents, grandparents, siblings, and such come to mind because, they are our family. We have to love them, even when they hurt us or break us or make us want to never speak to them again. Romantic love is different, because if we're not careful, if we take it for granted and lash out at it, it can be gone like that."

Luke snapped and it was like a knife plummeting into Marley's chest. He was talking about them. How she'd destroyed his feelings for her. Nausea bubbled in the pit of her stomach, and she pushed down the urge to vomit.

She needed to hear this. For Luke.

"Or is romantic love really any different?"

Wait, what? What did he just say?

Her mind couldn't process it quickly enough before he was speaking again. "Because *true* love, the kind you feel for your family, that's supposed to be unconditional. So, despite whatever hurtful actions your lover may commit, those feelings don't go away. No matter how hard you try not to think about that person, she's always going to be in your heart. Because that is what truly being in love is. It is forgiveness. It is unconditional. And it is forever."

Luke's gaze fell on her from across the room and he raised his glass. "To Brent and Kendall. Forever."

"Forever," the reception echoed.

Marley downed her appletini, trying to catch Luke's gaze again, but he'd already turned away to kiss Kendall's cheek and shake Brent's hand.

Marley ordered another drink from the bartender, more confused than ever.

Had that speech really been about Brent and Kendall, or had Luke been trying to tell her something?

The only way she could find out for sure was to ask him. But she had to catch him first.

* * * *

Luke lost sight of Marley after his speech, and an hour and two more Jack and Cokes later, he was ready to give up and go back to the hotel. There was no point in staying if he wasn't going to speak to Marley; he definitely didn't want to dance with anyone else.

"Okay, we need to talk."

Luke looked up as Marley sat down in the chair next to him, sipping on some neon green liquid and looking pretty sauced.

"About?"

She swallowed a large mouthful and set her glass down on the white linen table cloth. "About my letter. Your speech. Why you're messing with me."

"I'm not messing with you," he lied.

"Well, it sure feels like it and it isn't nice. I poured my heart out to you in that letter. The least you could have done is send me a fuck-off text."

Luke leaned his elbows on his knees, bringing him closer to her. "Is that what you want me to say? You want me to tell you to fuck off?"

"No, of course not, you dork." Marley's voice was higher and he thought she sounded a bit nasally. "I want you to tell me that you forgive me. That you missed me as much as I missed you."

"How much have you missed me?" he asked.

"Like stay awake every night listening to sad music and eating a crap ton of junk miss you."

Luke picked up her martini glass and moved it away from her reach. "How many of those have you had?"

"Two or three? I don't really remember."

Luke took her hand and pulled her to her feet. "Why don't we try sobering you up by dancing a bit?"

"I don't want to dance, I want to know—"

Luke pulled up short, looking sternly down into her petulant expression. "We will dance and when I'm ready, we'll talk. Okay?"

Marley hesitated, but when he started to let her go, she finally nodded. He pulled her out for a slow dance, shuffling slowly to "Because You Loved Me." Luke's arms wrapped around her waist as they swayed. When she laid her cheek on his chest, he relaxed.

They didn't talk, and Luke just let himself enjoy Marley's floral scented hair, the way she snuggled against him like a kitten, and most of all, he got lost in just holding her against him once more.

"Can we just stay like this?" she whispered above the music. "In this moment, can we just forget all the bad stuff, and can you just hold me?"

It was too easy to do that, to push the past from his mind and just enjoy Marley.

He just wondered if it was something he could really commit to and forgive her...or was he just fooling himself?

* * * *

The night flew by in a blur, and Marley knew she was still pretty tipsy as Luke kept his arm around her waist, leading her down the hallway to his hotel room. The Love Shack Hotel's hallway was quiet for a Saturday at eleven at night.

Or maybe that made sense. People this late were getting busy.

The thought left her giggling hysterically.

"What's so funny?" Luke asked, smiling down at her. She was glad he could still do that; she'd been afraid she'd never see it directed at her again.

"I was just wondering if you were bringing me back here so we can have make up sex?"

Luke shook his head as he pulled his keys from his pocket. "Actually, I'm bringing you back here so you can sleep it off and I make sure you don't aspirate on your vomit."

Marley leaned against the wall as the walls tilted, and he opened up the door. "That sounds so hot."

Luke chuckled and she held a finger up with a smile. "See? I can still make you laugh." The edges of her vision started to blur and she felt herself falling as she slurred, "I love it when you laugh."

Strong arms picked her up and she hummed as her eyes stayed closed. The sensation of floating surprised her, and she mumbled, "Am I flying?"

"No, sweetheart, I'm carrying you to bed."

"I really don't mind when *you* call me sweetheart. Other people do it and it rankles me."

"Rankles, huh? Pretty big word for such a drunk girl."

She didn't respond, as she'd already passed completely out.

When she woke up, she was so thirsty she started to get out of the bed, but there was an arm around her waist, anchoring her down. She looked over her shoulder, and could make out Luke's features in the sliver of moonlight. She was still wearing her silver bridesmaid dress, the silky fabric clinging to her.

A little drunk still, she was awake enough to realize that instead of sleeping in the other double bed, Luke had wanted to be with her.

A smile spread slowly across her features and warm tingles raced through her entire body.

She got up to get a glass of water, trying to be quiet as she moved around in the dark. She came back from the bathroom and as she stood beside the bed, she watched the light from the open window play across his features. He was truly sound asleep.

Before she could change her mind, she stripped off her dress, bra, and then panties, before crawling back in with him. She wanted to feel his warmth surround her once more, even if it was the last time.

She pressed her mouth against his throat, kissing him softly as her hand moved down, stroking him through his boxer briefs. She knew the minute he came awake, because his whole body stiffened, including his cock.

Marley gently pushed his shoulders until he lay on his back and kissed her way over his chest and down his stomach. The thing about buzzed sex was you were just loose enough to enjoy sex without worrying about the stupid stuff, like…well, she couldn't remember now.

She hooked her fingers into his boxer briefs and pulled them down, exposing his shaft. He didn't protest when she took him into her mouth, cradling his balls in her hand. In fact, besides his sharp intake of breath, she would have thought he was still asleep.

There was something about Luke letting her take control and do whatever she wanted to him that was empowering, sexy, bold. She started experimenting, listening to the sounds he made and learning what he really liked.

Before long, she was pulled up by her arm pits and rolled beneath Luke, whose dark eyes glittered in the moonlight. Apparently, he'd gotten tired of her teasing him.

His hand moved between her legs and against her lips he murmured, "My turn."

Marley ran her hands over his head as he followed the path of her body. Over her breasts, her ribs, her stomach. She sighed as his tongue dipped into her navel and lower, finding her clit with a wet, firm flick. She slid her hands up to play with her nipples as he sucked, licked and thrust his tongue inside her, making her whimper with frustration and desire.

"Please. Please."

Luke drew her hard bud into his mouth, making her cry out as fissions of electricity shot straight between her legs.

"Tell me what you want," he said, spreading her lips with his fingers and applying pressure, driving her crazy with need.

"I want you inside me…I want to be on top."

Luke rolled onto his back, lifting her with him.

As she climbed over him and rubbed her wet center on his tip, she put her hands on his chest for balance. Her back arched and she wiggled her way down his length until he was fully inside her. Biting her lip, she rocked her hips and the friction was excruciatingly wonderful.

His hands gripped her hips, impatient with her, and he started to move her back and forth over him, pushing and pulling her so fast that she found herself moving with his motions, picking up speed. The pressure inside her built and she curled her hands against his chest, little "ohs" getting higher and higher as she reached her peak.

Finally, she screamed, her body shaking and twitching as she came, a rush of liquid heat spreading through her limbs. She wanted to sink down on top of him, curl into a little contented ball and fall asleep.

Instead, she was almost lifted off him as he pumped up once, twice.

On the third time, he shouted and she held on, her muscles squeezing around him as he shuddered.

When she was sure he was finished, she slid off of him and lay against his side, her head on his chest.

She kissed his nipple, her eyes already drooping with exhaustion.

Through the fog of sleep, she heard him whisper something, and although she couldn't be sure, she thought it sounded a lot like *I love you.*

She tried to respond, to tell him she felt the same way, but her lips wouldn't move.

And then there was only darkness.

Chapter 27

The next morning, sunlight drifted into the hotel room. Marley woke up slowly and reached out an arm for Luke's warmth. When all she hit were cold sheets, she pushed herself up onto her arms and looked around the hotel room. All of his clothes were gone.

"Luke?"

There was no answer.

She climbed out of bed, putting on her bra and panties before sliding her silky bridesmaid dress over her head. She pulled her phone from the little clutch she'd had last night and texted him. Several moments passed, but there was no answer.

He wouldn't have left town though. Not without saying good-bye. Not after all they'd shared.

She took the hotel key on the nightstand and walked down to the honeymoon suite where Brent and Kendall were. Maybe Luke had just gone out to get them coffee or something.

Except why wouldn't he leave me a note?

Marley knocked loudly on the door and waited. When there was no movement inside the suite, she knocked again. Then she heard the stomp of feet on the floor.

"Hang on," Kendall grumbled inside.

The door opened and she squinted at Marley. "You realize this is the morning after my wedding, right?"

"Yeah, sorry, but does Brent know where Luke is?"

"Luke?" Kendall turned and called out, "Brent, have you talked to Luke?"

"He had to get back to work," Brent called from inside.

Marley didn't want to believe it. Sure, she'd known there was a chance that last night could have just been a one-time thing, but she hadn't really believed that. She thought they were more.

"So, he just left without even saying good-bye?" Marley said.

Brent stumbled up in a pair of boxers, but Marley didn't have time to be embarrassed. Luke was gone. She had to find him. To tell him to stay.

"I guess. He started a new job and he couldn't be late."

Marley's heart wouldn't stop pounding and she just kept nodding. "Okay, okay, sorry to bother you. I've got to go."

"Marley—"

But Marley ignored Kendall and ran, forgoing the elevator and ran down the stairs. She didn't bother putting on her heels until she reached the lobby, hopping on first one foot and then the other.

"Marley, what in the sam hill are you doing?" Turner asked.

"I've got a man to catch." Marley tossed the hotel keys onto the counter without stopping. "Thanks for the room, Turner."

Running out the door in the heels was torture, but there was no way she wanted to step on something sharp or disgusting in her bare feet. She kicked them off as soon as she got into her car and turned the key in the ignition.

She peeled out of the hotel parking lot and onto Omo Ranch, heading toward Sacramento. She'd get a flight to L.A. and track Luke down. She'd tell him if he wanted her to move, she would. She'd pour her heart out and if he told her it was too late, at least she'd have tried. Marley didn't care if he was trying to give her a hint by taking off; she would do anything to keep Luke and maybe if he knew that, he'd be able to forgive her.

She was taking the corners at sixty, pressing harder on the gas the minute it straightened out. Too late, she saw the Sheriff's car on the side of the road, and cursing a blue streak, she pulled over before he even flipped on his lights.

Marley started rummaging through her glove box for her registration, freaking out when she couldn't find it right away. Being pulled over was like getting caught by her parents sneaking out. Usually they liked to lecture her, and she just didn't have the time for that.

There was a tap on her passenger side window and she rolled it down. She couldn't see his face, just his uniform, belt and the pockets on his chest.

"I am really sorry, sir, I am looking for my registration right now, but I'm actually trying to catch someone before they leave town, so if you could please just give me a warning, I would be so..."

She stopped talking as the deputy squatted down, smiling at her from under his hat.

It was Luke.

"Grateful?" she finished, completely confused. What was Luke still doing here? And in an El Dorado County Sherriff's uniform?

"Now, why are you driving out of town like a bat out of hell again? I left you in the hotel to sleep. So what are you doing and who are you chasing?"

She stared at him, utterly speechless…until she exploded.

"What am I doing? Who am I…I'm chasing you, idiot! What are *you* doing? I thought you were gone! You just got up and left me after last night without even a note or a text—"

His brow knit beneath the tan Mountie hat. "I left a message with Turner that I had left for work and we'd talk later."

"You…left…a…message…with…Turner?" Checking her mirror to make sure there were no cars coming, she got out and rounded the front in her bare feet, ignoring the sharp rocks as she faced him. "You could have texted or left a note in the hotel room. Why couldn't you tell me?"

Luke didn't seem fazed at all that she was livid. "Actually, I couldn't find a pen or paper and I didn't have my phone on me last night, or this morning, so Turner seemed like the best choice."

She wanted to kick him right in the berries. Instead, she settled for his shin, which actually hurt her toes.

Luke rubbed his shin with his hand, shooting her a mock scowl. "Assaulting a police officer? Really?"

He was treating this all like it was a joke, and it hurt. Her eyes stung and she tried to fight back the lump in her throat. "This is funny to you? After what happened last night?"

The amusement left his face. "What do you mean? When she didn't answer right away, he reached out for her, and took a hold of her shoulders. "What happened last night, Marley? I want you to tell me."

"I…we…we made love and I…I thought… you said you loved me."

Luke's breath whooshed out. "I did say I loved you, and you fell asleep. Just passed out snoring after I'd put my heart on the line. That was cold, sweetheart."

That smile was back, proving he was messing with her, and this time, she hit his arm.

"I do not snore!"

Luke's hands slid down her arms and wrapped around her waist. "Yeah, you do, but I don't mind. What I want to know is if you have anything to say to me today."

This was it. Her chance to tell him everything that had been bubbling up inside her for the past four months.

"I love you. I was speeding after you because I thought you'd left without knowing how much."

She was suddenly crushed against Luke's chest and lifted off the ground as his lips crashed over hers. A thrill shot down her spine and she wrapped her arms around those broad shoulders, holding on for dear life.

He pulled away enough to mumble, "What took you so long, woman?"

Giddy laughter bubbled up her throat. "I was afraid that you'd tell me you didn't feel the same way."

Luke set her back on her feet, shaking his head. "I took care of you when you had snot oozing from your nose, and looked like some kind of swamp creature. Of course I feel the same way, dummy."

Marley glared at him. "I'm getting really sick of people calling me dumb."

"Then stop being dumb."

She grabbed him by those big ears and pulled his mouth down to hers, just to shut him up. Their kiss ignited something, and before she knew it, he had her pressed against the side of the sheriff's car, her legs wrapped around his waist.

Then something occurred to her and she pulled away from his kiss.

"Did Kendall and Brent know you'd taken a job with the El Dorado County Sheriff's Department?"

Luke cocked his head to the side. "Of course they did. Why?"

Fury laced through Marley as she realized they'd set her up. "Because they're a couple of bastards, that's why! They made me think you'd left town to go back to L.A."

Laughing, Luke smoothed some of her hair back from her face, leaving tingles in the wake of his touch. "I think they like a little drama in their lives."

"Not me. I am so over drama. No more crazy brides! No more forbidden love. From now on, I want a quiet, stress free life."

Luke pressed his forehead to hers. "I'll do my best to accommodate you."

Epilogue

One Year Later

"I can't breathe. I think my bodice is cinched too tight," Marley said.

Marley stood in the upstairs bridal salon in the newly renovated saloon. What used to be called Buzzard Gulch was now Sweetheart Meadows. The beautiful historical town opened with the start of the wedding season and had been booked solid every weekend.

Except this one. The minute she'd said yes to Luke, she'd known that this was the place where she wanted to say her vows.

Kelly huffed impatiently as she spread out Marley's train behind her. "It is not. You've just got wedding day jitters. Rylie, give Marley the bag again."

Rylie held up the brown paper bag and Marley took it gratefully, breathing deeply into it. She shouldn't be this nervous, but for some reason, she couldn't seem to chill out unless that stupid bag was covering her face.

Kendall came into the room, her eight-month pregnant belly proceeding her. "Uh oh. She needs the bag again? Should I get the car? Is she going to bolt?"

Marley glared at Kendall's joke. "You'd love that, wouldn't you, drama queen?"

Kendall laughed and slowly lowered herself into one of the empty chairs. She was wearing an empire waist bridesmaid dress in a periwinkle blue, while the rest of the bridesmaids were in navy, setting her apart as Marley's Matron of Honor. Kendall had convinced Brent that Sweetheart would be a wonderful place to raise a family, and since both of their best friends were living there anyway, Brent hadn't protested.

"Actually, I would not. You and Luke are too good together."

Marley smiled, silently agreeing with Kendall. Loving Luke was one of the easiest things she'd ever done, even when he was being bossy. Like when she woke up early one June morning, and he was standing in the kitchen with a box of Trix. On the front, he'd put a piece of paper in the corner that read, *Will you marry me, Marley? If yes, open the box.*

She'd almost ripped the box out of his hands, laughing when she found a velvet ring box sitting on top of the colorful cereal. She'd pulled it out with shaking hands.

He'd kneeled down, and after taking the cereal and the ring box from her, he'd said, "Marley, I love you and want you by my side for the rest of my life. Will you accept this ring and be my wife?"

Of course she'd said yes and launched herself at him, knocking him back into the Trix box that spilled over. They'd ended up making love on the painful balls of grain, but neither of them complained.

Until Butters ate his weight in colorful crunchy balls and they had to rush him to the vet where he passed rainbow-colored poo. Never a dull moment for them.

"You're ready now," Kelly said.

As Rylie pulled the old-fashioned mirror down and revealed the beautiful Maggie Sottero dress covering Marley's slender frame, and the wisps of blonde hair the framed her face under her veil, she dropped the bag. A wide smile split across her face, and she felt a hand take hers. Looking down into her mother's joyous face, she squeezed.

"I'm ready."

* * * *

Luke paced in front of the officiant, trying to calm his nerves. He stood at the edge of Sweetheart Meadows, overlooking the river below, where Marley and he had made love for the first time. He kept staring down the white runner covered in brightly colored wildflowers, and the faces of their closest family and friends, impatiently waiting for Marley to get out there so he could make her his wife.

Wife. God, I can't believe how happy I am.

"Relax, man, it's going to be great," Brent said, standing perfectly still at his best man post.

The music changed, and this was it. Luke stopped and waited, watching the door of the saloon. It finally opened and the bridesmaids started down the aisle, all holding large bouquets of yellow, pink, purple, and green.

Kendall, who held a leash in one hand and dropped pellets behind her for Butters, the official ring bearer. He surprisingly didn't seem to mind the black harness with the white bowtie on the back of his neck. The room laughed as the bunny hopped down the aisle, snacking on the little green logs all the way down to the special crate they'd set up for him. Kendall retrieved the ring, locked him inside and took her bouquet from Rylie, joining the rest of them beneath the arbor.

When the bridal march started and Marley and her mom came down the porch arm in arm, Luke's heart stopped. Everything and everyone melted away as he stared at his soon-to-be wife and the happiness transfixed across her face. He knew his expression mirrored hers and found himself walking halfway down the aisle to meet her. Cupping her face, he kissed her lips softly, until someone thwacked him on his arm.

Facing his future mother in law, he said, "What was that for?"

"For being impatient."

The audience erupted, and Luke sheepishly back pedaled to his place until Rose finally relinquished Marley to him.

The pastor started the ceremony, and when he reached the part where he asked for objections, Luke almost laughed, imagining someone standing up and—

"Oh, crap!" Kendall cried.

Every head turned toward her, including Luke and Marley.

"What's the matter?" Marley asked.

Kendall was hunched over, holding her stomach. "I'm pretty sure I'm in labor."

"What?!" Brent shouted, crossing to his wife. "Why do you think that?"

"Because my water just broke all over my shoes and my stomach feels like it's tied in knots!"

Without further explanation, Brent swooped Kendall up in his arms, and ran down the aisle toward the parked cars. "Taking the limo!"

"Son of a bitch!" Luke said.

"Sir, can we speed this along?" Marley said.

The officiant seemed stunned, but nevertheless pronounced them husband and wife.

"Are you thinking what I am?" Luke asked.

"Hell yes. I'm not letting them steal our thunder and our limo."

With a laugh, the two of them raced down the aisle after their friends.

"We'll see y'all at the reception!" Luke yelled.

When they reached the rows of cars, they found Brent arguing with the limo driver.

"Tony, get your ass in the driver's seat and haul us to the hospital!" Marley hollered.

Tony gaped at Marley for a half a second, then jumped into the driver's seat.

"Come on, guys, inside," Luke said.

Kendall shook her head, her face pale and sweaty. "What are you doing? You're going to miss your reception!"

Luke watched Marley take her friend's hand and squeeze it. "Nah, we just want to make sure you get there okay. Besides, in case the baby needs to be delivered, Luke's here."

Kendall and Marley looked at Luke, who appeared horrified and they laughed.

"I'm sorry we stole your limo," Kendall said.

"I don't care about the limo, dummy. We love you."

Kendall threw her arms around Marley with a cry while their husbands rolled their eyes.

"All right, all right, hugging later, hospital now," Luke said, ushering them inside.

When they were all inside, Brent held his panting wife while Luke took Marley's hand.

"You were sure cool about them hijacking our limo. I was expecting a crazy bride."

Marley snorted. "Remember I said I'd had enough of crazy brides."

"You did, but I wasn't sure I believed it. Especially since we might be late to the reception."

"No, we'll drop them off and get back in plenty of time." Her chin lifted stubbornly. "I'm not going to miss my first dance with you. We're going to do this, even if I have to drive the limo myself."

Luke held her close, holding back his laughter at her ferocity. "It's not exactly our first dance—"

"It is as husband and wife and I am not missing it." She kissed his mouth lingeringly, and he couldn't help his reaction to her. When he was eighty, he hoped that the simple brush of Marley's lips on his would still make him crazy in the best way possible.

Marley's fingers brushed over his chest, and she sent him a coy look from beneath her lashes. "Although, I will admit, I'm looking forward to what happens after the reception more than any dance."

He lowered his voice, and wiggled his eyebrows. "You mean the honeymoon? Me too."

She pushed at his chest with laughter. "No, you perv. I mean spending the rest of my life with you."

Luke kissed her long and lingeringly. "Don't try to act as though you aren't excited about the honeymoon."

"Fine yes, I can't wait to spend an entire week naked with you in the hotel room eating chocolate dipped strawberries and champagne."

"That's my sweetheart." His arms went around her, pulling her close until he felt the warmth of her breath on his ear.

"Yes, I am."

Acknowledgments

First of all, many thanks to my agent, Sarah Younger, for submitting my proposal for the Something Borrowed series, and always being there for me when I need you. To my amazing editor, Norma Perez-Hernandez for giving me this chance. To the staff at Kensington Lyrical for the support. To my husband and children, for learning with every book what "mommy's on deadline" means and being so understanding. To my parents, siblings, in laws, aunts and uncles, cousins, nieces, and nephews… thank you for talking about and reading my books. Love you all. My friends, who have been there through all the ups and downs, especially Hope Villano, Tina Klinesmith, Deana Gillingham, and Gayle Tominaga: You are amazing, strong women, and you inspire me. I want to thank my Rockers, who share my good news, read and review with gusto. You are the best. And last, but certainly not least, my amazing readers; never stop emailing, messaging, and posting to my timeline. You are my sunshine.

Kiss Me Sweetheart

Keep reading for a sneak peek at

KISS ME, SWEETHEART,

available in February 2018 from Lyrical Shine.

Chapter 1

Rylie Templeton sat at her desk, staring at the box of death by chocolate muffins she'd made that morning, and wondered if throwing one at Dustin Kent's head could be considered assault.

God, he was an arrogant son of a bitch. He leaned a broad shoulder against the door jamb, and watched her with one raised brow and a sardonic smirk across his full lips. He'd been working at Something Borrowed for just shy of a month, and managed to get under her skin in the worst way. Constantly mocking her with his fake compliments and flattery, as if she didn't know he was full of shit.

"You look very pretty today, Rylie. I love you in purple. It really brings out the green flecks in your eyes."

Rylie narrowed her very dark eyes at him. "My eyes are brown, asshat."

He pushed off and started walking toward her, a long stride that ate up the length of her tiny office in no time. He placed his hands on the desk and leaned over until he was almost nose to nose with her.

"Not true. Right in the center—"

She caught the finger he'd started waving in front of her face, tempted to bite it.

Not in a sexy way, of course.

She released him abruptly and stood. Why the hell would she go there, even in her head? Dustin wasn't sexy, and she had a boyfriend anyway.

"I know you are used to getting what you want from women, but your flattery will not work on me."

"Too bad. I was just coming to tell you that Kelly wants to see us in her office. Something about the Rolland/Marconi wedding?"

Rylie's heart almost exploded from her chest. This was it. She'd been waiting for Kelly to give her some of the higher profile clients, but most of them had gone to Marley because she'd been there the longest. But Marley's plate was incredibly full this summer, and Rylie had been praying for this chance since she'd watched Tonya Rolland, the governor of California's daughter, walk down the hallway into Kelly's office last week.

Then, the entirety of his words sank in. "Wait, why does she want *you* there?"

Before she could blink, Dustin snagged one of her muffins and bit into it, chewing slowly. The agony was killing her, until finally he swallowed. "I have a feeling the two of us are going to make this wedding very special."

"Are you kidding me? You and me?" Stepping around the desk, Rylie mumbled, "There has to be some kind of mistake."

Dustin followed behind her, talking in a low, suggestive tone. "Oh, no mistake, baby. Just destiny."

"Shut up." Rylie knocked on Kelly's office door, ignoring Dustin as he came up to stand beside her, bristling when his shoulder brushed hers. She had no idea why he irritated her so much, beyond the fact that he was an obvious womanizer and liked to manipulate women to get his way.

That was probably reason enough.

"Come in," Kelly called.

Dustin beat her to the doorknob. As he twisted it open, she looked up in time to catch his grin, his sparkling blue eyes.

"After you."

Rylie passed him and went to take a seat in one of the chairs opposite Kelly. "You wanted to see me."

"And me," Dustin said, taking the seat next to her.

Rylie gritted her teeth.

Kelly smiled and leaned forward, oblivious to the tension between them. "I'm sure you have an idea why I've called you both in here."

"The Rolland/Marconi wedding," Dustin said.

"Yes. They want to keep a very tight lid on everything, including the location. Close friends and family only, and no press. You two are to get everything ready so when they arrive, all they have to do is get dressed and walk down the aisle."

Rylie wasn't the type to rock the boat, but she couldn't help being irritated. She'd worked hard to get this account; she didn't need a partner, especially some playboy millionaire who didn't even have to work.

Taking a deep breath, she blurted, "Kelly, I know this is a huge account, but I can handle it on my own."

The office went dead silent, and Kelly sat back, her brow furrowed. "Dustin, would you please step out and close the door?"

"Sure."

Rylie's whole face felt like her skin was burning off. God, she hadn't meant for it to come out quite like that.

"Kelly, I'm so sorry—"

Her boss held up her hand and Rylie shut her mouth, waiting for Kelly to tell her she'd blown it.

"I didn't assign Dustin to this account because I thought you couldn't handle it alone. I know you can take on all of this and it would be spectacular."

Rylie waited for the *but* that was sure to follow that glowing speech.

"But, as both the bride and groom have no siblings, they have made their closest friends bridesmaids and groomsmen and asked for professionals to handle the positions of Best Man and Maid of Honor. Do you understand?"

And she did. Everyone at Something Borrowed, especially her friend Marley, had wondered why Kelly had hired a man after all these years. Now it was clear she'd been anticipating this request.

It still didn't explain why she'd chosen Dustin Kent. Even if he hadn't sold an app he'd designed in college and made millions on his own, his parents owned one of the biggest vineyards in the area and half the town of Sweetheart. The guy should be sleeping his way across the U.S. and Europe, not working as a professional groomsman.

"Yes. I'm sorry if I was rude," Rylie said.

Kelly's shot her an amused look. "Please. That is the first time you've ever questioned a decision I've made in what, four years? I think you've earned a question or two."

The tension Rylie hadn't known was there leaked out of her chest as she released a heavy breath. Kelly passed her a red folder, and held onto it until Rylie met her gaze. "I also want you to keep an eye on Dustin."

Rylie blinked at her a few times. "You mean spy on him?"

"No, not spy. I just want you to make sure that he'd doing his fair share of the work. I know how he likes to get one over on the other women here, but thankfully, you seem to be immune to him."

"I have a boyfriend," she said.

Kelly's lips thinned for a half a second until she forced a smile. Rylie wasn't surprised; she knew no one liked her boyfriend, Ashton Clark. Some were more polite about letting their feelings be known.

"Yes, I know. Will you send Dustin back in when you leave? I'd like to finish up telling him what I expect and then I'll send him back to you."

Rylie took the folder and left the room, making her way down the hallway to Dustin's office. He was sitting behind his desk, glasses slipped over that perfect nose making him look like Clark Kent. For a second she watched him, thinking she was due for a *Smallville* marathon.

Rylie shook her head. Dustin was nothing like Tom Welling, except for being insanely good looking, but beauty was only skin deep. Vipers were gorgeous too, until they bit you.

She knocked on the door frame and he looked up at her from his laptop.

"Kelly wants to finish talking to you," she said.

Dustin shut the laptop and stood up, stretching his arms over his head. Which, of course, lifted his button up shirt. She had to fight not to look down and see if any skin was exposed.

God, she was a terrible person.

"So, you didn't manage to get me kicked off then?" he asked.

"It wasn't about you. It was about me wanting to handle this on my own." *Plus, the commission alone would have changed everything for me.*

Dustin walked around the desk and actually chucked her under the chin. "Don't worry, baby. I promise that you're going to love working with me."

Rylie ignored the little flutter in her stomach and scoffed. "Just don't screw this up for me."

She left his office, her cheeks burning as his deep chuckle followed her down the hall. She hated that she'd actually been taken with him when he'd first started working there. Marley had told her he was a jerk, but he'd actually been nice to Rylie. Then, he'd started flirting, and teasing her, and when she'd walked by Marley's office one day to find him flirting with Sonora Star, one of their high profile brides, Rylie had known he was a dog. She could handle and tolerate a lot from a man, but she'd never trust a cheater.

Which was probably why she'd stayed with Ashton for so long.

She sat down at her desk in time to hear her phone beep. She checked the text message and winced.

Did u get BBQ sauce at the store?

Crap, she'd forgotten. Her heart sped up just thinking about how such a small thing could set Ashton off. Taking a deep, shaky breath she tapped out a response.

I'll pick some up on my way home.

There was no response five minutes later, and she knew things were going to be bad.

A tap on her door made her jump and Dustin threw his hands up. "Whoa, it's just me. Was going to see if you wanted to scout a few sites that the bride and groom have picked out?"

Rylie looked at the clock and calculated how long it would take to check out some places. With any luck, Ashton would be asleep when she got home.

"Sure, sounds good."

Meet the Author

An obsessive bookworm, **Codi Gary** likes to write sexy small-town contemporary romances with humor, grand gestures, and blush-worthy moments. When she's not writing, she can be found reading her favorite authors, squealing over her must-watch shows, and playing with her children. She lives in Idaho with her family.

Visit her on the web at www.codigarysbooks.com.

CPSIA information can be obtained
at www.ICGtesting.com
Printed in the USA
LVOW10s2334060817
544020LV00007B/193/P